THE EX

ALSO BY SHALINI BOLAND

The Birthday Party
The Honeymoon
The School Reunion
The Silent Bride
The Daughter-in-Law
A Perfect Stranger
The Family Holiday
The Couple Upstairs
My Little Girl
The Wife
One Of Us Is Lying
The Other Daughter
The Marriage Betrayal
The Girl from the Sea
The Best Friend
The Perfect Family
The Silent Sister
The Millionaire's Wife
The Child Next Door
The Secret Mother
Marchwood Vampire Series
Outside Series
A Shirtful of Frogs

THE EX

SHALINI BOLAND

Published by Thomas & Mercer, Seattle

www.apub.com

EU Product Safety contact:
Amazon Media EU S. à r.l.
38, avenue John F. Kennedy, L-1855 Luxembourg
amazonpublishing-gpsr@amazon.com

ISBN-13: 9781662529535
eISBN: 9781662529528

Cover design by The Brewster Project
Cover image: © Lauren Rautenbach / ArcAngel Images; © Chonlawut
© myboys.me / Shutterstock

Printed in the United States of America

This is for my friends who I've neglected recently (because of all the writing) but who I love dearly and who I will call this week!

Prologue

Your footsteps echo behind me, loud and relentless. It's killing me that I can't tell how close you are. The gravel path is torture on my bare soles, crunching into my skin, causing jagged bursts of pain, but I keep going until my feet finally hit the smooth, damp sand.

I think you're closing in – your breaths now merging with my own – but I cling to the hope that I can outrun you. That I can escape before you drag me back to darkness. My lungs burn and my legs ache, but I push myself onwards.

My feet pound the cold, damp sand as I sprint, the muscles in my legs screaming with pain as fear blurs my vision and sweat coats my skin. I don't know how much longer I can keep running. My heart is a jackhammer in my chest as I risk a glance back to see your shadowy figure not far behind. I was right! You're gaining on me. I feel the panic rising and it chokes me, but I force myself to keep going.

Do I keep heading along this deserted beach? It's a bad idea. You'll catch up with me. I know you will. You're faster, fitter. I don't think I can keep going. But if I stop – try to dodge sideways, double back, or fight . . .

'You can't outrun me,' you snarl, your voice dangerously, terrifyingly close.

I stumble in shock. You're almost upon me. A sob erupts from my chest. But I'm not giving up. I'm not stopping so that you can kill me. I won't let it happen. I can't.

Suddenly, I'm not running anymore as my feet are knocked from under me. Your hands are on my ankles. You must have lunged for me. I feel myself falling, my knee cracking as I land with a sickening thud on the hard sand.

There's a moment of silence before I find my voice and scream, praying that someone might hear me. 'Help!' I cry. 'Help me! Please!'

'Shut up,' you hiss as you crawl along my body until you're on top of me, the smell of stale alcohol and sweat tainting the clean ocean air. 'There's no one out here. I told you I wasn't going to let you get away from me again. And don't think for a minute that I believe the story you told me. If you're going to lie, you need to do better than that.'

'I wasn't lying,' I plead.

'Shut up,' you repeat, your breath hot on my face. 'I never want to hear your whiny little voice again.'

In what feels like slow motion, your cold hands wrap around my neck and I know there's no way I'll be able to fight you. You're going to strangle me. I kick upwards and tug at your clothes, but I don't seem to have any strength. I can't shake you off. You're an immovable object, and my attempts to escape are laughable.

'Please,' I croak. But the air is being squeezed from my lungs, and my throat is on fire. My vision blurs and I know I'm on the edge of blacking out. I don't want to die. My heartbeats thud in my ears, mingling with the roar of the waves as I desperately try to breathe. But I'm fading. It's already too late.

Chapter One

WILLOW

I duck into a café, my heart in my throat, my breath coming in laboured little gasps. Why can't my stupid brain give me a stupid break? It's exhausting. I wish I could be one of those people who doesn't care. Who just breezes through life with their normal everyday worries. But, no. I have to be this neurotic mess, always imagining the worst. Always terrified that my secret is about to be exposed. What was the point of doing what I did, if I'm still walking on eggshells? No point. No point at all. I may as well have walked off a cliff.

I take deep, calming breaths and try to get my bearings as the scent of freshly brewed coffee, vanilla and cinnamon makes my stomach gurgle. I've found myself in one of those cute, artsy cafés that has squashy sofas and paintings by local artists that you can buy. The sounds of chatter and laughter and the clink of crockery and cutlery are a welcome antidote to my anxiety, but it's not enough to dispel it altogether. It's the kind of place where it would be nice to meet up with friends or family . . . *if I had any friends or family*. I shove away a wave of self-pity and square my shoulders.

There's no need for any of that. I'm a strong, independent woman. I don't need anybody. I don't *want* anybody.

I was on my way home from finishing off a bathroom tiling job – a long morning spent on my knees, grouting – when I thought I felt someone walking behind me. Following me. I panicked and slipped down a side street – which is probably the worst thing I could have done – when, luckily, I spotted this café. I've never noticed it before. Wasn't even sure it was open at first. But now that I've found myself inside, I might as well make the most of it and order a coffee, even though the caffeine is more likely to add to my jitters than calm my nerves.

I join the snaking queue and stand behind a woman wearing a bright red coat, a couple of yellow leaves stuck to the back of her hood. I resist the urge to pluck them off. The menu is handwritten and hard to read, but I know what I want. When I reach the counter, the girl taking orders looks about twelve, with an oversized apron and a bored expression.

'Cappuccino to go, please,' I say, tapping my card.

The girl nods. 'Can I take a name?' she asks.

'Willow.'

The red coat lady takes her coffee and leaves, letting in a gust of cool September air when she opens the door. I keep glancing at the window, but there's no sign of the person I thought it might be. I think it was just me being paranoid. It's hard to shake it off.

While I wait for my order, my eyes skim the tables. A mothers' group has spread out across two sofas and an armchair, their babies asleep in their buggies as the mums chatter together and sip lattes. Retired couples enjoy their tea and pastries. A mother and daughter sit in a sea of shopping bags. And the rest are students or workers concentrating on laptop screens, earbuds in to block out the chatter. The road outside is still quiet. Nobody sinister is peering in. No faces I'd rather not see. I force myself to relax, to chant the mantra that calms me: I'm safe. I'm unknown. I'm safe. I'm unknown.

My coffee arrives with my name scrawled across the cardboard in blue pen. I take off the lid and turn to go, walking smack-bang into someone, my coffee cup smooshing between us as its contents erupt down both our fronts.

I yelp as some of the liquid splashes on to the back of my hand. Luckily, it's not too hot. I'm in my thick work overalls, which soak up most of it. But it's soaked through the T-shirt of the guy I knocked into.

'Jeez!' he cries.

I realise the café has gone quiet as everyone's attention momentarily turns towards us – the drama.

'I'm so sorry.' I turn to yank some napkins from the dispenser and start dabbing the man's top. 'Are you okay?'

'Just a few third-degree burns,' he gasps.

'Oh no! Are you really hurt?' I have visions of blistered skin and a trip to A & E. But as I stare up into a pair of really blue eyes, framed by dirty-blond hair, I'm relieved to see a teasing smile.

'I'll survive,' he replies. 'Not sure about my favourite T-shirt though. Thankfully the coffee's not too hot. Although I usually can't stand it lukewarm.'

I vaguely recognise the cartoon characters on his top. 'That's your favourite T-shirt?' I lift an eyebrow.

'Rude,' he quips. 'Yes, it's Rick and Morty, bought for me by my nephew, which is why I like it so much.'

'Are you guys okay?' one of the waitresses asks.

'Fine,' we reply in unison.

'Sorry about the mess,' I add, noticing the small puddle on the floor. 'I can mop it up.' I grab a few napkins from the counter behind me and start to crouch.

'No, don't worry, I'll do it, and I'll get you another coffee on the house. Cappuccino, right?'

'Are you sure? That's really kind. Thanks.'

'Get it to drink in,' the guy says to me. 'I'm sitting here.' He gestures to the table behind us. There's a laptop open on it next to a notebook.

I give him a quizzical look, not sure what he means.

'Join me,' he clarifies.

'Oh, no, that's okay. Looks like you're busy.'

'I need a break,' he replies.

My hesitancy must show on my face because he says, 'Just one coffee with me to relieve the boredom of my day and to make up for wrecking my favourite T-shirt.'

'You're guilt-tripping me into having a coffee with you?'

'Is it working?' he asks.

I roll my eyes. 'Okay. One coffee.'

'Great . . .' He tilts his head to read the smudged writing on my flattened coffee cup. '*Willow*?'

I nod and turn to dump the cup in the bin.

'I'm Gabe Walker, by the way.' He holds out his hand but I don't take it.

'Willow McAllister. I'm just going to wash my hands.' I hold them out for him to see. 'Sticky.'

There's a fresh coffee waiting for me on my return and I take it over to Gabe's table, blocking out the inner voice that tells me this is a bad idea. Annoyingly, his smile makes my stomach flip, something that hasn't happened in a long, long while. I look away quickly, taking a seat. I sip my coffee, its rich taste providing a brief distraction from my conflicting thoughts.

Any awkwardness soon melts away and the next ten minutes fly by as we start chatting. I learn that he's twenty-nine – a year older than me – and a graphic designer who's lived here in Highcliffe all his life.

'And what about you?' he asks. 'You've let me waffle on for ages. Where are you from? You're not local, or I would have seen you around.'

'London,' I reply.

'Oh? Whereabouts?'

I drain the last of my coffee and get to my feet. 'It's been nice chatting, but I have to get back.'

'You can't go already?' Gabe stands too, sliding his laptop into a sports rucksack. 'We haven't finished our conversation.'

'Sorry.' I almost trip over the chair in my haste to leave. 'I have a thing,' I lie. I don't have 'a thing'. I never have 'things'. I don't know how I could have let myself get so caught up in the moment. As though I'm living an ordinary life where I can meet cute guys and start to form attachments. What was I even thinking? I drop a pound coin on the table for a tip, and give Gabe a polite wave and smile without any eye contact.

'At least let me take your number,' he says, hastily zipping up his bag and following me as I head to the door.

I try not to imagine him taking my number and calling me for a date. The two of us growing closer over time and eventually becoming boyfriend and girlfriend. Having a normal life filled with love and happiness. Because those are not options open to me. Those are not the parameters I'm able to live within.

'Sorry, but I don't give out my number to strangers,' I reply, leaving the warmth and cosiness of the café.

Annoyingly and flatteringly, Gabe is still by my side. 'I'm not a stranger anymore,' he insists. 'Come on, just one date.' He swings his rucksack over his right shoulder and matches my strides.

I glance sideways to see a cheeky grin that's irritatingly hard to resist. 'Like it was "just one coffee"?' I ask.

'Exactly like that!' he replies. 'You have to admit the coffee was fun, aside from the whole ruining my T-shirt episode. Tell you what, if you come out for a drink with me, I'll let you ruin another one of my favourite tops with beer, wine or spirits – your choice.'

I snort, and somehow find myself giving him my number. Instantly regretting it.

Chapter Two
JASMINE

I've never had this feeling before. Never. The feeling that I've fallen into someone else's life. That everything is off balance and no one is who they're supposed to be.

The cool, late-September evening air ripples across my bare arms as I top up Katie's glass and laugh at something Tom says. I wasn't paying any attention to his words, but everyone else is roaring so I join in. The sound is harsh. Discordant. Their mouths open, red tongues curling, white teeth glinting under the fairy lights. Nausea churns in my gut as my husband Adam shoots me a dark look. A look I've never seen before tonight.

All I did was arrange a surprise barbecue for our one-year wedding anniversary. I invited a few close friends and workmates. People we love who were at the wedding. So why is he acting this way? Am I missing something? I had thought I was doing something nice. Something that would make him smile and kiss me. Something that would warm both our hearts. Instead, I'm bewildered by his coldness. At the undercurrents of reproach emanating from him, laced with – I can't believe I'm even thinking it – *anger*. It's incomprehensible. We've always been so close.

It's been two hours since Adam arrived home to find our house filled with people waiting to celebrate with us. Two hours in which Adam hasn't said a single word to me. To the untrained eye, he seems relaxed and happy around everyone. Smiling and chatting away as if nothing's wrong. But the subtle glares in my direction have turned my insides to jelly. What's going on?

Dressed in jeans and an olive-green shirt that matches his eyes, my husband appears handsome and at ease, his dark, wavy hair flopping over one eye, as usual. There's this funny little thing we do; whenever I reach over to push his hair back, he'll grab my fingers and kiss them. And we'll end up kissing properly. Not tonight though.

'What do you think, Jasmine?'

I realise Adam's friend, Tom, is talking to me.

'Oh.' I feel my cheeks heat up. 'Sorry, Tom, I zoned out for a second.'

'You're boring her,' Tom's wife, Katie, teases, knocking into his shoulder with hers.

'Not at all,' I reply. 'Just a bit squiffy from Louie's punch.'

'Yeah, Louie, what did you put in it?' my workmate Chrissie asks. 'All the dodgy leftover alcohol from last year's office party?'

'Cheeky mare.' Louie nods at her glass. 'I see it hasn't stopped you from dipping in. How many of those have you had?'

'Anyway.' Chrissie ignores his question, rolling her big blue eyes at him instead, before turning back to me. 'Tom was asking what you think about his new beard. Yes, or no? Katie isn't a fan, but we're all for it.'

'Only because you don't want to hurt his feelings,' Katie replies.

'It's very dashing,' I say diplomatically.

'You make me sound like someone from the 1800s.' Tom strokes his facial hair theatrically.

I'm trying to appear relaxed and engaged in the conversation, but my stomach is swirling with anxiety. I'm desperate for tonight to be over, but at the same time, I'm dreading any kind of confrontation with Adam. All evening, I've been wondering if it really is the party that's caused him to react this way. But how could that warrant this kind of coldness? I've tried to talk to him, but he's doing a good job of avoiding me, and I don't want to have any kind of drama in front of our friends.

Adam and I have been married for a year and together for two, and I've never seen him like this before. He's always been affectionate and loving towards me. Sometimes almost too attentive. It's what made me fall for him in the first place – his kindness. His desire to make sure I'm okay. I'd never had any boyfriend treat me this way before. They were all so casual and self-absorbed. It felt like Adam truly wanted to know the real me.

We first met at the hospital café where I used to work. He was visiting his dad who'd just had minor surgery and I messed up his drinks order. He was sweet about it and asked me out on a date. I was flustered, but smitten straightaway, and our relationship bloomed quickly. I was twenty-three and he was twenty-nine. Not a huge age gap, but he seemed so much more worldly than me. So grown-up, with his own business and his own home. Whereas I felt as though I was barely off the starting blocks. I was flattered that someone like Adam would be interested in me.

Those first few months were a whirlwind of happiness. Adam organised so many fun dates and trips away for us; he was always surprising me with flowers and chocolates, impromptu picnics and cute gifts. Nothing was ever boring. I had constant butterflies in my stomach whenever I thought of him.

When he proposed on our six-month anniversary, I was stunned but overjoyed. It may have seemed a bit fast to everyone else, but when you know, you know. And now, eighteen months later, he's still such a thoughtful husband, always checking in on me, calling me at work to see how my day is going, meeting me in my lunch break. Every day I pinch myself that such a perfect man exists, and that he's mine. Which is why tonight is so strange. So out of character.

I wish Adam's dad, Nigel, had been able to make it this evening. I'm sure he would have smoothed the situation. But sadly he had to attend the funeral of a close friend, in Basingstoke, where he's staying for a few days.

I float above the conversation, smiling, laughing and replying in all the right places, but my whole body is attuned to Adam. Right now, he's standing by the back door talking to Leo and Marc, a couple of his employees. Adam owns a painting and decorating firm and it's doing really well. He has a team of six right now, but he's been talking about expanding the business.

'You okay, Jasmine?' Louie asks quietly, turning his back to the rest of the group. He adjusts his glasses and peers at me worriedly. Louie works in telesales at the insurance company where I've been an admin assistant for the past fourteen months. But not for much longer because a group of us were made redundant last week, including Louie. We've been given a month's notice. It was a bit of a shock.

The job itself is fairly mundane, but I love the people I work with and I'm going to miss the camaraderie. Adam says he doesn't mind if I want to stay home for a while, that maybe we should start a family, but I'm not ready for that. I think I want to go to college or uni to train for a new career. I'm not sure yet.

'I'm fine,' I lie. 'How about you?'

Louie takes a sip of his drink and shrugs. 'Oh, you know. Looking for one of those mythical job things. Let me know if you hear of anything in sales.'

'I will,' I reply.

'It only took me eight months to find this one, so I'm sure I'll be fine,' he says glumly.

'You'll get a good reference,' I say. 'I can't believe they let you go.'

'Last in, first out. Single and jobless, what a catch. Anyway, sorry. Don't mean to be a Debbie Downer at your anniversary party.' He points to the patio where our other workmates, Tina and Chrissie, are dancing drunkenly to the Jackson 5's 'ABC'. 'Maybe we should join them. Dance our troubles away.'

'You go ahead, I'll be over in a bit.'

I watch Louie dance-walk over to them and get pulled into their mini-clique with squeals and over-exaggerated dance moves. Normally I'd be right there with them. I realise I'm chewing the skin at the edge of my thumbnail. I stop. This is ridiculous. I can't spend the rest of the evening feeling this anxious. I'm going to talk to my husband.

Through the sliding doors, I see him talking to his best friend Bertie. They're standing by the quartz island in our newly renovated kitchen, chatting away, both relaxed, swigging beer and laughing. Maybe I've been imagining the bad vibes. Please let it all be in my head. I should go in there, put my arms around Adam and kiss his neck. But . . . if he really has got the hump with me, I don't want Bertie to see any tension between us.

'Okay, guys!' my friend Naomi calls from the barbecue station. 'Lamb-and-mint burgers are ready!' She and her new boyfriend Curtis offered to be in charge of the food tonight and they're doing an amazing job. He's a chef, and it shows. Everyone's making a beeline for the grill, but Adam and Bertie are still in the kitchen. Maybe I should try to talk to my husband now, while everyone's distracted.

I head towards the open door and walk in, squinting under the bright lights. My heart sinks as Adam continues his conversation with Bertie without acknowledging me.

'Curtis's lamb-and-mint burgers are ready, if you're hungry,' I say, my voice weak.

'Starving,' Bertie replies. 'Can you bring us a couple of plates, Jas? Lots of ketchup on mine.'

This would be Adam's cue to tell Bertie to piss off and get it himself, but he doesn't. He just gives him an indulgent smirk and a slight head shake.

Bertie often makes snide comments at my expense and would probably enjoy the fact that things aren't all sunshine and roses between us. Adam says Bertie's been a 'joker' since they were at school together. That he hasn't really grown up. He says he's harmless and that his heart's in the right place. But I've never warmed to him. I think the reason he doesn't like me is that, before I came along, it was just the two of them, leading the single life. Now Adam spends most of his time with me, and I think Bertie resents it. I tried to be friends with him at the start, but I got sick of the snide remarks and so eventually gave up. Now I just tolerate him, for Adam's sake.

I don't want to give in to Bertie's request to bring them food, just because he was so rude about it, but I also can't bear to leave things like this. 'Do you want a burger, Adam?' I ask.

At my words, his hands clench at his sides. 'That's okay, Bert and I will get some grub.' He still hasn't given me any eye contact.

'Looks like you're off the hook,' Bertie says to me, flashing a grin as they walk past.

I stand in the empty kitchen feeling sick to my stomach, unsure what to do for the best. The doorbell startles me. I think everyone I invited is already here, so I wonder who it could be. I head through the narrow hallway, catching a glimpse of my reflection in the gilt-edged mirror. My long, brown hair is frizzing at the sides so I attempt to smooth it with my fingers. My lipstick has faded – I'll nip upstairs in a minute and reapply it. The bell rings again and I open the door to see a middle-aged woman with light-brown hair and iron-grey roots, wearing a pink dressing gown and a pair of green Crocs.

'Uh, hello,' I say.

'I'm your new neighbour,' she says. 'Carol. I moved in this week.'

'Oh, hello, nice to meet you. I was going to pop over to say—'

'Yes, well, the thing is, I'm exhausted and I'd like an early night, but your music and the shouting . . . is it going to go on for much longer?'

'Who is it?' Adam's deep voice sounds behind me and I step aside to make room in the doorway.

'Our new neighbour, um . . .'

'Carol,' she finishes.

'Oh,' Adam says. 'Well, you're welcome to come in for a drink. We're having a barbecue. I'm Adam Owens, and this is my wife, Jasmine.'

'I'm here because of the noise,' Carol says bluntly.

There's a short silence before Adam asks, 'Is that your dog barking?'

'What?' Carol's cheeks colour. 'Yes, Alfie's nervous because of all the people.'

'Tell you what,' Adam says. 'You stop your dog barking all hours of the day, and we'll turn down the music. Deal?'

'Well, like I said, he's only barking because—'

'Great, have a good night.' He cuts her off and heads back into the house.

I draw in a breath. Something is definitely wrong with my husband because he's never normally this rude. I have no idea what's got into him.

'I'm sorry,' I say to Carol. 'Of course we'll turn down the music. It's our wedding anniversary so we've had a little gathering, but we're not normally noisy neighbours.'

'That's good,' Carol replies. 'It's just with us being semi-detached and sharing a wall, I was worried.'

'Of course. No need to worry. Well, I'd better get back to my guests. But we'll keep it down.'

'It's fine,' she relents. 'As long as it doesn't go on too late.'

'It won't.'

She turns and retreats down the path.

I close the door and lean against it, trying to equate my Adam with the man who's been ignoring me all night and has just been breathtakingly rude to our new neighbour. But there's no similarity. What's got into him? I guess I won't find out until everyone's gone home.

The rest of the evening passes agonisingly slowly. People keep asking if I'm okay and I have to keep pretending that I'm fine. That I'm having a lovely time and nothing's wrong. Thankfully, Naomi has been occupied with keeping the barbecue going, so she hasn't noticed my discomfort. I'm glad, because she isn't exactly Adam's biggest fan. I think that's because I was annoyingly smitten with him when we first met. All I wanted to do was spend time with my new boyfriend, and I neglected her for a while. I think our friendship is finally getting back on track now. At least I hope it is. Seems like she and Bertie both had their noses pushed out of joint by me and Adam getting together.

At least everyone else appears to be having a great night. I try turning the music down a few times to keep our neighbour Carol happy, but the volume keeps creeping back up and eventually I give in. I feel a bit bad for her, but at least I know tonight is a one-off. We're not really party people, so she won't have to worry about noise in the future. It's just unfortunate timing that she's moved in this week.

Eventually, at just after midnight, the last stragglers – my workmates, and Bertie – leave in a drunken round of hugs and goodbyes. Adam and I have put on a good show that everything is all right, but when the door closes behind them, my stomach lurches with anxiety. Are we about to have our first-ever row?

I turn off the music and the house descends into silence. Adam walks past me and heads into the kitchen. I follow to see him take a roll of black bin liners from the cupboard under the sink.

'What a mess,' he mutters under his breath as he straightens up and tears off one of the liners.

I'm not sure if he's talking about the state of the house and garden, or our relationship. 'Adam,' I start, not exactly sure what I'm going to say.

He doesn't wait for me to continue, but instead strides outside and starts shoving bottles, paper plates, and cups into the bin bag, the glass clanking noisily. Normally he's a stickler for sorting recyclables from general waste, but not tonight. Everything goes in together – half-eaten burgers, used napkins, congealed salads, sticky beer cans.

'Adam,' I try again. 'What's wrong?'

His face is closed off and I worry that he's not going to answer me.

'Are you at least going to tell me why you're so angry?' I persist.

He keeps on with the task at hand, refusing to even look at me. 'If you don't know the reason, then you don't know me.'

I take a breath. 'I wanted to do something nice for our anniversary, that's all.' I pick up the roll of liners from the wooden garden table, tear one off and try unsuccessfully to open it out, but the edges are stuck together.

'"Something nice" would have been a romantic dinner – which, by the way, is what I'd planned, but I had to cancel it.'

'Oh.' I deflate even further at his explanation. 'I'm sorry I ruined your plans, but I didn't know. And I'd thought it would be a lovely surprise.'

Adam stops at the fire pit and turns to face me, his eyes glittering. 'Well, Jasmine, you thought wrong. It wasn't a surprise, it was a shock. The thought of you and our friends creeping around behind my back, whispering secrets and trying to keep me in the dark . . . that's not what I call "lovely".' He drops the almost-full bin liner on the ground, where the contents spill over on to the patio tiles. 'Please don't do anything like that ever again, okay?'

I'm so surprised that the breath leaves my body.

'*Jasmine?*'

I nod mutely and he exhales. My husband turns and walks away across the patio until he reaches the house, where he stops and turns. 'I'm going to bed,' he says. 'Sorry, but I'll be sleeping in the spare room tonight.'

My chest hollows out as I watch him go. *Happy anniversary to us.*

Chapter Three

WILLOW

I thought we were going out for casual drinks, but Gabe has booked a full-on restaurant date for this evening, which is panicking me slightly. It's harder to ditch someone partway through a meal than it is to slip out of a crowded pub.

It's been a week since I bumped into him – literally – at the café, and he messaged a day later to ask me out to dinner. I spent a few days going back and forth in my head as to whether or not I should accept his invitation, but in a moment of madness, I said yes.

Even right now, as I stand in front of the bathroom mirror, sweeping on my winged eyeliner, I'm tempted to call and cancel. But I know I would regret it. We clicked straightaway, and I realise it's been a while since I met someone who made me laugh, who made me feel seen. He's been the only thing on my mind this week and my work has suffered because of it. Thankfully my client – a woman in her sixties – was understanding when I used the wrong colour paint on her bedroom woodwork. It sucks that I'm going to have to go in on Sunday afternoon to redo it.

I've told myself to dress casually tonight, to keep things light. This date is nothing more than a little reward for managing to make it this far. This date is not the start of anything. It's simply a harmless flirtation, an enjoyable night out. A break from the calm oasis of my life. Because I can't let myself forget what's happened. What led me here to this place. If I do, then I'll be breaking the promise I made to myself. I gaze at my reflection and allow myself to remember the bad stuff, because I can't afford to let myself forget.

◆ ◆ ◆

The setting sun is just above the horizon, casting pink-and-orange hues over the bay as Gabe and I meet outside the Dolphin, a low-key spot set back from the beach. He looks better than I remember – tall, broad-shouldered, his blond hair tousled by the wind. He leans down to kiss my cheek and I catch the warm scent of his aftershave, mingled with the saltwater scent of the ocean.

'How did I not know about this place?' I ask as we walk side by side up the wooden steps. I can't tell if the chipped paint is shabby or chic. The decorator in me is itching to pick up a paintbrush and give the exterior a refresh, even though I can see its charm lies in its humbleness. 'It looks like someone's house, rather than a restaurant,' I add.

'It's a bit of a hidden gem.' Gabe glances at me, trying to gauge my reaction. 'It's been here for decades and has somehow resisted being taken over and done up. The owners are friends of my parents. I can only hope they never retire or sell up.'

'Are your parents local?' I ask.

'They were, but they retired to Spain eight years ago.'

'Nice,' I reply. 'Do you go out there much?'

He shrugs. 'We don't really get along, so . . .'

'Oh, sorry.' I regret asking about them and hope this doesn't ruin the tone of the evening.

He gives me a smile that immediately sets my mind at ease. 'No worries.' He brushes the back of my hand with his and I feel a jolt of electricity up my arm. I'm not sure if it was an intentional move on his part, but I put some space between us to stop it happening again. The man looks and smells entirely too good.

As we stroll in, I'm drawn to the easy-going vibe, the wood-panelled walls sticky with salt air and good conversation. The tables are lined with flickering candles and the gentle glow of string lights, the walls decorated with artwork, photos and seashells. I notice Gabe's warm expression and the soft twinkle in his eye as we settle into our seats at one of the best tables, overlooking the beach. The lapping waves outside mirror the furtive leaps in my chest and, despite the lingering doubts that shadow this date, there's no denying our mutual attraction.

'You look amazing, Willow,' Gabe says, holding eye contact.

My chest draws tight and I look down at my menu. 'Thanks.' Although I'm dressed casually in jeans and a black silk top, I took care with my make-up and hair, brushing my caramel bob until it shone, and I'm wearing my favourite silver earrings and necklace. 'You look good too.' I return the compliment to be polite, but I'm not lying. His pale blue shirt matches his eyes and sets off his tanned skin, the scruff on his chin giving him an edge.

He grins at me and I feel my cheeks heat up.

'Do you know what you want to order?' he asks.

I skim the menu, though nothing on it seems to register. The list of dishes blurs into an unreadable mess of letters. 'Not yet, no,' I answer.

'I know what's good here, if you'd like me to order for us both?'

My mind rebels at his offer, not wanting to cede control to someone else, even if it is something as trivial as what to eat for dinner. But I tell myself not to overreact. He's just being nice. So I shrug and nod. 'Sounds good.'

He orders the mussels to start, and I realise I was right to let him choose, as they arrive steaming and fragrant, loaded with garlic and white wine, with chunks of warm, crusty bread on the side, followed by a perfectly cooked sea bass.

'You weren't lying about the food,' I say, dabbing at my lips with a napkin.

'Told you it was good.' He mops his empty plate with a wedge of bread. 'Have to confess, I'm a bit of a foodie.'

'Nothing wrong with that,' I reply. I was anxious at the start of our date that I wouldn't be able to eat anything due to nerves, but Gabe is such easy company that it's crazy how quickly I've relaxed. 'I love the music in here,' I add.

'Yeah, Spanish guitar's the best.'

'Reminds me of being on holiday.' I close my eyes for a moment, letting the rich layers of harmony wash over me. When I open them again, Gabe is staring at me, his sapphire eyes soft and questioning. I blink and look away.

'So what music do you listen to?' he asks.

'All sorts really. But I like rock. The Black Keys, Pearl Jam, The Blue Stones.'

'Yes!' Gabe's eyes light up. 'Now we're talking. I saw Des Rocs in London last year.'

'No you didn't!'

He grins. 'He was amazing. We'll have to catch him on his next tour.'

My heart flips at his assumption that we'll still be seeing each other further down the road. For now, I allow myself the luxury of believing that it can happen.

Over the rest of the evening, we also discover a mutual love of reading and of classic films. And Gabe's sheepish admission of his obsession with goat memes leaves me laughing so hard I nearly knock over my wine glass.

Again, I question whether this is the right choice, if I'm being reckless, gambling with my fragile state by getting involved with someone. But Gabe's charm and humour unravel my worries, one laugh at a time. We bond over tangles of stories and shared quirks, passions and perspectives lining up with uncanny ease. Is it right to feel this happy? I almost forget myself, caught up in the lightness. It's been an eternity since I've known something so simple and good.

Dessert is a vanilla-scented crème brûlée, and our plates empty fast, the evening slipping through our fingers as we chat and joke. Gabe reaches across the table to lightly brush my hand again, the soft, warm touch sending a shiver down my spine. The spark unspoken, undeniable. *I am in so much trouble.*

When, finally, we've eaten more than is decent, we sip Irish coffees and Gabe calls for the bill. I pull out my credit card.

'Absolutely not,' he says.

'Let's go halves,' I push, not wanting to feel beholden.

'You can get the next one.'

'Who says there'll be a next one?' I ask, knowing full well that I'll say yes to another date.

'Well . . .' Gabe tilts his head and gazes at me. 'I think we had a good time, don't you?'

I nod grudgingly.

'And so,' he continues, a half-smile on his lips. 'Usually in these situations, if you both have a good time, then it makes sense to do it again.'

'I know, but . . .' I swallow. 'The thing is, I'm not looking to get into a relationship right now.' There, I've admitted it.

He shrugs. 'That's fine. It doesn't have to be a relationship. Just another date.'

'So you're happy to keep things casual?'

'More than happy.' Gabe smiles his devastating smile and I feel a perverse sense of disappointment that he doesn't want a relationship either. 'Although . . .' he adds.

'What?' I prompt, wondering what he might be about to say.

'I am a bit disappointed,' he finishes.

I frown and shake my head in confusion.

He nods towards my coffee. 'It's been over two hours and you haven't even tried to ruin my shirt.' He taps his chest with both hands. 'Come on, Cappuccino Girl, give it your best shot.'

'Ha ha.' I roll my eyes, while realising I love our easy banter.

As Gabe pays the bill, I gaze through the windows out on to the deck, and beyond to the view. The sun set a while ago, and now there's a fat full moon reflected in the rippling ocean. I see a figure in the distance, a girl walking alone on the beach, her dark hair gleaming in the bright moonlight. She glances our way briefly, but before I can make out her features, she turns away, walking steadily onwards.

Gabe follows my gaze. 'Everything okay?' he asks.

'Uh, yeah, just staring out to sea. The moon is amazing tonight.'

He nods. 'It really is.'

As we walk back together along the beach, Gabe reaches for my hand and I let him take it.

'You're freezing!' he exclaims, halting in his tracks to take my fingers between his, rubbing them together like he's starting a fire.

A tiny laugh escapes my lips. 'Your hands are nice and warm,' I reply, but I take mine back, letting them fall to my sides as I start walking again. He catches up, seemingly content to walk by my side without touching. I just don't feel quite ready for physical affection yet, even though a part of me is crying out for it.

When we finally make our way back to the street, I'm wrapped in a warm, giddy glow that cocoons me all the way home. Outside my block, Gabe gently kisses me goodnight on the cheek. I realise

I'm disappointed it wasn't on the lips. But I would have pulled away if he'd tried it, so it's probably best this way. Less awkward in any case.

'I'll call you,' he promises, his voice firm and confident.

'Okay,' I say as lightly as I can manage, though my voice wavers.

I linger in place like a question mark, watching him stride off along the pavement. His hands are burrowed deep in his jacket pockets, head tilted forward as if against an imaginary wind. He doesn't look back, and I stand, shivering in the chill of the evening, my heart warm with a jumble of emotions. Is this relief I feel? Dread? I hug myself and the alcohol swirls in my head, turning my thoughts into soft, blurry shapes.

After all my worrying about whether this was a good idea, I wonder if he'll even call.

Chapter Four

JASMINE

My heart bumps along with my footsteps as I walk up the carpeted stairs carrying a tray laden with all Adam's favourite breakfast foods – scrambled eggs, bacon, sausages, toast, beans, tomatoes and a large mug of extra-strong builder's tea. I'm hoping this will help fix whatever happened to us at the barbecue. I'm praying it was a blip and that we can both apologise and move past it. I never want to feel like that again. I just want my loving husband back.

He spent the night in the spare room and I haven't seen him yet this morning. I hardly slept at all last night, managing to doze off in our bed just as the sky was lightening and the birds had started singing. My eyes feel gritty and my face is dry and taut. I barely drank any alcohol at the barbecue, but my head is pounding like I have a class-A hangover. Added to that, I haven't eaten anything since yesterday lunchtime and my stomach is hollow, but I think I'd throw up if I tried to force anything down now. Even the smell of Adam's breakfast is making me nauseous. I'm sure once we've made up, my appetite will come roaring back.

I pause outside the door before giving a tentative knock and pushing it open. 'Hey, Adam,' I say softly. 'Thought you might like some breakfast.'

I blink and gaze around the room. The blinds are open and the sun streams in across the double bed, which is still made up. It doesn't look as if Adam's slept in it. Unless he got up and made it already. He must be in the bathroom.

I set the tray down on the end of the bed and return to the carpeted landing. Our house is small but perfectly formed with two upstairs bedrooms, a bathroom and an en-suite shower. There's also a little study nook with just enough room for a desk. With Adam's decorating firm doing so well, we could afford a bigger place, but he says we're better off putting our money into other properties and renting them out. So, wc have another small house, and we're about to buy a third. He says this is the quickest way to pay off our mortgage. We also own a one-bedroom flat where his dad lives rent-free. It's lovely that Adam's chosen to look after his dad in this way. Shows what a caring son he is.

We live in Guildford, a pretty riverside town in Surrey – not the cheapest place in the country. I was born and brought up here, but Adam's from Basingstoke. He moved with Bertie twelve years ago when they were nineteen. They had jobs labouring on a building site in the town centre and ended up staying. Adam now has his own business, while Bertie's a sales director at a builder's merchants.

I peer into the bathroom, but Adam's not there. Next, I check our room and the en-suite. Not there either. I look out of the bedroom window, dismayed to see our small driveway standing empty. His van is gone. Did he leave early this morning, or last night? It's Sunday, so he won't be working today, and he didn't have any plans that I know of.

I sit on my side of the bed, confused. I'm still not sure what I've done wrong. Lots of people plan surprise parties, don't they?

Adam's never mentioned that it was something he would hate. I apologised, but it wasn't enough. What should I do?

I snatch up my phone from the bedside table and check for messages, but there are none, so I call him.

'Hi, this is Adam Owens. I can't take your call right now so please leave a message and I'll get back to you.'

'Hi, Adam. Just . . . wondering where you are. Sorry I upset you last night. I didn't mean to. Please come home so I can make it up to you. I made you a nice breakfast! Hope you're okay.' I end the call reluctantly. Hopefully that should do the trick and he'll be back soon.

In the meantime, I retrieve the breakfast tray from the spare room and take it back downstairs, setting it on the island. I'm still not hungry, but I feel a little light-headed so I perch on a stool, nibble a corner of his toast and take a sip of his tea before checking my phone again. Still no messages.

I blow out a breath and gaze around the kitchen. I did most of the tidying up last night, but it's still a bit messy and the floor's sticky with spilled drinks and crumbs. I feel like curling up in bed and trying to get some more sleep, but what will Adam think if he comes home and I'm lying there feeling sorry for myself? No, I think I'll distract myself by cleaning up.

The minutes tick by and morning turns to afternoon with still no word from my husband. I've left him a couple more messages, but there's no point leaving any more. If he doesn't want to reply then what can I do? The house is now immaculate and I'm shattered and anxious.

Maybe something's happened to him. Should I call his friends? Or the hospital? Perhaps I should call his dad on the off-chance Adam's there. Then again, if he's not, I don't want to worry him. Nigel and I have always got on really well. He welcomed me as his daughter-in-law with open arms. He and Adam have a great relationship. That's part of the reason I was so drawn to my husband in the first place – the fact he's such a thoughtful son.

I pace the kitchen helplessly, swinging between fear that I've driven Adam away, and anger that he left without letting me know where he's gone. This is ridiculous.

I pick up my phone again, but this time I call my gran.

'Jazzy, love. How you doing?' It's good to hear her voice. Gran grew up in Southend-on-Sea and moved to Surrey after she got married, so she still has a faint Essex accent.

My throat constricts at the sound of her comforting voice. 'Hey, Gran. I'm okay.'

'You don't sound okay,' she replies. 'Tell me what's wrong.'

Gran is my dad's mum. He died from a heart attack when I was ten and she's more like a mum to me than my own mother, who I rarely see. After Dad died, Mum went a bit off the rails. She was out all the time, drinking a lot and hooking up with different men. I felt safer and calmer with Gran, so I ended up staying at her little terraced house more than at my own home. She's since moved into a warden-assisted flat, but she's still active and her mind is as sharp as ever.

'Honestly, I'm fine, Gran. Just rang for a chat.' I'm tempted to confide in her about Adam going AWOL, but I don't want her to worry about me, and I also don't want her to think badly of him. 'More importantly, how are you feeling?' I ask. 'Any better?'

She clears her throat. 'A bit better, thanks. This blasted cold is taking a while to shift though.'

Worry grips my chest. 'Do you need anything?'

'No, Sheila did a shop for me,' she replies. 'How was the surprise party?' she adds. 'Manage to keep it a secret?'

I swallow. 'Yes, I did. Everyone had a great time,' I reply. *Everyone except me and Adam.*

'Well, that's good. Sorry I couldn't make it. Didn't want to pass on my germs to everyone.' She pauses. 'So, you're not going to tell me what's up.'

'Just a bit tired and hungover.' I stare out through the sliding doors at a flock of starlings on the lawn, their blue-black feathers shimmering in the sun.

'Well, drink some water and have a little snooze,' she advises. 'Have you eaten today?'

'I had some toast earlier.'

'Well that's not enough, is it?' she chides. 'Make some proper lunch and you'll feel better.'

'I will, Gran. It should be me telling *you* to look after yourself!'

'We're a right pair, aren't we?' Gran chuckles. There's a muffled silence from her end and then I hear a wracking cough.

'Gran, are you okay?'

She doesn't reply, but the coughing sounds worse.

'Gran, shall I come over? Should I call the doctor?' My stomach clenches with concern.

'Hang on, love, let me get some water,' she croaks, coughing again.

I wait, my mind going into overdrive. What if her cold turns into something serious like pneumonia? Aside from Adam, she's the only family I have – apart from Mum, who doesn't really count as we barely see each other. I love Gran so much. I don't want to even contemplate her getting seriously ill.

'Ooh, that's better,' she says wheezily. 'Salt-and-vinegar crisp went down the wrong way.'

'Gran! You scared the life out of me.' I put a hand to my heart, relieved she's all right.

'Sorry, Jazzy love.' She chuckles. 'Anyway, when are you coming round next? I know you're busy, but it'd be a treat to see you.'

'Soon, I promise.' I usually visit at least once a week, but I haven't had the time recently and I realise guiltily that it's been almost two weeks since we last met up. I should have gone to see her today instead of calling, but I worried that in person she would have wrangled the truth about Adam from me as well as the news about my job. I don't want to tell her I've been made redundant until I've lined up something else. She'll worry otherwise.

'Work okay?' she asks, as if reading my mind. 'Still enjoying it? I liked that girl, Chrissie, you brought round to visit. She was a right laugh.'

'Yep, work's all good,' I lie, guilt tugging at my chest. 'And Chrissie's great. She loved you too.'

'Well, that's nice,' she replies, and I hear the smile in her voice.

Thankfully Gran changes the subject and starts telling me a funny anecdote about her neighbour. It's just what I need to take my mind off everything. I always feel better when we chat. Even on the phone, it feels like she's giving me a warm hug. I'm so glad I called. We talk for another twenty minutes or so until she tells me she has to go, as her old neighbour Barbara is at the door. I love the fact that Gran has a good social life. She's always meeting up with friends for walks, card games, book club and other activities. But, right now, I wish she was able to chat for longer.

'Say hi to Barbara from me.'

'I will. Now go and eat something, Jazzy love. I don't want you wasting away.'

Once the call ends, the house feels emptier than ever. The little flock of starlings takes flight suddenly, as though startled by something. It's such a lovely autumn day; the perfect weather to have gone out somewhere with Adam. Maybe a pub lunch in town followed by a walk along the river. Or a cycle ride in the forest. Instead, I'm here alone, going out of my mind. I toy with the idea of going for a walk anyway, but I just can't face it. I take Gran's advice and make myself a lacklustre salad, chewing half-heartedly, barely tasting a thing.

I push it aside and call Adam again, leaving another message:

'Can you just let me know you're okay? You don't have to talk to me if you don't want to, but I'm going crazy with worry here.'

I hang up and sit in pin-drop silence, willing my phone to buzz, but he doesn't respond.

The afternoon drags even more than the morning. I flick on a movie, but abandon it after fifteen minutes, restlessness gnawing at me. I take my Kindle into the garden, convinced my current thriller will take my mind off things, but I skim the same paragraph over and over without taking any of it in. Frustrated, I give it up and reach for my phone instead and fall into an endless scroll – reels, cat videos, interior-design hacks, hair transformations, feel-good reunions. Every happy ending a reminder that I'm stranded in limbo.

I know I should probably use the time more productively to research jobs and training opportunities, but instead I continue scrolling on autopilot until my eyes glaze over.

I sneak a peek at Bertie's feed, hoping for clues – maybe a story that might provide a clue to Adam's whereabouts – but there's nothing, and I'm certainly not going to contact the little tosser. He'd relish the fact that Adam and I have had a bust-up.

I hate the fact that Bertie and I have never clicked. As Adam's best friend, he could have been the brother I never had. It would have been perfect if the three of us got along, but Bertie didn't give me a chance. He's always been distant and suspicious. These days, I usually find ways to keep him at arm's length, but it's not always possible. Before Adam and I married it didn't feel like such a big deal, but now I guess I'll have to put up with him forever.

His worst offence was on our wedding day, when he stood up as best man and delivered that savage speech. At first I laughed, telling myself it was all just harmless banter. That best-man speeches are notoriously near the bone. Although, surely, the speech is supposed to roast the groom, not the bride. But then he congratulated me on 'fighting off the other gold diggers', implying I was marrying Adam for his money. As his meaning became clear, my face burned. There were a few nervous titters and I sank into my seat, humiliated. I hadn't warmed to Bertie before the wedding, but this only confirmed our mutual dislike of one another.

Adam stormed over to him after the speeches, pulled him aside and ordered him to apologise to me. I think his anger shocked Bertie who – miracle of miracles – seemed genuinely contrite. For a fleeting moment I thought maybe this would be the start of something better between the two of us. I wasn't too proud to let bygones be bygones. But no sooner than the cake was cut, Bertie slipped back into his old, obnoxious ways and I accepted that this would be how things always stood.

And yet, that wedding confrontation is how I know I chose well in marrying Adam. Seeing him stick up for me and prioritise my feelings over those of his oldest friend let me know that my husband would always have my back. Which is why his radio silence today is so confusing. So out of character. How can he have been gone all day? Is he genuinely angry with me? Is he doing it to punish me? Or has he simply lost track of time?

As dusk falls, a cold wind drifts through the garden, and I shiver in the chill air. It's still quite early, but maybe I should just give it up and go to bed, hoping that when I wake up, my husband will have returned. Although, will I even sleep? I stand, my body stiff from sitting hunched over my phone for so long.

It's properly dark now so I leave the garden and march inside, switching on the lights. I trudge upstairs to grab a sweatshirt. If he's not back by eight, I'll have to bite the bullet and call one of his friends. Maybe Tom or, at a push, Bertie. *Ugh*. Even the idea makes me grit my teeth. What a hideous day this has been. I yank my cosy blue sweatshirt from the wardrobe and pull it over my head, my chest tight with dread and longing. I just want to fix this, to hear his voice, to erase the knot of worry in my gut.

I'm halfway into a sleeve when a noise from downstairs makes me startle and freeze. My heart leaps with nerves and anticipation as the front-door lock clicks. The key turns once more, and relief floods me in a single breath.

At last, my husband is home.

Chapter Five

WILLOW

Climbing the front steps to my small apartment block, I spy my elderly neighbour, Elsie Kidd, up ahead, her arms weighed down with two bulky grocery bags she's hauled out of a neatly folded trolley-turned-shoulder-bag.

I hurry into the newly painted lobby to take the bags from her. 'Need help with these?' I offer.

She hesitates, then nods. 'Good timing, Willow.' She peers up at me over the rims of her tortoiseshell glasses. 'You look a bit less miserable than usual,' she adds.

A laugh bubbles in my chest as I realise that she's right. Ever since I started seeing Gabe, my life feels a lot brighter. I actually look forward to each day now, waking up with a spark of anticipation each morning. Not that I hated my life before, but I think I was just existing, getting through each moment. I was flat. Numb. Gabe has given me a reason to be excited about things again. I know it wasn't part of the plan to get into a relationship with anyone, but it just happened and I feel powerless to stop it. Addicted to the butterflies in my stomach, I'm torn between gratitude and fear that it's all too good to last.

Elsie's bags are impossibly heavy for someone who looks like a bird. 'Who do you have in here, Elsie? The rest of our neighbours?' I tease.

'None of your business,' she replies, but the smile in her voice blunts the edge.

We ascend the two flights of wooden stairs, her breath keeping time with her shuffling steps.

'Would you not think about moving to a ground-floor flat?' I ask, worried about what might happen if she slipped and fell while no one was around.

She pauses on a step, gripping the banister. 'And what do you think that would achieve?' she rasps. 'I'd grow weaker and weaker, wouldn't I? It would get harder to walk to the shops, and then someone like you would come along and say, "Why don't you get your shopping delivered?" Cutting out stairs is the slippery slope to being a bed-bound old woman. What is it you young'uns say? "Use it or lose it".' She cackles at this.

'I suppose so,' I reply with a smile, unable to fault her logic.

We finally reach her door, which is the one right next to mine, where she pauses as if considering inviting me in – a thing she's never done before. A flicker of mischief crosses her face. 'Why don't you—' she begins, but we're both startled by the sharp click of heels.

Turning, I see a young, dark-haired woman coming along the corridor behind us.

The woman looks up with a questioning smile. 'Hello,' she breathes. 'Do you live here? I'm Priya. Just moved in down the hall.'

Her greeting fills the small space with fresh energy, and I instantly warm to her, wanting to chat. But Elsie unlocks her door, brusquely snatches the shopping bags from me and retreats into her flat, closing the door behind her with a defiant clunk.

Priya stares at me, wide-eyed. 'Ok-ay,' she says. 'Did I say something to offend her?'

I shake my head. 'That's Elsie. When I first moved in, she ignored me for a year. Don't worry, she'll warm up to you eventually. I'm Willow, by the way. I live here.' I gesture to the door adjacent to Elsie's.

'Great,' she beams. 'I'm just at the end of the landing.' She points down the hall.

'Lucky you. You get that gorgeous sea view. I just get the alleyway and the car park.'

'The view really is spectacular,' she agrees. 'You'll have to come round and see it for yourself.'

'That would be nice,' I reply.

'Priya!' a deep voice calls from the direction of her flat.

'Oops, better go,' she says. 'My parents are helping me unpack. But they're a bit much sometimes. Had to nip out for a sneaky ciggie. Don't tell.' She puts a finger to her glossy lips before popping a mint in her mouth. 'I think we're going to be good friends,' she adds with a wink before turning to go.

I stand for a moment, flattered by her friendliness, but also unsettled by the abruptness of it all. I take the keys from my pocket and open the door to my apartment, stepping inside and gently closing the door behind me with a sigh. I slip off my work trainers, the wooden floor smooth and cool beneath my socks. The familiar scent of my apartment is a reassuring mix of lavender from my candles and the faint hint of coffee from my morning cup. But there's something else too, an aroma that I can't quite place. The air in here has felt different recently. Fresher.

Maybe that's because my life here is changing. So much that I almost feel like a different person. Someone I used to be a long time ago. After months of solitude, I've met a man that I like. Incredibly, we've been seeing each other for almost four weeks. And now it seems as though I might have made a new friend out on the landing.

As I head to the sofa, looking forward to putting my feet up, the air is thick with the possibility of these new connections. Yet, within this glow of anticipation, I feel the carefully woven threads of my life coming undone, leaving me . . . vulnerable. The glimmer of happiness I'm starting to feel is also tinged with the fear that my meticulously constructed existence might be unravelling.

Chapter Six

JASMINE

I take a breath, trying to gather my thoughts. Are Adam and I about to have an argument? I'm not sure whether to be concerned or defensive.

The front door slams, making me jump. 'Jasmine! Are you home?' At least he doesn't sound angry.

'Upstairs!' I call back. 'Hang on, I'll come down.' A quick glance in my dressing-table mirror shows dark circles beneath my eyes and a few angry-looking spots on my chin. My hair's a tangled mess so I twist it up into what looks like an even messier bun and smooth down my wrinkled sweatshirt. Please let us make up and put this episode behind us as an unfortunate blip.

Downstairs, my husband is in the kitchen pouring himself a glass of water. He looks up as I walk in. 'Hey,' he says.

'Where were you?' I ask tentatively. 'I was worried.'

He passes me the glass and I take it, gulping down the cool liquid. I hadn't realised I was so thirsty.

'Sorry,' Adam replies, pouring himself a glass and taking a sip. 'Should have told you I was going out.'

He moves around the large kitchen island, settling on to one of the stools beside me, and fixes me with a look that's hard to decipher. He said he was sorry, but his expression is somehow blank.

I lower my gaze. 'I'm sorry too,' I offer. 'I honestly had no idea you had a thing about surprises. I promise I won't do anything like that again.'

He nods slowly. 'I know I overreacted, Jas. I just hate the idea of you keeping secrets from me. Again, I'm sorry.'

'Okay,' I reply, relief tugging at my chest. 'Apology accepted.'

His jaw tightens, as though there's a deeper tension simmering beneath the surface.

Eager to bridge the gap between us, I rush to explain. 'But it wasn't really a secret. I was trying to do something special for you. It was supposed to be a *nice* surprise. Like you secretly planned to take me out to dinner. I just wanted to show you how much you mean to me.'

Adam's eyes narrow and a deep furrow forms between his brows as he replies in a clipped tone, 'That's not the same thing.'

'No?' I'm genuinely baffled. 'Why not?'

His voice grows more measured. 'Because your "surprise" involved making arrangements with all our friends behind my back.'

I feel a surge of desperation, willing him to understand. 'But . . . we were trying to do something nice for you.'

'I don't like secrets,' he says, gripping the countertop and enunciating each word.

'Okay, well, I know that now.' I still feel caught off guard by how my husband is reacting.

In a sudden shift, his shoulders sag and he stands up, facing me directly. 'Look, I never told you, but my mum didn't die. She left us.'

I manage a soft, stunned 'Oh' as his admission hangs in the room.

Adam sighs heavily. 'She was having an affair, and neither Dad nor I knew about it until she was gone. All we got was a note, and then she vanished from our lives.'

'No! That's awful.' I take his hand and squeeze it. 'I'm so, so sorry.'

With a bitter, almost resigned laugh, he adds, 'So that's another reason I don't like surprises.'

'Another reason?' I frown and then it clicks into place. 'Your ex.'

He gives a barely perceptible nod, his attention locked on some distant, painful memory.

When we first got together, Adam told me that his ex-girlfriend had left him without any explanation. She'd originally worked for him as a decorator. They'd moved in together, and then she just disappeared. No explanation. Nothing. He thinks she went off with someone else. This, coupled with what he's just told me about his mum, explains why he reacted so harshly last night.

'I hope you know I would never do anything like that,' I say.

He shrugs. 'Just don't tell Dad I told you about Mum. He doesn't like to talk about it. He felt betrayed. Humiliated. I think that's why he preferred that everyone thought she'd died.'

'I won't say a thing. Thanks for opening up to me. I'm touched.' I stroke his stubbled cheek and tilt my face up to kiss him. 'Did you ever try to find her?'

His face clouds over. 'No. And I never will. And, Jasmine, please don't ask me about her again. I don't like talking about it. I'm only telling you now so you understand why I reacted so badly.'

'Of course. Whatever you want. But if you do ever feel like you want to talk, you know I'm here for you.'

He nods, his eyes softening. 'You know I love you, Jas. Yesterday was just . . . I think I was overwhelmed and I took it out on you. I'm really sorry.'

'Nothing to say sorry for. Let's forget it.'

'I don't deserve you.' He wraps his arms around me and pulls me close. I feel his heart beating against my chest and I want to protect him, to let him know that I would never hurt him like he's been hurt in the past. I'm not like that. I need him to know that I'm a safe space. That he can tell me anything.

I understand why he kept his mum's disappearance a secret, but, as his revelation sinks in, I can't help feeling a little uncomfortable that, when we first met, we bonded over our parents' deaths. We talked about how terrible it was to lose a parent at such a young age. It was part of why I felt so drawn to him. All that deep sadness I carry, it's hard to explain to someone who hasn't been through it. And now he's just told me that that wasn't true. That the whole of our first, falling-in-love conversation was a lie.

I guess the truth of the matter is that we both lost parents and it doesn't matter how, but I wish he'd felt that he could have confided in me back then. That he could have been truthful. He's talking about hating secrets when all this time he's kept this huge secret about his mum.

'I bought a takeaway as a peace offering,' Adam says, tipping his head towards a couple of large, white paper bags on the countertop.

'I thought I smelled something nice,' I reply, my appetite zooming back. I knew I'd want to eat something as soon as we'd made up. We're not quite normal around each other yet, and I'm still processing his revelation, but at least we're talking civilly. 'Chinese?' I ask.

'Prawn noodles for you and lemon chicken for me.'

'Yum.' I fetch us a couple of bowls and run the hot-water tap over them to warm them up, my mind still ticking over what he just told me. 'Wine?'

He shakes his head. 'Early start tomorrow.'

'Shall we eat in here, or in the lounge?' I dry the bowls. 'Might be nice to cosy up in there. I could light a fire.'

'Here,' he says. 'It's nicer sitting at the table to eat.'

I nod. 'Okay.' I don't know why, but I'm nervous to ask him where he's been all this time. He hasn't volunteered the information yet, so it looks like I'm going to have to try to find out. I put the bowls on the table while Adam gets the cutlery and brings the food over.

'What have you been doing today?' he asks, beating me to it.

'Cleaning the house.' I gesture to our pristine kitchen.

'I can see. It looks good.' He nods approvingly, and trails a finger down my cheek, before reaching back and freeing my hair from the scrunchie I used to put it up. He runs his fingers through my tangled locks and steps back to look at me. 'That's better. You know how I like your hair to be loose.'

I pull at my hair self-consciously. 'It's getting a bit too long. I need to get a trim. Or maybe I should go for a shorter cut – what do you think?'

'Definitely not,' Adam replies. 'It's perfect as it is.' He gathers a large hank in his hands and gently tugs me towards him with it. 'No getting it cut,' he says softly, pressing his lips to the tresses in his hand. 'Did you go out at all today?' he asks, letting my hair fall and switching subjects abruptly.

I push my hair behind my ears. 'No. I chatted with Gran on the phone and then sat in the garden this afternoon.'

'Reading?'

I shake my head. 'Couldn't concentrate on my book so I ended up scrolling online,' I admit.

He rolls his eyes and sits at the table. 'You should delete those social media apps. Such a waste of time.'

'I like watching videos and seeing what my friends are up to.' I sit opposite him. 'Louie's hilarious on there. Anyway, you're on Instagram.'

'Only for work,' he replies. 'Clients like to look at the before-and-afters.'

'I suppose so.' I start removing the cartons from the bags, passing the rice over to Adam. 'So, where did you go today?' I finally ask.

'Met one of the guys from work at the golf club.'

'The golf club?' I echo. That's the last thing I expected him to say. 'I didn't know you played golf?'

His chin rises. 'Marc's dad's a member, so he invited me along. I was pretty good actually.'

'I wasn't criticising – just surprised, that's all.' I dump a large portion of noodles into my bowl. 'So, you were there all day?'

'Most of the day, yeah.' He says it lightly, but he isn't forthcoming about where he was the rest of the time and, for some reason, I'm nervous to ask. I also want to know if he left the house this morning or last night, but my heart pounds at the thought of questioning him further. Because something in his manner tells me it's not a good idea. I'm also getting the uncomfortable feeling that he might have stayed out late . . . not exactly to punish me, but to make me worry about him. To make me feel bad. Although, on second thoughts, surely I'm wrong about that. My husband has never been vindictive.

I take a mouthful of noodles, relieved this awfulness is more or less behind us now. But I still feel unsettled by Adam's revelation this evening and, more than that, by his reaction to the surprise party. Ever since we've been together, he's always been this straightforward, loving person, never one to play games or make me feel bad. That's why the past twenty-four hours has felt so disconcerting. But I guess all marriages go through their ups and downs. It was probably naive of me to expect plain sailing forever.

Anyway, whatever last night was, at least I now know why he was so upset, and thankfully he's apologetic about it. As I eat, I'm gradually beginning to feel more normal about things. I think it's probably best if we just put the whole awful episode behind us.

I smile at my husband across the table, and feel peace for the first time today when he smiles back.

Chapter Seven

WILLOW

'Happy anniversary,' Gabe says, as the waitress brings out a pink iced cupcake sporting a single silver candle.

'That's so cute!' I cry.

'Blow it out and make a wish, Cappuccino Girl,' he says, smiling across at me.

'We should blow it out together,' I reply, loving his little nickname for me.

Gabe has brought me back to the Dolphin for our one-month anniversary, which was totally unexpected. I never dreamed he'd be so thoughtful as to remember the date we met. Not this soon in our relationship anyway. But, I have to admit, it's been going better than I could have ever imagined. We've continued to connect on so many levels, and the man is so-o-o handsome I can hardly stand it.

We blow out the candle and I wish for my life to stay as happy as it is right now, and for the past to stay in the past. I look up and lock eyes with Gabe, wondering what he wished for.

'Dinner was delicious,' I say. 'Thanks for this evening.'

'You're welcome.' He looks as though he's about to say something, but then our coffees arrive and the moment is gone.

We're happy to sit quietly for a while, sharing the cupcake and sipping our drinks. That's another thing I love about him – the fact that we don't have to fill the silence with constant chatter. He's as comfortable as I am to just 'be'. I guess that's a recent thing for me, a side effect of living alone.

I catch Gabe's eye and we smile. 'You've got a bit of chocolate cake on your . . .' I point to the edge of his lip.

'I'm saving that for later.' He reaches for it with his tongue. 'There?'

'No, other side.'

'Here?' He finally licks it away.

'Yeah, gone. You look like a lizard,' I say with a snort.

He flicks his tongue back and forth in response.

'Nutter.'

'Charming,' he replies with a smirk. 'Are you around this weekend?'

I pause. There's nothing I'd like more than to see Gabe tomorrow or Sunday, but are things moving too fast? Maybe we should ease off a bit. The words leave my mouth before I can stop them. 'Yeah, I think so.'

'Cool.' His blue eyes light up. 'Thought we could go for a walk in the New Forest, or the beach, wherever you prefer.'

'Either sounds great.' I mean it. My heart lifts at the thought of us spending more time together.

'I really need to get outside in nature,' he adds wistfully. 'Work's a pain. And my flatmates are doing my head in.'

'You can come round to mine whenever you like,' I offer. 'It must be so annoying living with people you don't get along with.'

'I mean, they're okay,' Gabe amends. 'It's just, they're always there, making a mess in the kitchen and the bathroom, and they're so bloody noisy. It feels . . . claustrophobic.'

I give a sympathetic nod, realising how lucky I am to be able to live alone. 'I can imagine. Do you have to stay there? Can't you move?'

'Not yet,' he replies. 'But once my tenancy is up, I'm out of there.'

'You said work's annoying too?'

'It is, but I don't want to sit here moaning. Sorry.' He shakes his head as if clearing his brain of unwanted thoughts.

'I don't mind. Sometimes you just have to get things off your chest.'

'I guess you're right. It does help.' He tilts his head and stares at me for a moment. 'You're easy to talk to, Willow.'

'Thanks.' My cheeks are heating under his gaze. I look away and lean back in my chair, enjoying being the person that Gabe wants to open up to. After so long spent in my own company, or with passing acquaintances, it's good to be making a real connection with someone. Gabe is gentle and uncomplicated. He's just what I need.

My attention is captured by a figure striding along the beach, highlighted by an almost full moon in a clear black sky. I think it might be my new neighbour, Priya, and I get a strange feeling of déjà vu.

'Everything okay?' Gabe asks.

'Everything's perfect,' I reply, shaking myself out of my reverie.

'Perfection's good,' he says with a smile. 'I like you, Willow.'

My heart lifts again. 'I like you too.'

He drains his coffee cup. 'Shall we go?'

This evening he lets me split the bill with him, and we head back along the beach and up the gravel path towards my street, his arm slung around my shoulders. I'm looking forward to this hopefully being the night we sleep together for the first time. Gabe's been surprisingly gentlemanly about the whole issue of sex, hardly making any moves, aside from some deep kisses we've shared at the end of our dates. At first, I wanted him to be more forward, to ask to come up to my flat, but he said he's enjoying taking things slow. He said he doesn't want to mess things up, and I realise I like that about him. It's everything I've never had before.

At the end of my street, Gabe stops dead.

'Everything okay?' I ask.

He turns and dips his head towards me. 'Everything's great,' he replies, his lips finding mine.

I sink into his kiss, threading my fingers through his blond hair and pressing my hips against his. He kisses me back harder and I wish we were in my bedroom already. But then he pulls away.

'I should go, before we get carried away.'

'It's okay, you can carry me away.' I give him a smile.

'There's nothing I'd like more,' he says, running a finger down my cheek, 'but we're supposed to be taking things slow, remember?'

I want to tell him that taking things slow is overrated, and that I need him to come home with me right now. But I also don't want to come across as desperate. This is the part of relationships that I hate – the not knowing how to play things. Gabe and I seem to be on the same page about everything except this. But I tell myself that it's still early days. That it's better this way than him wanting to sleep with me and then losing interest. We're building a proper, solid foundation.

'I enjoyed tonight.' I take a step back from him towards my home. 'Thank you.'

'You're welcome.' He gives a mock bow.

I giggle and start moving away. 'Let me know about that walk.'

'Yeah. I'll give you a call tomorrow.'

I take a breath as I walk off, already feeling lonely in his absence. I worry that I've become too dependent on his company. That he's all I can think about. It's good he's not coming back with me tonight. I need to cool down. To really think about where this might be going, and if I can even risk that happening.

'Willow?'

I look up to see Priya loitering outside our apartment block, her infectious grin appearing, her dark hair spilling over her shoulders like silk. A cigarette dangles between her fingers.

'Hey,' I reply with an answering smile, happy for the welcome distraction. 'Was that you on the beach earlier?'

She nods. 'Yes, were you down there too? You should have come and said hello. I go walking on the shoreline most evenings. It's so relaxing, helps me sleep better.'

'Nice, I think I'll get into that habit too.' It's funny how we only met a few days ago, but I already feel totally at ease in her company.

Priya flicks ash from her cigarette. 'So, were you out walking, or . . . ?'

'I was actually on a date with this guy I've been seeing.' It bursts out of me before I know it, a revelation coated in the kind of hopeful naivety I thought I'd left behind a long time ago.

'Ooh, tell me all about it.' Priya's eyes shine.

We fall easily into conversation. I tell her about my night and gush about how wonderful it was, maybe oversharing, but she's easy to talk to, and it's impossible to hold back. She listens attentively, letting me ramble on as I mention how unexpected it was, how long it's been since anyone made me feel like this. She nods in understanding, leaning against the railing. Turns out she's been dealing with her own romantic ups and downs, but she doesn't go into detail. She takes a last drag on her cigarette and I watch the smoke coil into the dark air.

We linger on the pavement a little longer, shivering a little in the October air, neither of us making the move to go inside.

'I don't normally smoke,' Priya admits, 'but it's been so stressful, moving house and breaking up with my . . . oh, you don't want to hear all my problems. Sorry. I'm not going to bring you down after your date.'

'I don't mind,' I reply, interested in her life. I've been starved of real conversation for so many months that it's good to feel like someone might want to open up to me. 'You can talk about it if it helps. Or not, if you'd rather not.'

She sighs and tells me she's just extricated herself from a long, complicated relationship and that she's enjoying her independence, the freedom of answering to no one. 'I just think it's easier to be single,' she adds. 'Safer. Better for my mental health, anyway.' She gives a tiny laugh.

A chill slips under my skin. Suddenly Priya's words make my night seem fragile, a soap bubble ready to pop. My buried thoughts start surfacing and I can't help but think she might be right.

But if that's the case, then should I end things with Gabe before they get deeper? I know it would be the sensible thing to do. But I already know, with a beat of unease, that it's the last thing I want.

Chapter Eight

JASMINE

'I can't believe that's it,' Louie says, as we walk out of the ugly red-brick building where we've worked together for the past year or so. 'Our last day.'

Chrissie pulls me under the protection of her red umbrella. It might only be mid-October, but the cold rain feels as though we've been plunged into the depths of winter. 'End of an era,' she says, linking arms with me.

'A very short era,' Tina grumbles, tucking her black curls into the hood of her navy parka and opening her brolly – which Louie ducks beneath, giving her a cheeky grin.

'I know.' Chrissie bumps my hip as she swerves a puddle. 'But I feel like I've known you lot forever. Gutted we won't be working together anymore.'

'Same,' I reply, my stomach dipping at the uncertainty this redundancy has brought to my life.

'We should start up our own company,' Louie declares, taking off his rain-speckled glasses and giving them a wipe with his scarf. 'Then we could work together forever.'

'Doing what exactly?' Tina asks, rolling her eyes.

'Ooh, yes.' Chrissie stops in the middle of the pavement and someone behind bumps into me and swears. 'We could do something fun, like . . . like . . .'

'Excuse me,' the woman behind says, barging past.

'Rude,' Chrissie calls after her.

'Anyway,' I say as we start moving again. 'My car's parked miles away, over in Cabel Road, so . . .'

'Leave it there and get a taxi home,' Louie suggests. 'There aren't any parking restrictions. You can pick it up tomorrow.'

'I can't.' I dread explaining that I won't be joining them at our work's leaving do at the Coach and Horses. I couldn't face telling them earlier because I knew they'd kick up a fuss and try to persuade me to come. 'Sorry, but I'm not going,' I blurt out.

'*What?*' Chrissie screeches, coming to a halt again, to the annoyance of yet another hapless pedestrian.

'What do you mean you're not going?' Tina asks. 'You can't leave me with this load of reprobates.'

'Oi.' Louie gives her a mock glare.

'Why not?' Chrissie's blue eyes glitter with disappointment.

I sigh. 'Adam's booked a table at the Cavendish to cheer me up after my last day.'

'Didn't you tell him about the pub?' Chrissie says. 'Everyone's going.'

'He forgot,' I reply weakly. 'And I didn't want to hurt his feelings by telling him I couldn't go to dinner. Not after he did something so nice.'

'What about *our* feelings?' Chrissie pouts.

'He's invited too,' Louie adds. 'Call him and tell him to meet us there. You can go to the Cavendish another night.'

'Can we at least get into the pub to have this conversation?' Tina says. 'Because it's blowing a gale and my make-up's getting ruined.'

'You guys go,' I urge. 'Post lots of piccies.' But then I remember that I recently deleted all my social media apps so I won't be able to see their photos. I think Chrissie's profile is set to public, so at least I should be able to see her posts without logging in. I hadn't realised how much we all rely on social media to connect. It's weird not having it anymore. Adam says we should be more connected to the real world than the online world. That it's better for our mental health. I do agree, but the downside is that I feel a bit cut off from my friends. I can see where he's coming from though, as my scrolling habit had definitely been getting out of control. I'll have way more time for other things now, especially as I won't be working for a while.

'Surely you can come for one quick drink?' Chrissie wheedles.

I check my watch. 'Sorry, I'm already late as it is. I need to shower and change.'

She shakes her head and sighs. 'We'll miss you, Jas.'

I give them all a quick hug and start jogging back to the car, battling the wind and rain without Chrissie's umbrella to keep me dry. As I hurry along the rain-slicked pavements, and dart across the busy rush-hour roads, I try not to feel guilty about abandoning my friends on our final day of work together. Instead, I think about how lucky I am to be spending a romantic evening with my husband in a lovely restaurant.

So why do I feel nervous?

Chapter Nine

JASMINE

Opposite me, Adam's head is bowed as he concentrates on the menu, his hand pushing back a lock of dark hair that keeps flopping into his eyes. It's warm and serene in the Cavendish. Despite every table being booked, the atmosphere is hushed, the complete opposite of the Coach and Horses where my work friends will be commiserating with one another while doing their best to have a laugh at the same time. I wonder who's drunk, who's making a show of themself, what mini-dramas might be unfolding. Of course, it's great to be here with Adam, but I can't help the deep FOMO that's settling over me. It would have been fun for me and Adam to go there together, but he's not the greatest fan of my work friends. He thinks Chrissie's nosy, that Tina's stuck-up, and that Louie is a drama queen. He just doesn't know them well enough.

My attention is snagged by the family to our right who have started laughing at something one of their three teenage children is saying, and I wonder what it must be like to be part of such a nice dynamic. To grow up in such a warm cocoon of love, with parents and siblings. Of course, I'm speculating. They could be putting on a front. Pretending to be a happy family, when in reality they're—

'Jasmine . . . Jas?' Adam interrupts my musings. 'I think we should have the Mediterranean sharing platter. What do you think?'

I turn to my husband. 'Yes, sure, if you like.' It's not what I would have chosen – I'm in the mood for something with fries – but I'm happy to agree as it's only available for two people, so if I didn't share he wouldn't be able to have it.

'You don't sound too sure,' he grumbles. 'What are you looking at?' His gaze drifts over and he smiles. 'I'd like us to have that. A family, lots of laughter.'

'Same,' I reply. 'One day.'

'Soon?' he adds, his smile deepening.

'Umm . . .' I wish Adam had never caught me looking. I wasn't staring at them with the longing to have kids; I was staring with envy at the teenagers growing up in a big, loving family. Now, my curiosity has sparked a conversation I was hoping to avoid. I know Adam thinks it's the perfect time to start a family as he's mentioned it on several occasions, but I would really like to do something for myself first. I've wanted to broach the subject of my career ever since I got made redundant.

Back when Adam and I first met, I had a uni place to study nursing, but he suggested that we go travelling around Australia and New Zealand for a couple of months the following Christmas, so I deferred my place for a year and then never ended up going to uni. So I feel that now would be the perfect time to reapply.

I don't regret postponing my studies; we had an incredible time down under. Adam was the perfect boyfriend, taking charge and organising the whole trip, but also taking time to find out the places I wanted to visit. That blissful holiday was where we truly got to know one another – swimming, sightseeing, trekking, meeting new people. He charmed everyone we met and was always so attentive, introducing me proudly as his girlfriend. It made me feel so special and loved.

During those long, warm evenings, the two of us talked about everything. Our upbringings, our hopes for the future, his business goals, my dreams of becoming a nurse. I loved having someone to open up to. To plan with. It was exciting yet comforting at the same time. With Adam, I felt as though I could do anything, be anyone. I think I need to remind him of this. Of how we supported one another. How we connected.

I take a large sip of my wine. 'Remember when we went travelling?'

Adam's eyes take on a wistful expression. 'That was such a great trip.'

'I know. Can't believe it was almost two years ago.'

'Was it really?' He shakes his head. 'It would be good to go back someday. Maybe for our ten-year anniversary.'

'Definitely.' I take another sip of my drink, wondering why this conversation is making me so anxious. 'Remember, back then, we talked about our futures?' I say carefully. 'You wanted to grow the business, and now look at it – you're doing so well. I'm really proud of you, Adam.'

'Thanks, Jas.' He looks at me and smiles his true, warm smile. The one that made me fall in love with him in the first place. 'That means a lot,' he adds.

'And remember I told you how I wanted to get my nursing degree,' I say. 'I'd planned to do it a couple of years ago. Before we met.'

'Oh, yeah,' he agrees. 'It's funny how things move on, isn't it? How dreams change.'

'Thing is,' I continue, 'I'd still like to do that – study to become a nurse, I mean.'

He doesn't reply. Just looks back down at the menu and drums his fingertips on the table.

I continue, my voice taking on a firmer tone. 'So it would probably make sense to do it before we have kids.'

Adam lifts his head and raises an eyebrow. 'You still want to go to uni?'

My stomach knots and I don't know why, because surely this isn't anything to get worried about. It's just me having a conversation with my husband about what I'd like to do next. And it's not as if this is new information. 'Well, it makes sense, I guess.'

'I'm not sure it does,' he replies, a hurt expression crossing his features.

'I just mean that it would be harder to do it after we have kids,' I clarify. 'Harder to juggle kids and uni.'

'Ready to order?' I realise the waiter is now standing by our table expectantly.

'You'd better ask my wife,' Adam says with a smile. 'She's the one making all the decisions around here today.'

My heart thumps at Adam's underlying tone. He's trying to come across as jokey with the waiter, but the look in his eyes tells me he's upset by my admission.

The waiter smiles and turns towards me, not picking up on the subtext. Or, if he is, he's hiding it well.

'Umm, we'd like the sharing platter, please.' I point to the menu, my voice sounding feeble to my ears.

'You don't sound too sure,' Adam relents. 'Have something else if you'd prefer.'

'No, the sharing platter's good.' I offer him a smile that, thankfully, he returns.

Once the waiter leaves with our order, an awkward silence infects the atmosphere and I don't know what to say to break it. The last time things were this strained was at our anniversary barbecue last month. I thought that was a blip in our relationship, but Adam's whole demeanour is suddenly back to cold and distant, which has me swallowing hard and twisting the napkin in my lap, my brain scrambling for how to make things better.

I feel like he's waiting for me to speak, but when I open my mouth and start to ask if he's okay, he cuts me off. 'We've only been married a year, Jas, and you already want to go off to uni. Do you know how that makes me feel?'

'Oh. No, I didn't mean that.' My heart relaxes at his words, realising he's misunderstood me. 'I wouldn't be going off anywhere. I'd study locally. Of course I'd never want us to live apart.'

I'm waiting for him to realise that it's fine, that he's got the wrong end of the stick, but his expression remains fixed, his green eyes still glittering with hurt. He shakes his head. 'If you go to uni, then we may as well be living apart,' he mutters. 'Doesn't matter where you study. We'll never get to spend any time together. My work's already time-consuming. You'll be studying and working twenty-four-seven. Is our marriage really so bad that you want to spend all that time away from me?'

I reach across the table to take one of his hands in mine. 'Of course not. That's not why I want to . . .' I take a breath, trying to think of a way to express my needs without him taking it the wrong way.

'And how many years would you be studying?' he asks. 'I don't want us to be old parents. I don't want to wait five more years, or however long it would be.'

'We wouldn't be old,' I reply. 'We'd be in our thirties, which is still pretty young.'

'If that's what you really want to do, then I can't stop you,' Adam says, putting his other hand on top of mine, his tone softening. 'But you should take some time to mull things over. Think about what uni would mean for our marriage. There's no rush to decide what to do next. Enjoy the break. Most people would kill for some time to properly relax without worrying about finances.' He takes a sip of his drink and leans back in his chair.

'Okay. I'll definitely take some time to mull it over.'

'That's all I'm asking,' he says, a corner of his mouth quirking upwards.

'Just nipping to the loo,' I say, scraping my chair back and standing up. Stupidly, I feel as though I might be about to cry and I don't want Adam to see. I don't want tonight to turn into a drama. I head past the bar, tears blurring my eyes. I push open the door to one of the toilets and lock it behind me, exhaling and trying to get my emotions under control.

Is Adam against me working? Even if we were to start a family, I'd still want to work. I'm a person who needs to be doing things. Why am I feeling selfish for thinking this way? I take a tissue from my bag and blot the area beneath my eyes, catching the tears that won't stop coming. This is ridiculous – *stop crying*. I inhale and give my head a shake to try to dislodge all these worrying thoughts, but they keep on coming.

I know I should be grateful that my lovely husband is willing to take care of me while I work out what I want to do. But the trouble is, I already *know* what I want to do. I want a career, and I'm realising that Adam might not want that for me. Hopefully, once he sees I'm giving his concerns some consideration, he'll eventually come around to the idea of me studying. If not, I don't know what we'll do.

For tonight, I think the best idea is to change the subject and talk about things that won't cause any friction, like Adam's work, holiday plans, and what we're doing for Christmas. I square my shoulders and head back out into the restaurant, determined to salvage the evening. To get things back on track between us.

Chapter Ten

WILLOW

I ring the doorbell to Priya's flat, clutching a bottle of wine in one hand and a bunch of flowers in the other. I bought them from the local supermarket on my way home from work, and I'm regretting my choice as the blossoms look infinitely more wilted than they did in the shop.

A few seconds pass before the door swings open and an elegant woman stands before me. It's immediately clear that I'm underdressed in my black jeans and striped top. She has the same dark hair as Priya, expensively layered and cut, and is wearing a fitted knee-length hot-pink patterned dress with an emerald-green jacket. The combination should clash hideously, but on her it just looks stunning.

'Wow,' I say, trying and failing to sound casual. 'You look . . . amazing.'

'Thank you,' she replies with a warm smile. 'You must be Willow. What a beauty you are. Those eyes, and such thick hair. I'm Priya's mum, Urmila. She's told us so much about you. How lucky she is to have you in the same apartment block.'

I'm taken aback by her warmth, unused to so many compliments, and not sure how to respond. I've only known Priya for a week, so I don't feel as though I deserve all this praise.

'This is my husband, Ted. Priya's dad,' she adds as a tall, broad-shouldered man comes up behind her, running a hand through his thick grey hair. He's dressed in camel chinos and a rust-coloured sweater that looks like it could be cashmere.

'Ted Philips,' he says, shaking my hand. 'Nice to meet you, Willow.' His voice is expensive-sounding. 'It is *Willow*?'

'Yes, sorry, yes,' I stammer, then thrust the bedraggled flowers into Urmila's arms. 'These are for you.'

'Lovely, thank you,' she replies graciously, kissing both my cheeks, her rich perfume blending with the delicious aroma of Indian food. 'Come in, come in,' she cries.

Ted takes the wine, glancing approvingly at the label, and I thank all the gods I spent the extra tenner on a decent bottle.

Priya insisted on having me over to her place for supper to meet her parents. 'You'll love them,' she promised. 'If I invite them over, Mum will make us a feast.' I was happy to accept her invitation. I can't remember the last time I had a proper home-cooked meal.

'Willow!' Priya gets up from the plum-coloured velvet sofa. She's dressed in a green trouser suit and a violet silk shirt, her hair caught up in a ponytail. Despite her diminutive size, she looks like a supermodel.

'Wow!' I gush yet again. 'You look . . . Let's just say, you and your mum should be featured in all the fashion magazines. Like, all of them.'

'Shut up,' she says, laughing. 'Me and Mum like to dress up, that's all. I'm so glad you could make it. Mum's been cooking for days in preparation.'

'Your place is gorgeous,' I enthuse, glancing around the living room and contrasting it with my plain flat that comes up woefully short in comparison.

Priya's home is an explosion of colour and personality, every corner buzzing with a cosy vibrance. Indian rugs layer the wooden floor with bright patterns. Scatter cushions of every hue are nestled in the couch, and the soft yellow walls are adorned with striking family photos. In one, a younger Priya grins, her arm draped over an oversized teddy bear. In another, she's a gangly teenager standing beneath a wisteria-draped gazebo with her parents and an older boy who could be her brother.

Priya sees me staring. 'That's our house,' she says. 'Where I grew up.'

'It's so pretty.'

The aroma of spices fills the air, making my mouth water with anticipation. By the window, a table is set for four, a sumptuous red-and-gold tablecloth beneath dishes heaped with rich curries, fragrant rice, and warm naan bread.

'Let's get this bottle open.' Ted unscrews the cap in one swift motion. He has the same sparkle in his eyes as Priya as he fills the glasses with an extravagant pour, the wine sloshing dangerously close to the brim. He hands us one each.

'Cheers!' Priya says.

'Here's to new friends and neighbours,' Urmila adds.

'To new friends and neighbours,' we all toast, clinking our glasses.

'Can I do anything to help?' I ask.

'No,' Urmila says, shaking her head and gesturing to the small, square table. 'Come, sit, sit. It's all prepared.'

I settle myself opposite Priya and diagonally opposite Ted. Urmila hovers around the table, dishing up a mountain of food on to our plates before eventually taking her own seat next to me. I place the napkin on my lap and take a large sip of wine. It really is good.

Priya's parents clearly dote on her, babying her like she's a princess. I'm a little envious and wonder what it must be like to have that much love showered on you. Although they seem to have a similar generosity towards me, treating me warmly as if I'm a member of the family.

I take a mouthful of rice and butter chicken, savouring the blend of flavours. 'This food is incredible.'

'Told you Mum was a good cook,' Priya says. 'Try the potato curry, it's delish.'

'We're so happy Priya has a lovely girl like you living in her block.' Urmila's voice is soft and sincere. 'I can tell you two will be good friends. You will keep her from getting lonely, yes? You'll keep an eye on each other.'

I feel strangely on the spot, shifting in my seat under the weight of their collective gaze. But I'm not sure why. It's as if I've suddenly stumbled into a role I'm not sure how to play. I nod, trying to seem agreeable, but there's something unsettling about how quickly I've been cast as the solution to Priya's apparent loneliness. They watch me, expectant, waiting for answers.

'Uh, yes, of course,' I reply. Maybe, despite her outward confidence, Priya and I are more alike than I realise. Perhaps that's why they're so eager to set this up – two lonely girls in one cheerless apartment block. Or maybe they're vetting me to make sure I'm suitable company for their daughter.

'Mum.' Priya rolls her eyes. 'You're making me out to be a real saddo.'

'Not at all,' Urmila says. 'I just worry about you, that's all. Isn't a mother allowed to worry about her child these days?'

'What about your parents?' Ted asks me. 'Are they local too?'

'No, I, uh . . . sadly they're not around.'

Ted clears his throat. 'Sorry to hear that, Willow.'

'It's fine.' I blink rapidly and try to keep my voice light. 'I've been on my own a long time. I'm used to getting on with things.'

'I could tell you were an independent girl,' Urmila says. 'I'm sorry about your parents. Do you have siblings?'

I shake my head, desperate to flip the conversation back to them. 'How about you? Do you guys have any other children?'

'My older brother works for a big bank in New York,' Priya replies. 'He's the clever sibling.'

'Don't be silly,' Urmila says. 'You're both clever, you just haven't found your passion yet, Priya. It will come.'

I'm starting to feel under-equipped to deal with this conversation. I didn't think tonight would get so personal. But I guess it's reminded me why I've been keeping myself to myself for so long. Because it's too complicated, opening up to people. Telling them my history. *Lying to them.*

It's the same reason I worry about my relationship with Gabe. Because that's what it is now – a relationship. That first date at the Dolphin was just the start, and we've been out almost every evening since, despite me telling myself to take things slower. But, where he's concerned, I just can't seem to help myself. I'm falling for him, even though I sense there can be no good ending.

'Priya says you're a decorator,' Ted says. 'How did you get into that?'

'I did an apprenticeship and worked for a company for a while. Then, a couple of years ago, I decided to go freelance.'

'You don't normally hear of women decorators,' Ted says through a mouthful of naan.

'Dad!' Priya chides. 'Don't be so sexist.'

He holds his hands up. 'I'm not. It's just an observation. There are far more men in the trades than women.'

'He's right,' I say to Priya, dabbing my lips with a napkin. 'Which is why I decided to do it in the first place. My clients are all women, mainly single or elderly. People who'd rather not have strange men in their homes.'

'What a great idea!' Urmila claps her hands together. 'I love this. We're not your target market, but could we book you in?' She turns to Ted and starts talking about their garden room that needs a makeover, but I feel a bit uneasy about working for someone I know. It could get tricky if I did something they didn't like, or if they were to quibble over costs.

'We need to find something like that for Priya,' Urmila continues. 'A project. A passion.'

'I wish,' Priya says with a sigh.

'You will, darling,' Urmila reassures. 'And in the meantime, you can carry on working with Dad.' Urmila turns to me. 'Ted has a software company, but neither of the kids are that interested.'

'Ready-made company, and no one to take it over!' Ted grumbles.

'It's boring, Dad,' Priya teases, but I can sense some frustration beneath the comment.

'Yes, well, boring pays the bills.' Ted gives Priya a mock glare and then bumps shoulders with her playfully. 'And you also get very flexible hours, which you wouldn't get elsewhere.'

'That's true,' she agrees.

'You'll find your mojo again,' he adds. 'It's been a hard few months. You just need to regroup. You'll bounce back in no time.'

'That terrible boy was no good for you, darling,' Urmila says. 'Knocked your confidence.'

'Well, it's over now, so no need to worry. Anyway, Willow didn't come over to listen to my sob stories. Let's talk about something nice.'

'Of course. What about you, Willow? Any nice boyfriends?'

'Willow's seeing someone new,' Priya says, her eyes glinting. 'But she's being very mysterious about him.'

'Yes, well, it's early days. I don't want to start introducing him around until it turns into something. Which I'm not sure it will.' I say the words knowing it's gone way past that point. I just don't want to admit it out loud. 'Anyway, I like being single,' I add, trying to kid myself.

'Yes, it's great to be single when you're young,' Ted says. 'But as you get older, it's nice to have a bit of company.' He reaches across the table to take his wife's hand, and they gaze adoringly at each other.

'You guys,' Priya says indulgently. 'Honestly, it makes you sick, doesn't it?' She grins at me. 'Such a disgusting display of affection.'

'Twenty-eight happy years,' Urmila says.

'Lovely,' I reply, echoing Priya's smile. Although their relationship looks like a foreign language to me.

'So.' Urmila claps her hands. 'Let's drink to Willow's new relationship, and to a wonderful new relationship for Priya!' She beams and raises her glass in the air. 'And to no more Gabe Walker,' she adds as an aside.

Priya echoes her enthusiasm, but the blood whooshes in my ears. Did she just say Gabe Walker? Is that *my* Gabe she's talking about? What the hell? How does she know I'm going out with him? And why would she say *no more*?

'Are you all right, Willow?' Priya looks across at me with concern in her eyes. The three of them have raised their glasses in a toast, but I haven't even reached for my drink. I can't move.

I turn to Priya's mum, my voice trembling slightly. 'Did you say *Gabe Walker*?'

She wrinkles her nose in distaste. 'Yes, I thought Priya might have told you about him. That's Priya's ex-boyfriend.' She enunciates the last word with enough disdain to sink a ship.

Her words land with a thud.

'I'm sorry,' I say, my voice faltering. My throat is suddenly so dry I can barely swallow. 'Gabe Walker is Priya's ex?'

'Yes.' Priya laughs nervously. 'Don't tell me you know him!'

My stomach drops and my ears start buzzing. Is this some kind of sick coincidence? How the hell can this be true?

Chapter Eleven

JASMINE

'That's so lovely of you, but it's Gran's birthday next Saturday.' I swallow, feeling an all-too-familiar flutter of unease. 'I'd planned to take her into town for lunch. I thought I told you.'

'I don't think you did,' Adam replies, closing the dishwasher with a thud that makes me jump. It's Friday morning and we've been having a relaxed breakfast together before he heads to a job. It's one of those Sunday-supplement kind of mornings where you feel like you're in a lifestyle article. But now the spell has been broken.

I sit gingerly on one of the kitchen stools, worried this is going to turn into an argument. Adam has just surprised me with a mini-break to Bath next weekend, which would have been lovely any other time. But I can't miss Gran's birthday; she'd be so disappointed. I swear I told him about it, but he's somehow forgotten and booked this trip.

A tiny, insistent voice taps at my brain, trying to tell me that my husband has done this on purpose. That he didn't want me to spend time away from home without him, so he's booked this trip away. Just like he booked that meal last month so that I couldn't go to my work's leaving do. But the rational part of my brain is convincing myself that it's just me being paranoid. That he would never do something so . . . controlling.

'Anyway,' he continues, 'how can you afford to take her out? You're not working at the moment.'

I blink, taken aback by his mention of finances. 'I still have some wages left and a small pot of savings.'

'You have savings?' He raises a dark eyebrow. 'Since when?'

'Not much. Just some birthday money from Gran and the rest of my wages, like I said. Anyway, I won't be spending a lot. It's petrol money and some lunch, that's all.'

Adam's jaw tightens. He mops up toast crumbs from breakfast and opens the bin, dropping them in. 'How is this thing full again? I'm sure I only emptied it a day ago.'

I flinch at his angry tone before standing up and walking towards him. 'Do you want me to—'

'I'll do it.' He cuts me off and starts easing the rubbish bag out. 'Well, I've already paid for a nice hotel for the two of us. Are you saying you want me to cancel? I'm trying to do something nice and now you're saying you don't want to go. I actually can't believe this.' The rubbish bag finally comes free and he pulls the drawstring tight.

Dismay knots my stomach. 'If I could cancel Gran's lunch, you know I would, but she's so looking forward to it. I'm sure they'd let you rebook for another weekend. You know I'd love to go. Any other time would be amazing.'

Adam drops the rubbish bag on to the tiled kitchen floor. 'You know what,' he says moodily, 'don't worry about it.'

My mouth dries and I stand blinking at my husband. 'I'm sorry, I just don't understand why you're so upset at me wanting to treat Gran on her birthday.'

'You don't understand?' My husband shakes his head.

'Honestly, I don't. I was sure I told you about Saturday.'

'Well you didn't,' he snaps as he takes his phone from the pocket of his joggers, sits at the kitchen table, and starts swiping.

I'm nervous to say anything further in case I make things worse. I guess he must be going online to cancel the trip he booked. I feel bad, but I can't disappoint Gran. It wouldn't be fair.

'I've been thinking,' Adam says, changing the subject, his eyes still on the phone screen. 'It's probably best if we pause your car insurance while you're not working.'

My mouth drops open. Is he really threatening to stop me driving?

'Bloody thing won't let me do it via the app,' he mutters, 'but I'll call them in a minute and cancel. No point running two cars at the moment.'

'*What?*' Surely he's not serious. I had my own insurance policy, until he suggested last year that we get a family plan. He added mine to his as it was cheaper, and I thought it was a sensible idea. But now he wants to cancel it? My mind rebels, telling me that I could always get my own policy again. But then how would Adam react to that?

My brain is racing. How will I get to Gran's if I can't drive? How will I get to the supermarket and carry a big shop home? And I'm supposed to be meeting Naomi next week for a coffee in town. I couldn't make our last meet-up because I had the flu. Still feel a bit ropey, but I'm getting there. She'll be annoyed if I cancel again. I suppose I could catch the bus to town, but they're so irregular from here and they take forever.

Will Adam really cancel my insurance or is he bluffing? I'm hoping this is just his annoyance talking and when he calms down he'll apologise and leave me on the policy. 'If you're worried about finances, I'll get another job as soon as possible,' I add, my voice sounding faraway to my ears, my brain numb with shock.

'*You'll get another job?*' He puts his phone down on the table and gives me a look that's far removed from anything like the husband I know and love. Although, if I'm being honest with myself, I've been noticing differences ever since the barbecue. 'Thought you wanted to go to uni,' he says. 'But now you're talking about getting another job. I don't know where I am with you these days.'

I grip my left hand to stop it shaking. 'I did want to go to uni – I mean, I do – but if you're worried about money . . . I can get a job in the meantime.'

'I'm not *worried* about it,' he replies, 'but it's not exactly fair that I'm going out to work all hours, while you're chilling at home or swanning around having lunches. Don't you think that's selfish? What if it was the other way round?'

I don't quite understand his logic. On the one hand he's saying he doesn't want me to study or work, but on the other, he's criticising the fact that I'm not bringing in any money. But, maybe I'm missing something. I take a breath and try to keep my voice level. 'I don't have to take Gran to town for lunch, she could come here instead. I'd only planned to go out because I know you don't like people coming over at the weekend.'

'Oh, right. So it's my fault.' I flinch as Adam gets to his feet. 'Turn it around on me, why don't you? Have you heard yourself, Jasmine? I'm not the one who's unemployed, spending my secret stash of savings, rejecting a surprise weekend away and then acting like my husband's the bad guy. Honestly, I can't do anything right for doing wrong.' He inhales and then makes a show of breathing out to calm down. 'I'm going to work before I say something I regret.'

'Adam . . .' I stand, leaning on the table for support as my legs soften. 'Can't we talk about this first?'

But he leaves the kitchen, his boots heavy on the tiles, and I hear the jangle of keys followed by the slam of the front door, echoed by the slamming of my heart.

I sit back down heavily, my ears buzzing and my fingertips tingling. What just happened? I can't seem to make any sense of it. I get that Adam was excited to tell me about the weekend away that he'd booked, but it's Gran's birthday. He knows she's like a mother to me. He's always said he loves how close we are. And I know how important he considers family to be. After all, he and his dad have a great relationship, so surely he understands that I feel the same way about Gran.

Again, I wonder if there's something I'm missing. Did I do or say the wrong thing to cause this reaction? Maybe he really does think I'm taking the piss by not working. But that was what he wanted. I specifically remember him saying that I should take time to think about what I want to do next. To not rush into any decisions. Perhaps he's stressed with work, or maybe we're in some kind of financial difficulty that he doesn't want to tell me about. That could be it! Maybe I should ask him when he gets home. But I realise I'm scared to bring up a subject that might make him mad again.

I grasp my hand again to try to stop it shaking. My eyes fill with tears as I replay our conversation. As I wonder at how fast it morphed from an idyllic morning together to Adam threatening to cancel my car insurance. The past few minutes streak into my brain in brutal little snippets. His cruel expression, his angry outburst. This can't be happening. My husband can't be this person. Could he be ill? I've read about people who've undergone personality changes after suffering from a bump on the head or a brain tumour. Is that what's happening here?

I startle at the doorbell, my heart renewing its pounding. Could that be him, back to apologise, maybe? But why wouldn't he use his keys? Maybe it's a delivery. Opening the front door is the last thing I feel like doing, but it could be the curling wand I ordered for Gran's birthday. I don't want them to bother the neighbours with it, or take it back to the depot.

The doorbell rings again, which is unusual for delivery guys, but I force myself to move through the hallway and open the door.

A middle-aged woman with sandy hair stands on the path, but she's not carrying a parcel. She's not wearing a coat either, and it's quite chilly out. She's wearing a patterned dress and a pair of Mary Jane shoes and she seems vaguely familiar.

'Can I help?' I ask.

'Hello, Jasmine.'

'Sorry, do I know you?' I wrap my arms around myself against the chill wind that's sweeping into the hall.

'Carol,' she says.

I give her a blank look. Maybe she's selling something. I haven't got the mental energy for this.

'From next door,' she adds.

I frown and then it clicks into place. It's the new neighbour who was complaining about the noise at our barbecue. Great. This is all I need. 'Sorry, I didn't recognise you.' She was in her dressing gown last time I saw her.

'I dyed my hair,' she says, patting it self-consciously. 'Did it myself and I know it's turned out horribly, but I refuse to pay a hundred quid at the hairdresser's.'

'No, it looks . . . good. Is there something you need?' I realise I'm being curt. Rude, almost. But I don't have the capacity for politeness right now.

'Yes,' she replies. 'I was wondering if you'd mind if I put up some trellis on the fence. I want to grow some clematis, but it's your fence, so I thought I'd better ask first.'

'Sorry?' I actually have no idea what she's talking about and I wish she'd just go away and leave me alone.

'Are you okay, love?' Her brow wrinkles with concern.

'What?' I snap.

'Are you okay? You look a bit—' She glances down at my hands and I realise they're still trembling, so I clench them tight, then clasp them behind my back.

'I'm fine.'

'Okay, good. So, about the trellis?'

An unwelcome tear slides down my cheek. I swipe at it with the back of my shaky hand, mortified.

'Oh, love, you're not okay, are you?' She puts her hands on her hips and tilts her head to the side.

'What? No, I'm fine. It's just the wind making my eyes water. So annoying.'

To my horror, Carol steps into the hall and puts an arm around my shoulders, leading me into the house. 'Come on. Let me make you a cup of tea,' she says briskly.

'Oh. No, that's okay, I'm . . . I have to . . .' I desperately try to think of an excuse as to why she shouldn't be making me a drink, but my mind is still reeling from my argument with Adam and we're already in the kitchen.

'Oh,' she says, glancing around. 'Now this is nice. What a lovely big room, and there's so much light. I should do this with my kitchen.' She heads over to the sink and starts opening cupboards, quickly laying her hands on the teabag jar.

'Honestly, there's no need to—'

'Nonsense.' She cuts off my protests. 'I was about to make myself a cuppa at home anyway. It's much nicer to share one with a neighbour, don't you think?'

I'm too numb to protest so I just sit on a stool and watch helplessly as she proceeds to make a horribly milky cup of tea to which she adds two heaped teaspoons of sugar. I hate sweet tea.

'Here, drink this,' she says sliding the mug across the island towards me. 'It will help with the shock.'

How does she know I'm in shock?

'Now, what's happened?' she asks, tucking her hair behind both ears.

I put my hands around the mug, enjoying the warmth on my cold fingers, although there's no way I'm putting that vile concoction anywhere near my mouth. It's nice of her to be concerned, but I'm not about to open up to a stranger, even if she is my neighbour. *Especially* as she's my neighbour. Adam would get even more annoyed if he thought I was spreading our private business around.

'Honestly, I'm fine. You were saying something about trellis,' I prompt. The quicker we have this cup of tea, the sooner she'll leave, and then I can figure out what to do about my husband.

But my heart almost grinds to a halt as I hear the key turn in the lock.

Adam's back. And I'm here with Carol, drinking tea. My heart starts thumping as I realise he's not going to like this one bit.

Chapter Twelve

WILLOW

While Gabe's at the bar getting our drinks, I find a booth in the picturesque pub that's all stone walls, wooden beams and twinkling lights. It's another one of his favourites, a local place I've never been to before. Since I met him, he's been pulling me into a whirlwind of new experiences, taking me out to all his favourite haunts. It's as though I've stepped out of normal life and into a new, exciting reality where everything is brighter and clearer. Like I was living in greyscale and now it's all Technicolor. But I'm worried it's all an illusion, a shimmering mirage about to evaporate. Priya's parents dropping the bombshell that Gabe is her ex has made me doubt everything.

To stop my brain from spinning out, I check my emails on my phone. There are a couple of new enquiries from people who'd like decorating quotes. I've already got another three quotes that I haven't got around to writing up yet. I normally do them over the weekend, but I spent most of it either with Gabe or thinking about Gabe. I'm doing that classic thing of letting a boy take over my life. And since yesterday's dinner with Priya and her parents, I've been too preoccupied with thoughts of the two of them to concentrate on my job.

I look up as the man in question finally comes over, setting two Cokes on the table. As he came straight from work, we're both driving tonight. Around us, couples chat, families talk over each other, and a group of friends play cards by the fire, laughing loudly. It's busy for a Wednesday night. Gabe slides in opposite me with a heavy sigh that's unlike him. He checks his phone like he's waiting for some news, maybe a message from someone more important than me. As he scrolls, the glow of the screen reflects in his eyes.

'Everything all right?' I ask, taking a sip of my drink. It's sweet and cool, a welcome distraction from my nagging thoughts.

He hesitates. 'Yeah, just work stuff, you know.'

I wonder if that's the truth. This is the first time since we met that things feel slightly off-kilter between us. I can't tell if it's me or him. But I guess it's probably me, because I have this big thing I need to ask him, the words burning on the tip of my tongue even though I'm nervous to speak them.

'Work?' I say instead. 'What's up?'

'Just my boss being a dick.'

'Aren't they all?'

Gabe shakes his head. 'He's pissed off because I didn't stay late enough tonight. I worked till seven, but apparently that isn't cutting it.'

'I hope you're not in trouble because of me,' I say. 'We didn't have to go out tonight if you were busy.'

'God, no.' He reaches across the table and takes my hand. 'This isn't about you. This is about my idiot boss asking my work colleagues why I'm not in the office tonight at . . .' he checks his phone screen, '. . . eight thirty. If he's got a problem, he should talk to me about it, not criticise me in front of everyone.'

'I'm sorry, that doesn't sound great.'

'You've got the right idea, being self-employed,' he says, draining a third of his drink in one go. 'Anyway, enough about my crap. How's your week going?'

I pull a face.

'Oh, that good, eh?' Gabe smiles and shakes his head. 'What are we like?'

The booth we're sitting in is cushioned and comfortable, but I keep shifting in my seat, unable to shake off the nervousness that prickles through my skin at the thought of bringing up Priya. At the sickening thought that this could be the last time I go out with Gabe.

It might not have been very long, but I already feel as though we're in a fully fledged relationship, and he's constantly telling me how much he likes me. If he still harboured feelings for Priya, then why would he have asked me out in the first place? Perhaps I'm letting my imagination run away. Finding problems where there aren't any.

'Something strange happened last night,' I begin, forcing a light tone, my voice steadier than I feel.

Gabe sets down his phone, his eyes locking on to mine with genuine interest. 'Now I'm intrigued,' he says, a smile playing on his lips.

I wait for him to take a sip from his drink, the liquid disappearing down his throat, before telling him what I learned. 'So, you remember I said I was going to my neighbour's place for dinner?'

He sets his empty glass on the table. 'Yeah. I was working late so we couldn't go out anyway.'

'Well, her parents were there and they mentioned her ex-boyfriend.'

'Someone you know?' he asks, raising an eyebrow. 'Don't tell me he's your ex too?'

'No. He's you.' I scrutinise his expression, searching for any flicker of emotion that might reveal something.

'Sorry, I don't understand,' Gabe says, a frown etched across his features.

I realise I'm making a hash of telling him. 'My neighbour's name is Priya Philips.'

Gabe blanches, but recovers himself quickly. 'You went to dinner with Priya?'

'Yes.' I purse my lips. 'And her family.'

'So Priya's your neighbour?' he asks.

'That's what I'm trying to tell you.' I swallow.

'*Priya*,' he mutters. His eyes widen and then he chuckles. 'Well that's weird.'

'I know, right.' I'm so tense, waiting for him to tell me about her.

'You know it's ancient history, though,' he says, taking my hand across the table. 'It's definitely over. I can't believe you live in the same building as Priya. What are the odds?'

'Hmm.' I'm not sure what to make of his reaction. He seems quite nonchalant about it. Like he doesn't really mind. Is that how he truly feels? 'She's only just moved in down the hall, and I actually really like her. Which makes this . . .' I point at myself and then him, '. . . a bit awkward.'

'No shit,' he says, leaning back in his seat and exhaling. 'And you've been worrying about this all day?'

I nod.

'You should have called me straightaway, last night.' His fingers drum the table. 'What did they say about me? Do I even want to know?' He gives a nervous laugh.

'Nothing. Just that you were her ex. Why? Did it end badly between you?'

'Not at all. It just fizzled. Did you tell her we've been seeing each other?' he asks.

'Well, no. She was there with her parents. It would have been weird.'

'Yeah, I can see that.'

'But, of course, I will have to say something,' I add. 'I was sure I mentioned her to you over the weekend.' I watch him again closely for a reaction.

'Definitely not,' he replies. 'You said you were going to dinner with your neighbour, but you never mentioned her name. I'd have remembered if you did. *Obviously*.'

His eye contact is so strong, his smile so honest, that I'm certain he's being sincere. I'm relieved he no longer has feelings for Priya, but it still feels odd that she's his ex. Of all the places in Highcliffe, Priya lands right in my lap. It's like the universe is trying to mess with me, and I can't quite shake a gnawing sensation in the pit of my stomach.

Gabe changes the subject back to his work, but I barely register his words. I nod in all the right places, pretending to hear, all the while absorbing the impossible connection between the three of us.

On the drive home, my thoughts swirl like a dark cloud being pulled about by an ill wind. How did Priya end up living where I do? I can't help but wonder if she might have orchestrated the entire thing. My mind races, replaying the conversation over and over again, examining Gabe's words from every angle. It bothers me. Their past feels too close for comfort. Gabe acted like it was all history, but can I really be certain? My anxiety creeps up a level, heavy and insistent, as if someone is whispering doubt into my ear.

I switch on the radio to drown out the noise in my head. Music floods the interior, upbeat, joyful, but still I squirm under the weight of all these spiralling thoughts.

I'm almost too distracted to notice the headlights that appear suddenly and hover in the rear-view mirror like unblinking eyes. I glance up again. Is that car following me? I can't quite tell. I change lanes instinctively, but it follows, sticking close as I turn down one road, then another. I slow down to let them pass, but they linger. Too close and too persistent.

My pulse quickens and I turn off the radio. This would not be a good time for my eighteen-year-old red Peugeot van to break down. It's been making odd noises recently, and I pray that it's going to get me home safely tonight. I could really do with getting something newer, but I'm strangely attached to it. Maybe I'll just get a full service. Hopefully that should give it a few more years of life.

I glance again at the rear-view mirror, my heart in my throat, but the car veers off at the next lights. Relief washes over me, but only for a moment. I drive faster, as if trying to outrun this restlessness that's taken hold of me. Will I ever be able to relax, or will I be looking over my shoulder forever?

Finally, I reach my street and turn into the car park at the rear of my building. I switch off the engine and sit for a while, the van engine ticking as it cools. Trees swish above me, and raindrops spatter the windscreen. I think a storm might be coming.

I exit the van and walk around the building towards the front entrance, but the familiar alleyway feels menacing tonight, the lamps casting long, sinister shadows, my footsteps too loud on the concrete.

I hear something, suddenly – a rustle of movement behind me. I stop, look back, see nothing. Paranoia has seeped into my bones, and I can't shake it. I hear it again, closer. Shivers shoot up my spine as the sound grows louder, nearer. Someone is walking behind me. I quicken my pace, my breaths coming hard and fast.

I whirl around, startled by the nearness of footsteps to see a young woman brush past me without even a glance, unaware of my pounding heart. I stop for a moment, wiping sweat from the back of my neck and getting my breathing under control.

This is ridiculous. I've let this thing with Priya and Gabe spook me. I need to be less mistrustful and learn to accept things at face value again. Priya being Gabe's ex is nothing but an annoying coincidence, and there's nobody following me. I need to calm down and get a grip.

Chapter Thirteen

JASMINE

My pulse races and stutters. I try to work out my next plan of action after I hear the front door open and close. Adam's back already and I don't know why. But I do know that he won't be happy about our neighbour Carol being here. He'll be furious that I'm drinking tea with her after he specifically said he didn't want me 'swanning around and socialising'. Only, it's not my fault that our neighbour's in our house. She practically invited herself in.

I leave Carol in the kitchen and head out into the hall, praying she doesn't follow. 'Hi,' I say to my husband, hoping I don't look or sound too panicked. 'Did you forget something?'

To my surprise, given how angry he was only minutes earlier, Adam cups my face and kisses me. 'Jas, I'm so sorry about earlier. I should never have lost my shit like that. Of course you should take your gran out on her birthday. I was just disappointed about the weekend away, that's all. I'll rebook it for another time. Are you okay?'

'Umm, yes, I'm fine.' My heart is thrumming with anxiety at what he'll think when he sees our neighbour here. I try to sound breezy. 'Carol from next door has come round to ask about the fence.' I tilt my head in the direction of the kitchen.

'She's in there?' he mouths, his expression clouding.

I nod and roll my eyes to show him that I don't want her here either.

He strides past me into the kitchen, and I follow him, dreading what he'll say when he sees that we're drinking tea together. But there's no trace of the mugs or the tea things. She must have put them all away, which is strange. Not that I'm complaining. She's done me a favour.

'Hello.' She nods at Adam and gives him a tight smile before turning to me. 'If you could let me know about the trellis, I'd be grateful.'

'No problem,' I reply.

'Trellis?' Adam asks.

'I just popped over to ask you and Jasmine about attaching some trellis to the fence.' Carol gestures towards our joint boundary line. 'I'll let her tell you.' She sweeps past us and leaves the house, closing the front door behind her with a click.

'What did you invite her in for?' Adam's brow furrows, his voice sharp.

'She invited herself. She wanted to show me something to do with the fence.'

'Well I don't want that nosy old bag thinking she can pop round whenever she wants,' he snaps, his irritation bubbling to the surface. 'Such a pain in the arse. Why can't people mind their own business?'

'She's okay,' I say tentatively, immediately regretting my words as they hang in the air between us.

'Oh, right, getting all pally with the neighbours while I'm at work,' he sneers. 'Here I was wanting to come home to see if you're all right, and you're all cosy with creepy Carol, like our fight doesn't even matter to you. Honestly, Jasmine, sometimes I wonder why I bother.'

'I'm sorry,' I murmur. 'Honestly, I didn't want her here either.'

'Didn't look that way to me,' he retorts, his voice laced with accusation. 'I thought I'd be the bigger person and apologise. More fool me. You don't look sorry at all. The minute my back's turned, you're inviting people over.' He exhales heavily, his hands clenching and unclenching by his sides. 'I don't want you talking to her again. If the doorbell rings, you ignore it, okay?'

My eyes are wide, my mouth dry. I can barely breathe. Is my husband really stopping me from talking to our neighbour? Or is he forbidding me from answering the door at all?

His eyes narrow. 'I said, *okay*?'

I nod repeatedly, unable to speak.

'Good.' He sighs, a mixture of relief and exasperation. 'Jesus, Jasmine. It's a good thing I came home. You need keeping an eye on.'

I know I should push back on what he's saying. Tell him he's being unreasonable or illogical. But the words are stuck in my throat and I don't want to make him any more angry. How have I found myself in this situation? And what am I going to do to claw my way out?

Chapter Fourteen

JASMINE

'It's been ages!' Naomi cries, sweeping me in for a hug. Strands of her thick chestnut hair tickle my nose, carrying the faint scent of vanilla shampoo that I always associate with her.

'I know, I'm so sorry.' I pull back to let her eyes meet mine. 'Bloody flu had me flat on my back. I'm only just dragging myself upright.'

She gives me a sympathetic nod. 'You need to get fit, start taking echinacea, especially now it's the start of flu season. Curtis has put me on to this amazing supplement. It's a bit pricey, but it's so worth it. Honestly, I've barely had a sniffle. I'll send you the link.'

'Amazing,' I say, knowing for a fact that I won't be ordering it as my bank account is currently on life support. I can't afford anything pricey now that I'm not working. Adam gives me enough for groceries, but that's about it.

I head for a cosy booth, relieved that Naomi has offered to get our coffees as I only have enough cash for one espresso. I sink into the red leather seat with a sigh. I'll have to sip my drink slowly as I can't afford to get the next round in, which is crazy. I hate being a mooch and feel mortified that I can't pay my way. I'd considered cancelling again because of my lack of funds, but I figured that might end our friendship for good. Naomi already thinks I'm an unreliable friend, and she's not entirely wrong. But it's not because I want to be. My stomach clenches with anxiety and I try to breathe through it. To concentrate on the here and now. On being out in town with my best friend.

She returns, balancing two steaming white mugs on a tray next to two delicious-looking pastries. The foam on my latte is a heart – like it knows I need a bit of extra love right now. I hold the mug in both hands for a moment, willing my pulse to calm. Focusing on the warmth seeping into my cold fingers, on the relaxed chatter around me.

I met Naomi four years ago at the busy hospital coffee shop where I used to work. We were both twenty-one and it was our first day on the job. Naomi took to it like a duck to water as she'd been in hospitality since she was eighteen. I, on the other hand, was terrible from the start, mixing up orders, dropping crockery and getting into fights with the demon coffee machine that would always glitch whenever I approached it. Naomi covered for me a lot back then, and I'm sure I would have lost that job without her.

'So,' I say, 'tell me about you and Curtis. How's it all going?'

She wrinkles her nose. 'Badly,' she admits, tapping her fingertips against her mug.

I frown. 'What? Why? Last time we met, you two were perfect.'

'Yeah, well, that was a couple of months ago.' She takes a sip of her latte. 'His new job's a nightmare. He's always working.'

'At the restaurant, right?' I take another tiny sip of my coffee.

Naomi nods. 'Head chef now, so I literally never see him. Well, maybe twice a week, if I'm lucky. But he's so knackered that I barely get a word out of him.'

I reach across to touch her hand. 'I'm sorry,' I offer. 'Have you talked to him about it?'

'Yeah, but . . .' She shrugs. 'What can he do? It's his career. He's chasing his dream. I can't exactly tell him to give it up just because I miss him. We've only been together a few months.'

I wish I could offer her some encouraging words, but my mind is blank. 'Maybe things will get better once he settles into the job . . .'

'Maybe,' she echoes, but her smile is brittle.

'How's *your* work, Miss Manager?' I ask, trying to shift the mood.

Her eyes brighten. 'Good, actually,' she replies with a smile. Naomi still works at the hospital café, but she was made manager last year. She's one of the youngest members of staff, but is also one of the most efficient, so I'm not surprised they promoted her. 'The best part is getting to boss Cherry Fart around,' she adds.

I snort-laugh at this, memories of the old team flooding back. Cherry Fart was the name we gave to Gerry Galbraith, an insufferable mansplainer who used to talk to us as if we were five years old. The nickname came about when he called across the café to ask if there were any cherry farts left, instead of cherry tarts. Naomi and I could barely stop laughing all day. Childish and silly, but it was moments like those that made the job fun. 'I can't believe he's still there,' I reply. 'Has he got any better?'

'Worse. He still goes around acting like he's the CEO of the whole hospital. I'd feel sorry for him if he wasn't such an arse. Anyway, how's Adam?'

I try not to take offence that she's mentioned my husband in the same breath as saying 'arse'. I know she's not his biggest fan, and I push away the fleeting thought that perhaps she was right for saying I should be wary of jumping into marriage so quickly.

For a moment, I almost unload my own troubles – the way Adam's smile has creased into impatience, how he snaps at me for tiny things. Part of me would like to be more honest. Would like to tell her that my marriage isn't turning out how I imagined. But what if I unburden myself, and it just turns out to be a blip? What if Adam is simply stressed out at the moment, and he goes back to being his normal, loving self? I swallow my words, keeping myself in check. I can't bad-mouth Adam to her when she already doubts him. I need her to like my husband, otherwise it will be impossible for us to stay close friends.

'Adam's great,' I say, my lips tightening. I let my gaze drift to the swirling foam in my cup. There's something sad about the way the heart shape is already dissolving at the edges. I tuck a strand of hair behind my ear and force myself to smile. Because maybe, if I can pretend everything's okay, then it just might be.

Chapter Fifteen

WILLOW

After my conversation with Gabe, followed by the traumatic car journey home, I'm finding it impossible to fall asleep; my bed feels uncomfortable, my body's hot and tense, and my brain is whirring like a machine on fast forward. Thankfully, sometime in the early hours, exhaustion pulls at my eyelids, and I tumble into an uneasy sleep filled with restless dreams where Priya's eyes are cold and accusing, and Gabe's hands are outstretched, reaching for me, but I can't quite grasp them. The scenes shift and collide. Everything is disjointed, an Escher drawing of my troubled emotions. I wake with a start, the half-light of dawn creeping through the window, uncertainty still gnawing at the edges of my mind.

Thursday morning passes in a haze. I go through the motions at work, trying to lose myself in my brush strokes as I paint my current client's hallway. Gabe texts around lunchtime, asking how I'm doing, and I text him back that I'm good, wondering if he can sense the lie between each letter of my reply. Priya messages in the afternoon, but I leave it unread, my stomach knotting tighter at the thought of what I have to tell her. Part of me knows I'm overreacting to the whole thing. But I can't help the way I feel.

The secrets I carry are too consuming to allow room for other complications. If Priya wasn't my neighbour, it would be simpler to just ghost her, but, either way, I like her too much to do that.

After work, I'm far too wound up to go to my apartment, so I wander the streets, my phone on silent in my pocket. I'm relieved not to bump into Gabe out for a run or Priya picking up some shopping. The street lights seem to blink at me like knowing eyes, and I walk until the tension in my body gives way to fatigue.

I realise that I can't go on like this. That I won't feel better until I tell Priya the truth, even if it's the last thing I ever say to her. She's bound to find out about Gabe, so it's best coming from me. I take my phone from my pocket and send her a text before hurrying home.

The minutes crawl until I hear a tentative knock on my door.

'Come in,' I say, gesturing towards the worn grey sofa that has become a reluctant stand-in for a proper lounge. As Priya steps into my living/dining/kitchen space, I take a furtive glance around the room – the sofa, plain wooden table and four chairs, a dated kitchenette, bare walls, minimal personal touches – and I feel a rush of embarrassment. After seeing the beauty of Priya's apartment, I want to apologise for my flat's lack of character. To explain that this isn't to my taste. But I've been here for two years already, there's no reasonable justification for its blandness, so I stay quiet.

Though I pride myself on my decorating skills and flair, I've never bothered to transform this impersonal space into a home. Mainly due to lack of inspiration. That, and I'd never planned on inviting anyone over. Besides, I rented the flat fully furnished so it's not like I got any choice in the furniture. Although I realise a nice throw, some cushions and artwork could have cheered up the space a bit. The only nod to decoration are the scented candles that help relax me. I probably have enough money in the bank to indulge in some interior decor. I just haven't had the desire. It might not be aesthetically pleasing, but I love my little flat anyway.

I wanted this evening to feel relaxed, but the thought of Priya's past relationship with Gabe lingers like an exhale of smoke in the air. My fingers tap nervously on the arm of the sofa as I wait for the kettle to boil – a jittery countdown to an unwanted conversation.

'Herbal or regular?' I gesture to the kettle.

'I don't mind,' she replies, sitting on the sofa.

After dinner with Priya and her parents a couple of nights ago, I've been a bit of a mess, my mind lurching from one possibility to the next. I couldn't find the words at the time to tell them I'm currently dating her ex. It would have been too tricky to say it in front of her parents, not to mention the fact that my brain was paralysed with shock at the news. So I've invited her round this evening to tell her.

'Thanks so much for dinner the other evening.' I pour tea into my only two mugs. There were four in the set I originally bought, but two of them broke. I should probably buy some more. 'Your parents are so nice, and the food was absolutely delicious.'

'Mum and Dad loved you.' She slips off her shoes and curls her feet under her. 'I knew they would.'

'Well, the feeling's mutual,' I reply, pulling one of my two dining chairs over to sit opposite her, the steam from our newly poured tea curling between us.

'Were you okay, though?' she asks. 'Because you left quite early. I know Mum and Dad can be quite intense. Especially Mum, she just wants the best for me, and she loves meeting my friends, and because you live down the hall, they wanted to matchmake our friendship if that makes se—'

'Oh, no,' I interrupt her worried explanation. 'Your parents are lovely. They were so warm and friendly. Honestly, I thought they were great.'

Priya puts a hand over her heart and exhales. 'Oh, that's a relief. I thought we might have scared you off with all the food and the family stuff!'

'No, not at all.' I pause. 'It was a great evening, honestly. But there is something I wanted to mention—'

'I knew it,' she cries. 'I knew something was up when you left early and then you didn't respond to my messages. I was so happy to get your text this evening.'

'Look,' I begin. 'There's something I didn't tell you on Tuesday.'

'Okaaay . . .' Her expression grows wary.

'The reason I left early is because . . . well, your mum mentioned that you'd had a bad break-up, and then she said your ex's name.'

'You mean *Gabe*?'

'Yes,' I reply.

'You said you didn't know him,' she says, frowning.

'I know I said that, but . . .' I wince. 'It isn't strictly true. You see, the reason I didn't want to say anything is because . . .'

Priya's dark eyes widen. 'Don't tell me . . .'

I nod. ''Fraid so. Your ex-boyfriend is the guy I'm currently seeing.'

Her eyes flick away from mine for a moment before she takes a sip of tea, the steam curling around her face like a secret.

'Priya, did you hear what I said?' I ask, my voice catching on the edge of apprehension.

She gives a tight-lipped smile, dismissing my worry with a casual wave of her hand. 'It's fine,' she says, her tone light as if discussing some mildly inconvenient chore. 'I'm way over him.'

'Are you sure? Because your parents seemed to think that—'

'Oh, you know what parents are like – always fussing and . . .' Her voice trails off. 'Oh, no, sorry, I know yours aren't . . .' She presses her fingers to her forehead as she remembers that my parents aren't around.

'Don't worry, I know what you mean,' I reply.

'I'm such an idiot,' she mutters before gazing back at me. 'Honestly, Willow, I'm fine with you seeing Gabe, although, I should probably . . . No, never mind. Obviously, it's a bit weird and a bit . . . unexpected, but it is what it is. I'm just glad that's all it is, and it's not anything I did to upset or offend you.'

I'm relieved, but also taken aback by her acceptance of the situation. Does she really not care that I'm dating her ex? She seems as unfazed by it as Gabe was when I told him.

Priya continues to sip her tea, reiterating with a smile that she's over him. But is she being one hundred per cent truthful? I've never seen her anything other than breezy, seemingly without a care in the world. Although her parents made it quite clear that the happy-go-lucky Priya I know isn't the only version of her. According to them, she's also lonely, going through a tough time. Is that because of her and Gabe's split? I can't exactly ask her without things becoming even more awkward. And if her bright personality is covering up her true feelings, then how do I know that she really is okay with me seeing him? She might be seething on the inside. Or devastated.

Her voice cuts through my racing thoughts. She sits upright now with curiosity in her eyes, leaning forward. 'That night when we chatted outside the building and you said you saw me down at the beach, were you at the Dolphin?' Her words hang in the air, loaded.

I nod slowly, a heavy sensation rising in my stomach.

Priya shakes her head. 'That's where he used to take me on our dates,' she says. 'And don't tell me – I bet the first time you went, he suggested you have the mussels to start followed by the sea bass.' She rolls her eyes.

A hot flush crawls up my neck as I shrug and nod in agreement.

'Ugh. That's exactly what Gabe suggested we order on *our* first date.' Priya sits back with a disbelieving huff.

I look at her, trying to work out if she's being a bitch about it, or if she genuinely finds it upsetting. Either way, this feels super-uncomfortable. And, of course, I don't like the idea that he's done the same things with her.

Priya's eyes fill with concern as she sees how her revelation has upset me. 'Oh, Willow, I'm sorry. Don't read anything into that. Highcliffe's a small place so there are only a handful of restaurants he could take you to. I just . . . I shouldn't have said that. My big mouth always gets me in trouble. It wasn't meant as a dig at your date. I know him too well, that's all.'

Her reassurances land too late because my mind is already spinning in tight, anxious loops. Was she purposely reminding me that she did it first? Trying to sabotage our relationship, digging up doubts like buried landmines beneath our fragile, new connection? All of Gabe's and my special moments suddenly seem smaller, diluted, a repeat performance. It makes me feel icky, like a warmed-up version of something left over. Did he do the one-month anniversary cupcake with her too? I daren't ask.

'Please don't take it to heart, Willow. He's not worth it.' She reaches across the scuffed wooden coffee table for my hand and squeezes it briefly before I ease it away.

Priya's delayed concern appears genuine enough, but I feel it closing around me until I can't breathe. The room seems smaller, like the walls have edged inwards. I also don't like the fact that she's bad-mouthing him in front of me. Does she genuinely not like him anymore? Or is she trying to turn me against him for some other reason? Maybe she's jealous. Maybe she wants to get back with him. This is definitely not how I expected this conversation to go. I'd hoped I was going to come out of this with more clarity, but now I don't know if I trust my new neighbour. And I also don't know if Gabe is the person I thought he was.

Am I being unfair to her?

Maybe.

Are Priya and I even friends yet? I haven't known her long enough for us to be BFFs like her parents wanted. But I liked the feeling of being welcomed into their family. I loved the warmth of their interest in me. That they thought I was someone worth knowing.

The question is, is Gabe worth giving all that up for? Because how can I keep seeing him while being close friends with Priya? I can't exactly talk about him with her, like you're supposed to do with friends.

Should I end things with Gabe? But what if Priya really doesn't care that I'm seeing him, and I give him up for nothing? The truth feels slippery, and I can't get a grip on it. Gabe calls me his Cappuccino Girl. We laugh at the same absurd things. I wish I didn't like him so much. It would make things so much easier.

And now I'm uneasy about this woman in my flat who I thought was an uncomplicated new friend. Is she genuinely over their relationship, like she says? At least I've got things out in the open now, but I can't imagine this is going to help our fledgling friendship.

Am I really going to have to choose between Gabe and Priya? Or should I go back to my hermit-like ways and ditch both of them? Take a leaf out of my next-door neighbour Elsie's book and shun all new people. Things were certainly easier before I made these new connections. But the idea of losing either one of them fills my heart with despair. I feel genuinely bereft at the thought of it, and have to blink back the sting of tears waiting to be sobbed. I didn't realise how lonely I was before I met them.

I open my mouth to say something to deflate the tension, to let Priya know I'm not annoyed, but the words don't come. I feel stuck.

Chapter Sixteen

JASMINE

The February rain cuts straight into me as I step off the bus on to the sodden pavement. It's Saturday and Adam's working this morning so I've come to the other side of town to visit my gran. Her warden-assisted flat has a front-row view of the park and a bus stop right outside the door, which is handy for Gran who can go anywhere for free with her bus pass. She never learned to drive, though a few of the residents in her block have cars and are as active as they were thirty years ago. Gran's often part of an OAP convoy with trips to bingo, the local shopping mall, the cinema and other events.

The bus stop is also handy for me since I'm no longer insured on my car. Adam didn't follow through with his threat to cancel the policy; instead he simply waited for it to run out, which it did last month. Then he casually said there was no point renewing it. I probably should have argued, but I guess he was the one paying for it.

Gran buzzes me into the building and I take the stairs, rather than wait for the lift. She greets me at the door with a huge smile, her cheeks flushed pink from the central heating. 'Ooh, it's great to see you, Jazzy love. But you're looking a bit peaky. Everything all right?' She pats my cheek and pushes my hair off my face to get a better look at me.

'I'm fine, Gran. Bought you some of that walnut cake you like.'

'Now we're talking,' she replies, taking it off me and heading into the kitchen, humming one of her favourite showtunes – '*You'll Never Walk Alone*' from *Carousel*. Gran is on the lively side of seventy-nine, vibrant and full of energy, with hair as brown as mine (thanks to a box of Clairol) and eyes as sharp as her sense of humour. She likes to say that the only thing wrinkled about her is her stockings.

I follow her through and sniff. 'Have you been smoking in here again, Gran?'

She wafts at the air with one hand, and frowns. 'You can't tell, can you?'

'Gran, it smells like an ashtray in here.'

'Oh dear.' She opens the back window that looks out on to the residents' garden, letting in a wintry blast of air.

'They'll kick you out if they find out you've been smoking inside,' I chide.

'No they won't,' Gran retorts, flicking on the kettle. 'That Marilyn is a lazy so-and-so. If she reports me to the management committee, I'll report her right back.'

I snicker. Marilyn is one of the wardens. She's nice enough, but always does the bare minimum around here. I've had to have words with her a few times about the state of the hallways, and the faulty lock on the main entrance door.

Gran and I chat about this and that as I move around the flat, doing a few odd jobs for her while she sits with a cup of tea and a slice of walnut cake.

'Can you put these up next?' she asks, handing me a couple of framed watercolours of the ocean.

'They're lovely, Gran.' I admire the prints and then turn them around to examine the fixings.

'You know how much I love the sea,' she replies. 'I miss it. When I was a nipper, every weekend, we'd go down the pier, paddle in the shallows and get an ice cream after. I wish you could have grown up with that kind of childhood. You can't beat the sea air.'

'Sounds idyllic. But I had you, Gran, so I feel very lucky.' Gran more or less raised me, never once complaining that her life had been taken over by a needy child. Gratitude stings the backs of my eyes. I owe her everything.

'Go on with you.' Gran's eyes are glistening too, until she blinks and sniffs. 'Anyway, I got these prints from Harvey's. They were half-price. Couldn't resist.'

She's talking about the local garden centre where she and her friends sometimes go for Sunday lunch as it's such good value for money. 'Tell you what,' she says, leaning forward with a twinkle. 'There's some dishy widowers there at the weekends. Me and Sheila had some fun. She calls them "Harvey's hunks".'

I laugh. 'Are you looking for a new husband, Gran?'

'No, course not. No one could replace my Derek. It's just a bit of harmless flirting. Reminds us we're not dead yet.' Her laughter turns into a hacking cough and I feel a wave of panic.

'You need to get that cough seen to, Gran. Have you been to the doctor?'

She waves my concern away with a flick of her wrist. 'It's just the change of seasons. I always get a little cough this time of year. It's nothing.'

'Well, if it hasn't gone by next week, then I want you to see your GP, okay?' I make a mental note to remind her about it.

'Fine,' she agrees.

'And you should cut back on the cigarettes,' I add.

'I only smoke the mild ones,' she replies. 'Now, Jas, would you mind putting up some shelves for Sheila next door? I know it's a bit much to ask, but—'

'Shelves? Of course. I could do it next time I come.'

'Can you do it now, if you're not too pushed?' Gran asks.

I check my phone and see that it's still only 10.40 a.m. Probably enough time to get it done. I like Sheila. She's a good friend to Gran. 'Yes, sure,' I agree.

We leave Gran's flat and walk the three or four paces along the corridor to knock on her neighbour's door, which opens almost instantaneously. 'Thought I heard you two laughing,' she says. Sheila's a sprightly eighty-year-old with white hair and an infectious smile. 'Have you come to do my shelves?' she asks, skipping the pleasantries.

'She has,' Gran replies, shooing me inside before following and pulling the door closed.

'Oh, you are good, Jasmine.' Sheila turns to Gran. 'Wendy, you're so lucky to have your granddaughter living close by. I can't believe my lot are all down on the south coast now. I only get to see them a few times a year.'

'I do feel very lucky having Jas nearby,' Gran agrees, taking my hand and kissing it.

I get to work straightaway, measuring the space for the two shelves Sheila wants above her sideboard while she makes us all tea and brings out a plate of custard creams. 'Would you not think about moving down to be with them?' I ask Gran's friend.

'You're as bad as they are,' Sheila replies. 'My Jim's always begging me to move down, but they've got their own lives there and they'd all feel obliged to spend time with me. Last thing I want to be is a burden. Anyway, I'd be lonely without all my friends.'

'You wouldn't be a burden,' I chide. 'You're great company. The reason they want you down there is because they love you.'

'You're very sweet. But, no, aside from missing them, I like my life here. Lots going on, as your gran probably tells you.'

'You might want to move these pieces, before I start drilling.' I gesture to a collection of framed photographs and porcelain figurines that sit on the sideboard, unchipped and perfectly arranged, as though waiting for a visit from royalty.

'Good point,' Sheila says.

She and Gran carefully remove all the pieces while I mark the screw holes on the wall in pencil. As I'm working, Sheila and Gran break into song, for my benefit. They've got cracking voices and I'm loving their rendition of '*Oklahoma*'. But Gran's cough soon reappears and Sheila makes us all another cup of tea.

Once the shelves are up, and Gran and Sheila are done admiring them, Sheila presses twenty pounds into my hand and asks if I'd be free to do some other odd jobs from time to time, like putting together flatpack furniture or clearing out cupboards. She mentions that she has lots of friends who'd pay me too.

'You don't need to pay me,' I protest.

'Nonsense,' Sheila replies. 'Now what do you think about the odd-job idea? I know you're already working, but this could earn you a little extra.'

I still haven't told Gran I was made redundant, which isn't great, I know. But she's spent years looking after me, worrying about me, scrimping and saving for me, so I want her to relax now. To know that I'm secure and happy. Even though I'm not.

'Well, Jas?' Gran asks. 'What do you think?'

I want to agree, but I know that Adam wouldn't approve of me taking time out to do this. He'd take it as a slight that he can't support me, or that I want to spend time away from him, which makes no sense, because he's at work all day while I'm at home doing nothing but housework.

'You should do it,' Gran pushes. 'Could be a good little earner.'

'I'll give it some thought,' I reply, knowing that I'll do no such thing. The repercussions of even mentioning the idea to Adam would be too high.

As I retrieve my coat from Gran's flat, she asks me again if everything is okay. The desire to tell her my worries is so strong, I can feel the words on the tip of my tongue. I would love nothing more than to let all my troubles come pouring out. But as Gran stifles another cough, I remember that it would be selfish of me to pile this kind of stress on her. I need to sort this out myself.

Not for the first time, I wonder whether I should have confided my fears to Naomi when I saw her in town. Perhaps if I'd opened up at the time, she could have helped me figure out what to do. But, back then, things weren't as bad as they are now. I had no idea how much worse everything was going to get. And now, I think it's too late to tell her. We haven't spoken properly in two months and I feel bad that I wasn't a good enough friend when she was going through issues with Curtis. She was understandably upset when I kept fobbing her off. It wasn't that I didn't want to see her. It's just the situation with Adam has meant that I daren't.

On the bus ride home, I think about the money Sheila gave me. Her two crisp ten-pound notes sit like a prize in my purse, though I know Adam would scoff at the amount. He doesn't like me earning anything. But getting cash from Sheila and her friends, in return for doing odd jobs, would be different. It would be rewarding in a way that has nothing to do with money. It would allow me some independence again, some social contact beyond what Adam dictates.

Last month, I suggested to him that I should look for a part-time job to take the pressure off him, so he didn't have to carry the burden of our finances by himself. He accused me of not having faith in him. If he knew about Sheila's offer, I don't know how he'd react. I wish I did. I wish I could predict his emotions. Sometimes he's so loving and sweet that I think I've imagined his terrifying outbursts. But his moods have gradually worsened to the point that I know for sure it's not my imagination.

The journey home takes longer than expected due to a diversion caused by roadworks. I check my phone for messages, dreading one from him. Dreading none. He said he wouldn't be home till one, but sometimes he changes his mind and comes home earlier. Even when he is in a good mood, he expects the house to be in perfect order, lunch or dinner ready and my day completely devoted to the home. I left the breakfast things out this morning as I had to rush to catch the bus to Gran's. I'm praying I get in before him so I get the chance to tidy it all away.

Please don't let him be back before me.

I'm not sure exactly when it happened, but there's now an understanding that I'll only visit Gran once a month. And, as I saw Gran two weeks ago, I shouldn't have visited her today. Which is why I didn't tell Adam about it, because it's not worth the argument. But if he discovers I went there without telling him . . . I don't know what he'll do. It's not the first time I've snuck out to see her, but it's getting harder and harder on my nerves. I'm not sure how long I can keep doing it.

Adam's grandparents died when he was young, so he can't relate. I tried explaining that Gran is like a mum to me and that she looks forward to my visits, but Adam just brushed it off by bringing up the fact that she has a great social life and doesn't need me fussing around her. But our relationship isn't like that. Gran and I are close. We need and enjoy each other's company. Adam just doesn't get it.

I consider phoning, telling him I've been to Gran's, so that if he does get home first at least he's not blindsided by my absence. But if I do that and he's not home, then I'll be making him angry for nothing. My ears are buzzing as I get off the bus, open my umbrella and head towards home. I don't even feel the icy rain on my fingers or the easterly wind cutting into my cheeks. All I can think about is whether or not I'm going to see Adam's navy VW van parked in the drive when I get home.

My heart slams against my ribcage as I turn the corner into our street and peer through the rain to find out whether our driveway is empty or not.

Thank God.

His van isn't there.

I unlock the front door and step inside, not quite trusting that he isn't home, despite the absence of his van. I dump my bag in the hall and hurry to tidy up the breakfast things. I hear myself breathing loud and fast. My hands shake as though they're possessed, and I drop a mug on the tiled floor, swearing as it smashes, sending shards of pottery in all directions.

It's almost 1 p.m. What if he comes home right now while the bed is unmade and the mug is in pieces? He'll go mad. I pause and listen for an engine. For his van door slamming. I can't hear any telltale sounds but that doesn't mean anything. I leave the smashed mug for a moment and rush to the living room at the front of the house where I peer through the window, my pulse racing.

He's not there.

I have time.

Just breathe deep, calm down, and get it done. I manage to pull myself together just as a text comes through from my husband.

> Running late. Be home around two. Can you do me a fried egg sandwich when I get in? Thanks. Love you xx

The relief is so deep, so overwhelming, that I let out a strangled sob. Why am I living like this? My mind steeped in anxiety and fear. My days a combination of boredom and terror, with only fleeting moments of relief, like this one right now. But what can I do to change it? I have no money, no job, no other home. And Adam would never let me go. Not without a fight. I'm trapped and I can't see any way out.

Chapter Seventeen

WILLOW

I'm painting a hallway in the tasteful shade of Farrow & Ball's *Stony Ground*. My client, Tansy, a forty-something divorcee with blonde hair and sharp features, stands at the bottom of the stairs of her Edwardian house, her arms crossed, a thoughtful expression on her face. I glance up as she surveys the space, her deep-red jumper creating a stark contrast against the neutral tones of the hallway. The walls are now smooth and rich, reflecting the light from the windows and making the space feel bigger and brighter.

Tansy, who's full of opinions, is thrilled with it. She's also full of advice, especially about my relationship with Gabe. I somehow found myself opening up to her about my situation with him and Priya, which is most unlike me. But I've desperately wanted to talk to someone about it, and Tansy is far enough removed from my life for me to feel comfortable telling her what's been happening.

'Don't you dare let your neighbour put you off your new boyfriend,' she chides, her gravelly voice a balm to my anxiety.

'But won't it be weird?' I ask, loading my brush with fresh paint. 'And isn't it a bit of a no-no? What about "girl code"?'

'I thought you said you met him before you met her,' Tansy says, folding her arms.

'Well, yes. I did meet him first. I spilled my coffee over him at the café' – I smile at the memory – 'and then I met Priya a month later.'

'So, like I said, you met him first,' she reiterates. 'That's definitely allowed under Girl Code: Article 2, Subsection D.'

I turn to give her a grin.

She winks back at me. 'Stop worrying about her, and worry about you. Do you know how hard it is to meet a decent man? Almost impossible. And the ones you do meet, at our age' – I let the fact that she's grouping us in the same age bracket slide – 'well, they've all got history. They're all weighed down by a tonne of baggage. Just like we are.'

I can't disagree with her.

'So, when you meet a good one, you do everything you can to hold on to him, okay? He deserves a clean slate. So do you.'

'I suppose.'

'No "suppose" about it. You cling on to that man and fight every bitch who tries to separate you from him.'

I laugh at this, glancing over as she continues to lecture me on relationship dos and don'ts. She speaks with a lightness of tone, but I can tell there's a tinge of bitterness beneath the advice. A bitterness to which I can relate, but I don't tell her about all that.

'Look, Willow,' she says, sitting down on the stairs and resting her elbows on her knees. 'I really like you and I don't want you to make the same mistakes I did – trusting the wrong people, being too nice, putting every damn person ahead of yourself. It was only when I started standing up for myself and doing what was right for me that my life started getting better.'

'I'm glad things are going well for you now,' I reply.

'You're sweet,' she says. 'Look, I'm not advocating being a horrible human. I'm just saying, don't be a doormat. Don't shove your happiness aside through misplaced loyalties.'

As our conversation rolls on – and she brings out tea, cake, and even offers wine, which I decline – she seems more determined to convince me to give Gabe the benefit of the doubt, speaking about her past mistakes, but with the tentative brightness of someone who's finding her confidence again. It's actually quite inspiring and I realise that maybe she's right. Maybe I should stop worrying about who's been with who and just focus on myself and Gabe. After all, everyone has a past. Maybe I should just own mine, but not let it hold me back from my future.

'Thanks for coming to my Ted Talk,' she finally says, her mouth quirking upwards. 'Sorry for going on, but I couldn't help myself. Can you tell I live alone?' She laughs.

'I appreciate all the advice. Honestly, Tansy, it's been so nice to talk to someone about this. You should charge me for your time. Ever thought of becoming a counsellor?'

'Ha! You're very kind, but I'd be terrible at it. I'm no good at following the rules. I'd end up getting struck off, or going to counsellor jail or whatever it is they do to the ones with no filter.'

By the time I've finished for the day, I've convinced myself that I am going to continue seeing Gabe. It's 4 p.m., so I load up my van and start the engine, optimistic that I'm making the right decision, my stomach filled with butterflies at the thought of seeing him later. Of actually giving this a proper go.

I float through the journey home, stopping for groceries and ticking off errands that had been buried under the avalanche of my anxiety. By the time I turn into my road, I'm bubbling over with relief and excitement. I want to tell Gabe everything, reassure him how happy I am that we met and that I don't care about his past relationships. That they're irrelevant.

I enter my apartment block and almost fly up the stairs, keen to shower and make myself look good for when I message Gabe, in the hope that he's free to come over. I reach the second floor, my heart buzzing with hope as I put my hand on the landing door to push it open. But I'm completely floored when, through the glass, I spy a familiar figure standing at the entrance to Priya's flat.

It's Gabe.

It stops me dead in my tracks, and I remain frozen, just watching, unable to look away. They haven't noticed me yet. Gabe is wearing a navy wool jacket and jeans. He has his back to me and Priya's face is blocked by him. He's saying something to her, but his voice is too low for me to hear. His body language is relaxed, as if it's the most natural thing in the world for him to be there.

I take a single quiet step to the side, my movements slow and calculated, trying not to be seen or heard. The short distance between me and them feels like a chasm. My optimism is splintered, my thoughts chaotic, crashing into each other, trying to make sense of what I'm seeing. I watch them a second longer, a moment that stretches into eternity. Has he been coming here to see her all along? Was I just fooling myself this whole time, thinking I was different, that *we* were different?

There's an ache where my excitement was a moment ago, and I can't breathe for the confusion. Then, suddenly, they both laugh – a quick, light sound that flies to me like an arrow. It jolts me back to my senses. I need to get out of here. I need to not be seen by them.

Every muscle in my body tells me to move, to flee, to get away before they notice me standing here like a complete idiot. But then I watch helplessly as Gabe steps across the threshold and into Priya's flat. The door closes behind them, crushing any confidence I'd just built up. I feel a rush of raw emotion, a wave of disbelief, and then the blow of reality.

My heart pounds in my ears, and I turn and bolt back down the stairs, tripping over my own feet in my hurry to escape into the cold, grey evening, out into the rain that's just starting to fall. I slump against the wall of the building, drawing in deep breaths that do absolutely nothing to calm the disappointment that clogs my throat and pricks my eyes. What a fool I've been.

Chapter Eighteen

JASMINE

Adam's upstairs in the shower while I'm in the middle of laying the table for our ritual Saturday breakfast together. We didn't have it last week as Adam was working, so I've made an extra-special effort with it today, squeezing fresh orange juice and adding all the trimmings to his full English. I'm wiping a watermark off one of the knives when the doorbell rings, the sound echoing through the house like an alarm. My heart thuds. Should I answer it? Normally Adam gets the door if he's home, but he can't exactly do that right now. The bell rings again, its chime stressing me out to the point of nausea.

I'll have to answer it. It's too early for the mail. Maybe it's Carol from next door needing another chat about the garden or something. She's hasn't been put off by Adam's rudeness or my subtle attempts to dissuade her from coming over. She doesn't seem to pick up on social cues at all. Despite that, I kind of like her. She's never explicitly said anything, but I get the feeling she knows something's up between me and Adam, and she's on my side. Hopefully, it's her at the door, and I can just say we're having breakfast and to come back during the week – when Adam's at work. But then her red setter, Alfie, starts barking, and I hear Carol through the wall, shouting at him to be quiet, so it can't be her at the door.

I lay down the clean knife and turn the heat down on the grill as I make my way to the front door and pull it open with some trepidation.

'Hey, Jasmine!'

I'm completely taken aback to see three of my ex-work colleagues on my front step. I haven't seen them in five months. Not since my last day of work when I had to ditch them to have dinner with my husband. It's a treat to see their friendly faces, but I'm also panicking as to why they're here. Adam isn't going to like his Saturday morning being interrupted. I hope I can put them off somehow.

'Hey, Jasmine,' Chrissie says, her eyes shining. 'Thought we'd surprise you with coffee and Danish pastries!'

Louie waves some paper bags at me, while Tina presents me with a cardboard tray stacked with five coffee cups, saying, 'We figured if you're too busy to come to us, we'd come to you.'

'Oh, guys,' I say, caught between happiness and dread, 'that's so nice of you, but Adam and I are just about to—'

'Jasmine?' Adam walks up behind me and my stomach lurches.

I turn towards him, worried how he'll react. He's bare-chested, a towel wrapped around his waist. 'Hey, Adam, the guys from my old work are here with coffee, but I told them that—'

He puts his hands on my shoulders and kisses the side of my head, his hair dripping from the shower. 'You brought coffee?' he says to them, his eyes bright and welcoming. 'Perfect timing. We were just about to have breakfast. Come in and join us. I've been saying to Jasmine that she ought to invite her friends over more often. Honestly, she's such a hermit these days.'

'Great!' Chrissie grins at me and steps into the hallway, Louie and Tina following, bringing in the fresh morning air.

'Let me just run up and get changed,' Adam says. 'Back in a mo.'

I show my friends into the kitchen, my heart racing from Adam's lies. Why did he feel the need to tell them that? Probably because he knows that he's been treating me badly and he doesn't want my friends to worry about our relationship. I'm surprised he invited them in. When I heard his voice behind me, I was certain he was going to try to get rid of them.

'Something smells amazing,' Louie says, heading over to the stove where he pokes about to see what I'm preparing. 'Full English? Yes please.'

'I'm sure there's enough to go round.' I smile despite my uneasiness. It feels so good to have my friends here. They're like a light in the darkness. 'Can you grab some more plates?' I point to the cupboards. 'Cutlery's in this drawer.'

'She's bossing us around again,' Louie says.

'Just like old times,' Chrissie adds with a grin.

'I am not!' I retort, feeling a glimmer of my old self shining through. I turn up the grill and flip the bacon and sausages.

Chrissie immediately launches into a lively update, telling me that she's been working for a new company in insurance sales. It's been busy, but she seems thrilled with it all. She says she might be in line for a promotion soon. She's beaming as she talks, clearly caught up in the whirlwind of her career. 'You know, there are a couple of openings if you're interested, Jas,' she adds. 'I could have a word with my manager, if you like?'

'What's this?' Adam comes into the kitchen, and hugs me from behind, kissing my ear.

Chrissie turns to him. 'I was just saying that—'

'What about you, Louie?' I ask, feeling bad for interrupting her, but not wanting to give Adam any excuse to have a go at me later. The last thing I need is for him to accuse me of fishing for a job offer.

Thankfully, Louie jumps in and says he's moved back in with his parents to save money while he tries to get his new business off the ground.

'What business?' I tip the quartered mushrooms into the frying pan and sprinkle salt over them. 'You said you wanted to start working for yourself. Now I'm intrigued.'

'It's, like, all online,' Louie explains, waving his arms dramatically. 'Skincare products. We're even doing celebrity endorsements!'

'Sounds fascinating,' Adam says, loosening his hold and fetching the ketchup and mayo from the fridge. He rolls his eyes at me over my friends' heads. He's being mean and wants me to join in, but I can't respond because my friends are all looking my way.

Oblivious, Louie continues. 'I'll show you all the product line in a minute. You'll love it. You can even come on board, if you like?' He's smiling but there's something a little defensive about the way he talks, like he's expecting me to shoot him down. Honestly, it sounds a bit like a pyramid scheme, but I don't want to be negative and burst his bubble. Instead, I nod encouragingly. 'Sounds amazing, Louie.'

'It really is.'

'I think everything's ready now,' I say. 'I'll just get the orange juice from the fridge.'

'I'll get it, Jas,' Adam offers. 'Sit down, everyone.' He gestures to the table.

'What about you, Tina?' I ask, dishing everything up on to warmed serving platters.

Tina sits, her eyes shining. 'You'll never believe it, Jasmine, but I got re-employed by our old company.'

'What? Really?'

'Didn't even have to interview!' she adds. 'It worked out great! I got to keep my redundancy money, had a month and a half of pure freedom, and then I got re-employed on a higher salary. Sorry, guys.' She looks so pleased with herself that I can't help but laugh along with her. She and Chrissie have this amazing confidence, just like when I knew them at work, and I'm envious of how bold and carefree they seem to be. I feel like such a mouse in comparison.

'Jammy cow,' Louie retorts, smiling to show there are no hard feelings.

'How about you?' Chrissie asks. 'I can't believe we haven't seen you since last year. You must be busy. What have you been up to?'

'That's my fault,' Adam replies, taking a seat directly opposite me. 'She's been helping me out with my business. She's been a godsend actually. Don't know what I'd do without her.'

'Aww,' Tina says. 'That's so nice.'

'Doing what?' Chrissie looks from Adam to me.

'All sorts,' Adam answers for me again. 'Helping with the accounts, taking bookings, doing quotes for customers.'

Chrissie scrutinises my face while Adam is talking and I do my best to look relaxed.

Of course, everything Adam is saying right now is a lie. I haven't been doing any of that. But he can't exactly tell them that he's been guilt-tripping me into not seeing my friends, not getting a new job, not applying to uni. That I have no car insurance, no income and no social media. That I'm basically a prisoner in my own home. They'd be horrified.

Thirty minutes later, Adam makes the excuse that he and I are going out, but that we'll all have to get together again some time. They thank us for breakfast, and we thank them for the coffee and Danishes.

Knowing that they're leaving, and I'll be alone with my husband, sends my pulse skyrocketing. My head is woozy and my toes and fingertips start to tingle as I hug my friends goodbye, clinging on as though each one of them is a lifebuoy.

After the front door closes behind them, a silence descends on the house. The hairs stand up on the back of my neck as I wait for the coming storm.

'What the hell was that?' Adam says, his voice dangerously quiet. 'Why was my Saturday morning interrupted by a bunch of fuckwits? I work hard during the week. Is it too much to ask for some peace and quiet at the weekend?'

'I was going to send them away,' I reply, trying to sound as conciliatory as possible.

'Sure you were,' he sneers, striding away into the kitchen. 'And how would that have made me look?'

As I follow him, I don't dare mention the fact that he had his mates over last night to play video games. He can have his friends round, but I can't have mine. How does he think that's fair? How can he justify treating me this way?

'Did you arrange for them to come over today?' he asks. 'Have you been calling them? Meeting up with them behind my back?'

'No, of course not.' I place a tentative hand on his arm. 'I would never do that.'

'I don't believe you.' He jerks his arm away. 'I don't think I can trust you anymore, Jasmine. God knows I've tried, but you keep letting me down. It's too much.'

I stay silent, wondering what this means. Hoping and praying that he might be about to suggest a separation or a divorce. If the idea comes from him, then I'll be free to leave. Please let that be what he wants. Because there's no way I could ever suggest such a thing myself. He wouldn't allow it.

My hopes are quickly squashed.

'I'm going to have to put a tracker app on your phone,' he says. 'It's the only way to know you're being honest with me. That you're not secretly going out to meet your friends while I'm at work. I honestly didn't expect this from you, Jasmine.'

'A tracker app?' My heart plummets. If he does that, then I won't be able to sneak off to visit Gran as often, and I can't bear the thought of that.

'Yeah,' he replies. 'It's a good idea, right?'

I don't reply.

'Jas?' he pushes. 'It's a good idea, right?' He enunciates each word to let me know that I need to agree.

'Yeah. Yes. Sure. It's a good idea.'

His shoulders relax and he holds his hand out for my phone. He already knows the password so I let him install the app. What other choice do I have?

He glances around the room slowly, taking in the state of the kitchen island and the dining table covered in leftovers and dirty plates. My friends offered to help clean up, but Adam laughed and said not to be silly. That the two of us would do it later.

'Your friends, your mess,' he says now. 'I'm going upstairs. Make sure it's all spick and span by the time I come back down.'

I nod mutely as he leaves the room.

His heavy footfalls on the stairs are like drumbeats sounding a death knell, and the creaking floorboards overhead make me feel like the ceiling is pressing down on me, squeezing the air from my lungs. I know I have to do something. I can't carry on living like this. The only way I could possibly leave him is to move far away where he can never find me. But I have no money and no transport. My phone now has a tracker app. And, besides, more importantly, I could never leave Gran.

With a lightning bolt of clarity, something suddenly occurs to me – Adam said his ex-girlfriend left him without a trace. The one he used to work with. Is that because he treated her the same way he's treating me? Did he put her through the exact same fear and anxiety that I'm experiencing right now? I'd previously thought that she was a terrible person for leaving him with no word. For hurting him so badly. How could she do such a cowardly thing? I remember promising Adam that he needn't ever worry about me. That I would never do something so callous. I smile grimly to myself. *Never say never*. Because now my sympathies have switched. I can totally see why his ex had to leave. She was given no choice. Did she do a moonlight flit to escape from him? I envy her so much. If it weren't for Gran, I'd do the same thing.

Chapter Nineteen

JASMINE

'Straight there and straight back,' Adam says, his voice low and clipped, his gaze drilling into me like he can see my rebellious thoughts. He stands in the doorway, his jacket slung over one arm, rays of morning light tracing the sharp angles of his jaw.

I force a bright smile. 'Of course,' I chirp. Then I add, with practised cheer, 'I'm actually looking forward to coming home and trying out this new chicken-and-squash cacciatore recipe I saw online. Can't wait for you to taste it tonight!' My default setting around Adam these days is upbeat and happy. The breezier I sound, the more relaxed he is. My acting skills are getting better.

'Sounds good,' my husband replies with a satisfied nod, the corners of his mouth inching upwards for a fraction of a second. 'Your cooking's much better these days.'

Twin coils of relief and dread twist in my chest. Ever since he put the tracking app on my phone last month, I've been restricted to the house, scared to go anywhere aside from the supermarket or any other place that he deems necessary. Adam floated the idea of getting online food deliveries to 'save time', but I've managed to put him off by saying that the problem with online shopping is that the sell-by dates aren't great and I prefer to pick out my own fresh fruit and veg. He reluctantly agreed, but I don't know how much longer he'll go along with it. Any day now, I'm expecting him to put his foot down and insist on home deliveries only, which will confine me to the house even more.

A couple of times, I bravely – or stupidly – left my phone at home to go visit Gran, and another time I left it to go to the doctor's. But I was so anxious at the thought of Adam arriving home to find me gone that I almost threw up from the stress. I wish I were braver.

Today, Adam has asked me to take some paperwork over to his dad for him to sign as he has a crucial meeting with a development company who could potentially give him a lucrative contract. I'm excited to get out of the house on a legitimate errand. One I'm not terrified that Adam will find out about. Instead I can relax on the bus journey. Daydream about a different life.

'Jasmine . . .' Adam grasps my wrist, jolting me out of my reverie. 'I mean it when I say no detours, okay? Take the bus to Dad's, then come straight home.'

I nod, my heart pounding, my wrist on fire where he's squeezing and twisting it so hard it feels as though the bone might snap.

'Yes, of course,' I whisper, trying not to let any traitorous tears fall. I've learned the hard way that Adam does not like tears. He says that I'm only crying to guilt-trip him. That it's manipulative and selfish.

He lets go of my wrist and I blink and sniff. 'I think I might be coming down with a cold,' I lie, resisting the urge to rub my throbbing wrist or even look at it.

'You better sleep in the spare room tonight then,' he replies. 'I can't afford to get ill right now. Too much on at work.'

I pretend to look disappointed. 'Okay.' I sigh. 'I'd better go if I'm going to catch the 8.40 bus,' I add, stuffing the paperwork into my tote.

'Careful with that,' Adam snaps. 'Don't crease it.'

'Sorry,' I reply meekly.

We leave the house together, Adam getting into his van, while I set off down the road towards the bus stop. I jump as Adam beeps his horn and waves as he passes me, rounding the bend and disappearing from view. Out here in the bright, chilly April air, I feel as though I can finally breathe again.

Now that I'm alone, I stop for a moment and push up the sleeve of my coat to examine my wrist. I wince at the reddish welt forming where he grabbed me. This isn't the first time he's been rough. There are already a couple of bruises on my forearm from previous 'discussions' when he wanted to make a point. I pull my sleeve back down and quicken my pace. I don't want to miss the bus.

I make it there with a few minutes to spare, and hover on the periphery of the crowded shelter, lost in my thoughts. I have a soft spot for Adam's dad. He's always been lovely towards me, cracking jokes, drawing me into their conversations. I've never truly managed to get over losing my own father at ten years old. Always wondered how different my life might have been if he was still here. So, having Nigel has been a blessing. Almost like having a second dad.

I glance up as the bus doors hiss open and the queue surges forward. Inside, toddlers chatter and squeal, mums juggle prams, and pensioners shuffle to empty seats. I plant myself by the window, watching rows of familiar brick houses slip past, with their neat hedges and aloof cats. I gaze at pedestrians going about their daily lives, and I wonder if they're happy, if their lives are carefree and simple, or if they're guarding terrible secrets. Like me. My stomach rises and dips with the constant anxiety that I've grown used to.

Thirty minutes later, I ding the bell next to my seat and make my way down the aisle to the exit, where I step down on to the pavement and glance up to see my father-in-law, walking down the road.

'Nigel!' I cry, surprised but pleased to see him.

'Hello, Jasmine,' he replies warmly. 'Adam called to tell me which bus you were getting. Said it would be nice to meet you at the bus stop. I was fetching the paper anyway,' he adds, waving a rolled-up tabloid.

'Oh, that *is* nice,' I agree, leaning in to kiss his clean-shaven cheek, pushing away the thought that Adam only called his dad to meet me because he didn't trust that I would come straight here.

'Well, this is a treat,' Nigel adds as we walk side by side. 'Don't often get visitors on a Thursday morning. Actually, don't get visitors any mornings!'

'You know you're welcome to come round to ours whenever you like,' I offer without thinking, hoping Adam won't object to the invitation. He and his dad get on well, so I'm sure it would be fine.

'Thanks, Jas. That's nice to know, but I wouldn't want to be a bother.'

'Don't be daft,' I reply. 'We love having you over.'

Adam's dad retired to Guildford from his home town of Basingstoke five years ago and lives in one of Adam's properties, a one-bedroom flat near the river. Nigel loves it as it's close enough to town that he can walk there, plus he's happy to be living much closer to his son – and to me, I hope.

We turn into a pretty side street lined with trees, their branches almost bare, and stop outside Nigel's building. He reaches into his pocket for the keys and lets us inside. We head to the rear of the overheated entrance lobby and come to a halt outside the door of his ground-floor flat. While he's fiddling with the lock, a thought flashes into my brain. One that makes my head swim.

'You coming in?'

I realise I'm standing like a lemon outside the door while he's waiting expectantly.

'Oh, yes, sorry, Nigel.' I remove my coat distractedly, my mind spinning through the pros and cons of my idea. I must be mad for even considering it. It could backfire hideously. But the alternative is to carry on like I am, and I genuinely don't think I can take much more.

'Fancy a brew?' Nigel asks as we step inside. He takes my coat and hangs it on one of the hooks by the door. I follow him into the small contemporary kitchen – Adam renovated the whole flat before his dad moved in. 'I usually have a cup of tea while I read the paper,' he adds. 'It'll be nice to have a natter for a change. Sit down.' He gestures to the small wooden table next to the wall, two folding chairs tucked at either end.

'Tea would be great,' I reply distractedly as I pull out a chair and sit.

Nigel switches on the kettle and makes us both a mug of tea while chatting about the neighbour above who plays his music too loudly, and about his run-in yesterday with a rude cashier at the bank. He reaches up to a shelf for his classic-cars biscuit tin – the one that Adam got him last year for Father's Day. 'Sorry, I've only got Digestives,' he says. 'An oldie but a classic, bit like me.'

I grin and help myself to one of the crumbly biscuits as he proffers the open tin. 'Lovely,' I say, taking a bite. I reach down and take the papers from my bag – not sure what they are, something to do with the flat, I think – and pass them to Nigel, still wondering whether or not to follow through with my idea. I've always got on really well with Adam's dad. He's sweet, kind. I know he genuinely thinks of me as family, so I like to think he'd listen to my worries and maybe offer to . . . I don't know, to help somehow. I only hope he believes me.

'Thanks.' Nigel sits down heavily opposite me and places the paperwork on the table in front of him. 'I better not spill any tea on this lot.'

'No,' I agree, trying to keep my voice steady.

'So, how's everything with you two? Saw Adam a couple of weeks ago and he said you're going to be starting a family soon.' His eyes light up. 'That's exciting news. Looking forward to being a grandad.'

I can't believe Adam told his dad we're starting a family. Actually, I can believe it. My own wishes don't seem to be of any consequence at all. 'Well,' I reply carefully. 'I hope you will be a grandad, one day.' My heart starts twanging in my chest. 'I'd really like to go to college first, though. Study for a nursing degree. But . . .' I swallow, my throat dry as dust. I take a sip of tea and continue. 'Adam's not keen on me going to uni.'

'He wants a family.' Nigel chuckles. 'You can't blame the lad. He's building a little empire. Wants kids to pass it on to. You'll make a great mum, Jasmine.'

Nigel's words aren't the comfort he thinks they are. Saying that he thinks I'll make a great mum makes me think of my own mother and how she accidentally fell pregnant with me. How she never really wanted a child and how I've felt that resentment all through my life. It hurts to know I stood in the way of her living the life she wanted, and it's not something I would want to put a child through. If I ever become a mother, I would want that child to know how loved they are. How wanted. Like my dad. He always let me know how cherished I was to him.

I begin, my voice small, 'I—' My throat closes around the words. 'The thing is, I'm . . . struggling a bit.'

'Struggling?' Nigel echoes, his eyes filling with concern. 'Struggling how?'

I take a breath. 'With my marriage.'

My father-in-law frowns and I think I might have made a terrible error in judgement. I push on anyway. 'Adam . . . he's not always nice to me.' I swallow. 'Sometimes . . . well, I'm a bit scared of him. I don't know what to do about it.' I exhale and hope with all my heart that my father-in-law will help me. Will throw some kind of lifeline to get me out of this dark whirlpool that's sucking me under.

Nigel stares down at his hands folded on the table. But when he looks back up at me, I see allegiance to Adam harden his gaze. 'Jasmine,' he says, voice steady, 'Adam's your husband. It's really not my place to interfere in your marriage.' He clears his throat. 'He can get a bit . . . passionate when he's talking, sometimes. But I know for a fact he loves you. Worships the ground you walk on.'

My stomach tightens. I clutch my mug of tea, knuckles whitening. 'It doesn't always feel that way,' I whisper, swallowing back tears. 'He's—'

Nigel cuts me off. 'Start that family,' he suggests. 'That'll give you something to focus on. Stop you worrying about everything. You've probably got a bit too much time on your hands.' He shifts in his seat, glances at the papers and reaches for a pen from the shelf behind him. He scribbles his signature once, twice, three times. 'There . . . I've signed the pages he's marked. He's a good lad, looking after his old man, and looking after you. He's a provider, is Adam. You shouldn't forget that.'

His loyalty seals the room in ice. I give a forced smile, stand, and tuck my hair behind my ear. 'Well, I'd better get back. Lots to do,' I mumble, taking the proffered paperwork and slipping it into my tote, fingers trembling with disappointment.

'Good of you to bring it over, Jasmine,' he replies, businesslike.

'No problem,' I reply, echoing his tone and stepping into the hallway. A further chill envelops me as I slip on my coat. I press my bag against my side, heart pounding in my hollowed-out chest as a new fear starts to hit. 'Nigel,' I begin. 'Our conversation just now, can you—'

'It never happened,' he interrupts. 'You're just having a bad day, that's all.'

I nod my thanks, relieved he won't relay my disloyalty to Adam while at the same time feeling as though a stone has dropped into my stomach. I realise now that Nigel was the worst person I could have spoken to. Of course he wasn't going to side with me against his son. What was I thinking?

Outside again, the spring sun hangs pale above the rooftops, and I tuck my chin against the cold, wondering how much longer I can keep pretending – and whether I'll ever be able to escape my husband.

For the hundredth time, I wish I'd opened up to Naomi when I had the chance. Maybe I could sneak off to her apartment somehow. Explain the real reason I've been unable to meet up with her – surely she'd be sympathetic. But even as I'm having the thought, I know I'll never do it – I couldn't handle a possible rejection, not to mention the fact that if Adam found out . . . I shudder. Maybe my only hope is to speak to Gran. Even though I swore to myself that I wouldn't burden her with my worries. I can't see any other way out.

Chapter Twenty

WILLOW

After the shock of witnessing Gabe go into Priya's flat, I ended up walking in the rain to try to gather my thoughts. But the weather's getting worse so I'm forced to return home, still without any clarity. As I round the corner, I stop short. *There he is.* Gabe stands under the faded canopy outside my building, his broad shoulders slightly hunched against the gusting rain that shrouds the pavement. I pause in my tracks, my heart pounding. He hasn't spotted me. Reluctant for him to see me yet, I keep my distance, my mind churning with the thought that, maybe, if he confesses to having seen Priya and explains why he went into her apartment, if he tells me the truth before I have to ask for it, our relationship might somehow be saved.

For a brief moment, I allow myself to study him – even in the cold drizzle, he looks so good it makes me catch my breath. He's wearing the same navy jacket and jeans as when he went into Priya's flat an hour ago. But I'm puzzled – if he was up there earlier, why is he waiting outside the building now?

Standing frozen as the rain continues to pelt me, soaking my hair and clinging to my lashes, I waver between anxiety and relief at the chance to clear things up with him so soon. Suddenly, I can't contain it any longer: curiosity overwhelms me, and I march up to him through the rain-soaked gloom.

Gabe's face lights up with a smile as he sees me heading his way, but it falters when he catches my hard expression. 'Willow,' he begins. 'You're soaking.'

'Why are you out here?' I ask brusquely.

Confusion clouds his features. 'I wanted to surprise you, but you weren't home yet, so I thought I'd wait.'

'Been here long?'

'Um, not too long, no. Are you okay? You seem a bit . . .' He hesitates, searching for the right word.

'A bit what?' I reply, struggling to sound civil.

'Annoyed. Have I done something wrong?' Gabe runs a hand through his hair, then scratches his cheek.

'I don't know, have you?' I ask, my voice rising as frustration shakes my words. Maybe I'm coming across as a bit unhinged, but I'm sick of second-guessing everything. I want to know if he's being straight up, or if I'm being played.

'Okay, what's going on?' he asks warily.

Taking a deep breath and steeling myself, I blurt out, 'I came home earlier and saw you go into Priya's flat.' My words hang in the damp air as I brace myself for his explanation.

He looks at me, startled for a moment, and then his shoulders relax. 'Oh, that. Yeah, she saw me waiting out here and asked if I could take a look at her sink. It's blocked.'

'You went into her flat to unblock her sink?' I hear the scepticism in my voice.

'I'm well aware how it sounds,' he counters. 'But what else could I do?' He shrugs. 'I know it's a bit awkward that she still likes me, but I feel sorry for her.'

'She still likes you?' I cry, feeling a sting of jealousy at his words. 'That's not the impression she gave me. She seemed fine with us seeing each other. She said you two were over.'

Gabe pauses and he blows on his hands and rubs them together for warmth. 'Can we go inside to talk about this? It's freezing out here.'

'Fine,' I agree reluctantly, nodding toward my building's entrance. I'd prefer to have this conversation in private anyway, and I'm soaked through to the skin. My heart races as I turn the key and grip the doorknob, my palms slick with rain. I open the door and usher him inside, the sharp chill of the evening replaced by the quiet warmth of the lobby.

As we walk up the stairs in silence, I'm not sure what to believe. Past deceptions rise to the surface, casting shadows over his words. I can't help fearing the worst. I mean, the woman is gorgeous, why wouldn't Gabe want to 'unblock her sink'. But if that's the case, then why start something with *me*?

We reach my floor and walk past Priya's flat. I glare at her door, frustrated by the whole situation. I open my door and usher him in, removing my sodden coat and hanging it on the hook. 'I need to change out of these clothes,' I say, gesturing to my dripping work overalls.

Gabe nods and I disappear into the bedroom, shedding my clothes and pulling on a pair of black joggers and a pink sweatshirt. My skin is still damp, but at least I feel a bit warmer. I grab a towel from the airing cupboard and start drying my hair as I head back to the lounge.

Gabe flops down on the sofa. 'Sit with me.' He pats the space next to him and I reluctantly do as he asks.

Why does he have to smell so good? Like rain and cedarwood. It makes me want to kiss him. It would be so easy to do that, to forget all the crap and lose myself in the moment, but I'm not going to do that. I shift away a few inches and lay the damp towel over the arm of the sofa. After my optimistic afternoon with Tansy, I feel so deflated, so incredibly bleak. But I haven't really been with him for long enough to feel this disappointed.

'I don't think I can do this, Gabe,' I say, staring ahead at the blank TV.

'Are you serious?' he asks.

'It's just all too weird with your ex living down the hall, and you popping in to fix her sink. I mean, maybe if she didn't live in the same building it wouldn't be so . . . complicated.'

'So we'll both just ignore her,' he says swiftly.

'I can't just ignore her,' I retort. 'She lives down the hall. I see her almost every day.'

'Okay, well not *ignore*, just be polite . . . civil. And I'll act the same way. I really like you, Willow. We can't let someone else break us up. Not when there's nothing going on between me and Priya.'

It's nice to know that he feels this strongly about us. That he doesn't want to accept me calling it quits. But I still feel uneasy about the situation.

Gabe must see the hesitation on my face because he gives me an earnest look that's hard to resist. 'I promise, there's nothing to worry about with Priya,' he reassures. 'As far as I'm concerned, she's history, and I really want to keep seeing you.'

'If she's history, why did you go into her flat today?'

'She asked for help,' he says, a vein of desperation running through his voice. 'Like I said, I felt sorry for her. I know I should never have agreed to it. I just wasn't thinking straight.'

'I understand that,' I say softly, 'but the whole thing just feels overwhelming. I don't think I've got the mental energy for any of it right now.'

'Even though we get on really well? Even though you're my Cappuccino Girl?' he adds, flashing a hopeful grin.

I can't help a bittersweet smile escaping at that – those silly little words. They're supposed to make me feel special, but right now they only add to the heaviness in my chest. I don't want this situation. I don't have the bandwidth to deal with complicated relationships. I thought Gabe and I were going to be straightforward and simple.

For a fleeting, hopeful moment, Gabe reaches out and lightly touches my arm. Instantly, I recoil, not wanting any contact. This is hard enough already. 'I'm sorry, Gabe. I think you'd better go.' I stand abruptly.

'I promise I'll never go into her flat again. Like I said, I'll be polite but curt with her. Then, hopefully, she'll get the message.'

'I'm sorry, but no.' I walk over to the lounge door, wanting him to leave now that I've made up my mind.

He shakes his head, dispirited, and stands slowly.

Much as I want to heed Tansy's advice that I should give things a go with him, that was before I saw him and Priya together. I can't live with this kind of uncertainty in my life. Tansy was right when she said I need to put myself first. And I think the only way I can do that is to say goodbye to Gabe.

I walk him into the hall and watch him leave.

Immediately after I close the door, a torrent of uncertainty floods my mind. Have I made a terrible mistake? Have I pushed away the person I like most in the world?

I have to remind myself that I was fine before I met him, and I'll find my footing again afterwards. It might just take a little time to adjust to the disappointment.

As I head back to the empty lounge, my phone buzzes with a message. It's Gabe, saying that he's not giving up on me. For a swift instant, a spark of hope flickers in my chest, but I shut it down straightaway – that's the slippery slope towards heartache.

I should probably block him, but I can't bring myself to do it. Not just yet.

Chapter Twenty-One

JASMINE

The front door slams behind my husband as he leaves for work, and my body goes limp. I collapse on to a kitchen chair and sit, coma-like, for a few minutes. These days, I feel as though I'm holding my breath when he's at home, and I can only exhale after he departs. It doesn't feel much better when he's gone though. The only bright spot is that spring is finally here and so I can spend time in the garden rather than being cooped up in the house all day.

I stand and head upstairs and into the bedroom, where I strip the bed. I take fresh, ironed linens from the airing cupboard and meticulously remake it. Adam has decided that it's nicer to sleep in clean sheets every night. I don't disagree – it's definitely nice. However it's a chore to wash and iron sheets, duvet covers and pillowcases every single day. Ditto for fresh towels. Basically, I have to make sure that, by the time Adam returns home, there are no dirty clothes in the wash basket and nothing left in the washing machine or tumble dryer. It must all be clean, dried, ironed and put away.

I'm sure he's giving me these chores to ensure I don't have any time to myself. But I'm getting pretty quick at getting things done. I'm not an idiot. I've found shortcuts.

Once the bed is made, the duvet smoothed and cushions plumped, I open the wardrobe and take out my favourite fake-fur jacket, and I peer out the window to double-check the driveway is empty, before sitting on my dressing table stool with the jacket on my lap.

Adam's obsession right now, aside from his work, is starting a family. We've been trying for a few months, which is bad enough, because I have to fake enjoying sex, when I feel like I'm dying each time he touches me.

He's getting frustrated that it's taking me so long to conceive, and he announced last week that he wants us to visit a fertility expert. I told him that it's proven that the best thing for conception is to be relaxed, happy and unstressed. Of course I made sure not to hint that it's me who's stressed. Instead I massaged his shoulders and told him he needed to relax about his work and not get so wound up.

This has worked in my favour as, since then, he's been extra-specially nice to me, checking that I'm happy and calm. Suggesting that we have a weekend away by the sea to unwind. But I'm not falling for the nice-guy act. I'm not dropping my guard. Because I know that one wrong move on my part will bring out his real personality. So I've been faking happiness, pretending that I adore being a domestic goddess, and that he's the love of my life. When the reality is that I hate him with a passion. I *loathe* him.

I still can't believe that we managed to spend two years together without me seeing a glimpse of his true self. How did he hide it from me for so long? How did such a seemingly beautiful relationship turn into this sham of a marriage? Was he keeping his anger and meanness bottled up all that time, love-bombing me to disguise his true intentions? Or is his personality change a recent thing? It's not exactly something I can ask him.

I turn the left sleeve of my jacket inside out and carefully pull apart the satin seam. A couple of months ago, I unpicked the stitches and created a Velcro opening with a little lined pocket, which I now open.

I need to stop Adam from booking an appointment with a fertility expert, because the reason I'm not falling pregnant is that I'm on the pill. There's no way I'm bringing children into this nightmare of a marriage. Not if I can help it. If I do, he'll try to trap me in it forever. So I'm hiding contraceptives in the lining of my jacket. I dread to think what would happen if he ever found them. It's better than the alternative though.

I remove the blister pack and pop a pill in my mouth, enjoying my act of defiance, before replacing the packet and returning my jacket to the wardrobe.

As I close the wardrobe door, I'm startled by my phone ringing. My first thought is that Adam has somehow seen what I've just done and he's calling to scare me. But I shake my head; it's probably just a spam call. I look at the screen to see an unknown number. I hesitate, then decide to answer it.

'Hello?'

'Hello, is this Jasmine Owens?' A woman's voice, professional-sounding.

'Yes, who's this?'

'I'm calling from the Royal Surrey Hospital. Your grandmother, Mrs Wendy Cartwright, was brought in to A & E early this morning. She's currently being seen by the Same Day Emergency Care Service. But she's asking for you to come in.'

'Gran!' I cry. 'What's wrong with her? Is she okay?'

'You'll need to speak to the team.'

'Can I speak to them now?' My brain is spinning out.

'It's best if you come in,' she replies.

I'm shaking as I try to locate a piece of paper and a pen to write down the directions. 'I'll be there as soon as I can,' I say before hanging up.

My heart pounds as I stare blankly around the bedroom. A *team*? What's wrong with Gran that she needs a team? I should gather a few things to take with me, but I'm too panicked to know where to begin. Might this be something to do with her cough? She told me her GP had given her the all-clear. Could she have been lying? My eyes sting as I stumble out of the room. My breathing is shallow as I hurry down the stairs, my only thought to get to the hospital – to get to Gran – in case . . . in case . . . I can't even think the words.

At least I'm dressed, but I haven't brushed my teeth or washed my face. I don't care. I don't have time for that. Frantic, I almost trip over my own feet as I grab a set of keys from the hook by the door, then my denim jacket from the hall stand, my mind racing to figure out what I'll say to Adam. What excuse I'll make for not being home. I'll text him from the hospital once I know more. Surely he'll understand that this is an emergency. He can't be so cruel as to keep me from Gran while she's ill, can he? I consider leaving my phone at home so he won't see that I'm out. But I quickly dismiss that idea – the hospital or Gran might need to get in touch.

I tug on my jacket as I pull open the door, then stride to my car. My fingers fumble uselessly as I unlock it and climb inside. A single, salty tear drops from my eye and lands on my lip as I start the engine. *Please Gran, hold on. Please.*

I reverse out of the driveway and then slam on the brakes, remembering with a sinking heart that I'm no longer insured to drive. *What should I do?* The bus will take too long, and I don't know if I have enough money for a taxi. I can't worry about insurance right now. I need to get to Gran. It's a good thing my car hasn't sold. Adam recently advertised it on Facebook Marketplace, but, thankfully, it hasn't garnered any interest yet.

As I turn out of our road, I can barely see through the blur of tears, but I have to concentrate. Can't afford to be pulled over by the police for driving erratically. I inhale deeply and try to pull myself together. The woman from the hospital wasn't specific about the state of Gran's health, so maybe she's not that bad. Maybe I'm worrying over nothing. She could have had a fall and twisted her ankle, or some other minor injury. I should have pressed for more details. I should have insisted.

I'm so preoccupied that I almost forget to switch lanes when the hospital turn-off finally appears. I then drive into the wrong entrance of the car park and get beeped at by an irate man in a minivan. Finally, I find a space and turn off the engine. I check my face in the mirror, take a tissue from my pocket and dab away my tears. I don't need Gran to see what a state I'm in.

It's crowded as the doors open to the Emergency Care Ward, and it takes every ounce of self-control not to shove past the people in front of me. I dart around them as soon as I can. My weary legs carry me to the front desk before giving out. I'm exhausted and breathless and terrified, and I clutch at the counter for support.

A nurse looks up at me. Her face says patience while my blank stare says panic, and she sighs before giving me a kind smile. 'Can I help you?'

'Yes,' I gasp, trying to find the air to finish the sentence. 'My gran. She's here . . . she's been brought in. Wendy Cartwright. They said . . . they said she was asking for me.'

The nurse types something into the computer. Her nails are short and clean, and her expression is unreadable as she looks from the screen, back to me, and then to the hallway. She does this three times, and with every glance, my fear ratchets up a notch. I open my mouth to plead with her, to beg her to just tell me what's happening, when she finally speaks.

'You're her granddaughter?' she asks.

I nod. 'Yes, she's my gran.'

'I'm glad you're here,' she replies. 'But you've just missed the doctor's rounds.'

'I came as quickly as I could.'

'I'm afraid the cancer's progressed,' the nurse says gently. 'She doesn't have much time, so it's good you made it.'

My ears start ringing and I'm not sure I've heard correctly. 'Sorry, *what*?'

'Your gran's cancer has spread. She doesn't have long. It's good that you'll be with her.'

'Cancer?' The word sounds foreign on my tongue.

'You didn't know?' Her lips purse as she looks down at her screen. 'She was diagnosed with lung cancer last year. Didn't want any treatment.'

'No! That can't be right.'

'I'm sorry, love.'

'When you say she doesn't have much time, are you talking months? Weeks?'

She gives me a sympathetic look.

'What, *days*?'

'Maybe hours.'

I shake my head. This can't be happening. 'Where is she?'

'Third cubicle on the right.' She points down the corridor. 'Press the buzzer if she needs more pain meds. We'll make her as comfortable as possible.'

I nod my thanks, and head off in the direction she sent me, stopping in front of a blue curtain. My hands shake as I pull it back.

I hardly recognise the frail woman in the bed. Her skin is waxy, a ghost of its usual warm glow. I only saw her a couple of weeks ago. How can she have deteriorated so fast? I sink into the chair at her side, taking her hand in mine and kissing it over and over. She stirs and opens her eyes, blinking at me. I force a smile and squeeze her hand gently.

'Jazzy, love,' Gran whispers.

'I'm here.' My throat is so tight that I can barely get the words out. 'I'm here, Gran. I'm not going anywhere.'

Her eyes slide shut, and her fingers relax in my hand. I'm about to call for the nurse, thinking that she's slipped into unconsciousness. But she speaks again, so softly I can hardly make it out.

'Are you in pain, Gran?' I ask.

'My beautiful girl,' she replies.

I can't hold the tears back. They spill out of me, drop after drop, soaking my cheeks and my chin and my shirt. I don't know what to say. My eyes sting so badly that I have to close them. 'I'm sorry, Gran. I'm so sorry.' I bury my head in her hand, smelling Palmolive soap and something else, something bleak and antiseptic. 'You'll be okay. You'll be okay,' I murmur.

'Sorry, Jas. Wish I could be here for you . . . a bit longer.'

'Don't leave me, Gran,' I plead. 'Please. Not yet.'

'You'll be fine, Jazzy love,' she rasps. 'You're a good girl. You can do anything you want, you know. You're stronger than you think.'

'I'm not, Gran. I'm really not.' I shouldn't be saying this to her. Not now. I should be more comforting, more reassuring.

Her eyes open wider at my admission, and she seems suddenly more alert. 'Listen to me, Jasmine Cartwright' – she's using my pre-married name – 'I didn't raise you to be scared of anything or anyone. You're my Jazzy and there's nothing you can't do, okay?'

I blink at her words. Does she suspect about Adam? Or perhaps she's just giving me a general pep talk about life. I never did end up admitting the truth to her about my marriage. I told myself so many times that I would, but when it came to it, I just couldn't find the right words. Couldn't bear for her to worry about me. And now it's too late.

'Why didn't you tell me you were ill?'

'No point,' she gasps, her momentary alertness fading. 'Wanted to spend my last months enjoying life. Don't like people fussing. Didn't want you to . . . worry.' Her chest rattles alarmingly. I realise we've both been keeping secrets from each other.

'If I'd known, I could have helped,' I cry. 'I would have thrown away those bloody cigarettes for a start.'

Gran gives a reedy chuckle. 'Well, that would have ticked me off.'

I stroke her hand and bring it to my cheek. 'You can't leave me, Gran.'

'Not leaving,' she murmurs. 'Always be *here*.' She presses her palm against my heart, as she exhales.

Chapter Twenty-Two

WILLOW

I sit cross-legged on the sofa in my pale pink dressing gown, eating a bowl of soggy cornflakes, chewing without tasting, checking my phone for messages. Gabe has left three texts and two voicemails since last night, but I haven't replied to any of them. I note the time, realising it's been fourteen hours since I broke things off with him. I feel really deflated about everything. I keep telling myself that it's normal to feel like this after a break-up – even if we were only seeing each other for a few weeks – but it doesn't make it any less painful. It's my own fault. I should have trusted my initial instincts and never got involved in the first place.

It's Saturday today, which is bad timing as I could really do with some work to take my mind off things. I guess I could call Tansy, see if she minds me coming in to carry on with her hallway, but I don't like messing clients around. And, in my experience, they're not keen on me going in over the weekend. Plus, she'll want to hear all about Gabe, and when I tell her my decision to end things, I don't think she'll agree.

Through the gap in the curtains, a blue sky taunts me with its cheerful brightness, but I guess I should be grateful it's stopped raining. I groan and drag myself up off the sofa. I think I'll get dressed and go out for a walk, try to shake off this lethargy and gloom.

I take a quick, hot shower, followed by an icy cold jet leaving my skin tingling and my senses more alert. Back in the bedroom, I dry myself, pull on some clean underwear and socks, and blast the hairdryer through my damp locks, not bothering to comb them. My eyes trace over the mess of clothes tossed carelessly across the room and I rummage around on the floor, picking out a pair of jeans and a sweatshirt which I pull on, along with my trainers and quilted jacket. Finally, with a shaky determination, I leave the flat and make my way down to the seafront.

The brisk sea air fills my lungs and I purposely avert my eyes as I stride past the Dolphin restaurant perched above the beach. All I can think about is that Gabe took Priya there first, and how she told me about it with such nonchalance. Why *did* she tell me that? How insensitive. *No* – I have to stop my mind wandering back there. Instead, I force myself to take slow, deep breaths, trying to anchor myself in the beauty of the day instead of the ache in my heart.

It's a busy Saturday morning, the seafront teeming with life – dog walkers chatting in groups, rhythmic joggers pounding the shoreline, families and couples having animated conversations as they amble along, some clutching cardboard coffee cups that have me reminiscing about how Gabe and I first met. But I'm doing it again – letting my mind drag me back to the man I'm trying to forget.

That's when I see him. A familiar face, accompanied by a woman with long brown hair, their presence suddenly slicing through my fragile composure. They're standing at the shoreline, chatting. When our eyes meet, he does a quick double take, his gaze flickering with instant recognition.

What should I do?

Is this real? Or am I having a bad dream?

He frowns, then smirks, and my stomach hollows out. My heart pounds so hard, I worry it's about to burst. I shake myself out of my frozen state and quickly turn away before he can approach me or attempt to say anything, the lingering shock sending me fleeing home in a rush, terror pulsing through every stumbling step. I throw a couple of panicked glances over my shoulder, but I don't see him.

Back in the building, I nearly collide with Priya on the narrow staircase. Her eyes, usually so warm and bright, now brim with concern as she takes in my rumpled hair, crumpled clothes, and the barely contained tremor in my hands.

'Willow, are you okay? You look as though you've seen a ghost.'

But instead of accepting her support, I lash out with a mistrustful snap – a desperate attempt to shield myself from more hurt. 'I'm fine!'

'Of course.' She holds up her hands. 'I'm sorry if I said something wrong.'

After what Gabe told me, I don't think Priya has my best interests at heart. I can't trust anyone right now. And she's the last person I want to speak to after my encounter at the beach. 'Sorry, I don't have time to talk,' I say, through gritted teeth, attempting to slide past her, but she isn't moving aside.

In a hushed tone, as if weighing every word, she tries again. 'I'm really sorry about the Gabe thing. I promise you there's nothing to it. I'd really like us to keep being friends.'

'For goodness' sake, Priya, it's not all about you and Gabe, you know!' She thinks I'm upset about her being Gabe's ex. I can't tell her that my fear is nothing to do with that. It's something far worse.

'Of course,' she says, contrite. 'I'm so sorry. If you want to talk about it . . .'

'Why would I want to talk about anything with you?'

She takes a step back, up on to the landing, her mouth open in surprise at my rudeness.

This isn't who I am. I never speak to people like this, but I think I'm in shock. In fact, I think I might be about to throw up. I push past her and hurry along the hall to my flat, fumbling with the key and shoving the door open. I race to the bathroom, slam the loo seat up and heave my guts into the bowl, my whole body shuddering and trembling, my eyes watering.

I pause before vomiting again. And again. Until my stomach is empty, this morning's cornflakes and coffee swirling away as I flush the toilet. I stand shakily and bend over the sink, angling my head under the tap and rinsing my mouth.

'Knock, knock.' A quiet voice sounds from out in the hallway. *My hallway*. Priya has followed me into the flat.

'Can you leave please?' I call out, wanting to tell her to piss off, but not having the courage to be that rude.

'I need to make sure you're okay first,' she persists.

'I'm fine,' I repeat, but the words don't sound convincing at all.

Her face appears around the bathroom door. 'No you're not, you just threw up.'

'I ate something dodgy.' I rinse my mouth again and wipe my face on the towel.

She cocks her head and raises an eyebrow.

'Why are you here?' I snap.

'What's happened?' she asks. 'I can tell you've had some kind of upset or shock. I'm not going until you tell me.'

There's no way I'm telling her the real reason I'm in such a state, so with a bitter edge to my voice, I mention that I saw Gabe going into her flat yesterday.

Her face flames and I feel vindicated for all the paranoid thoughts I've been having. 'I'm sorry you saw that,' she murmurs.

'I bet you are,' I reply quietly.

'Not like that,' she says, leaning against the doorframe. 'I didn't want to say anything before, because we don't know each other very well and I didn't want you to think I was making things up.' She sighs and pulls at her lower lip. 'I'm just going to say it, and you can believe me or not . . .'

I wait for her to continue, but my mind is still back down on the beach. That double take, the smirk on his face imprinted on my brain. It was so shocking that it hardly seems real. I need to shove all that aside now and get this thing sorted out with Priya. I don't have the mental energy to deal with both issues. And, even though I know this reappearance from the past is the most pressing thing right now – the thing that's made me sick to my stomach – I can't deny that Gabe is still important to me. If he's telling the truth, then I owe him a second chance and he could be the key to helping me move on. To keeping me safe. What Priya says now could help me clarify things.

'Gabe is still in love with me,' Priya says. 'He wants us to get back together.'

I hear the words, but it takes a few seconds for them to sink in. Silence hangs between us, the bathroom tap dripping behind me.

'Gabe wants to get back with you?' I repeat slowly, each word steeped in disbelief.

'Yes.' She nods once. 'I'm so sorry, Willow. I know how much you like him.'

'That's funny,' I begin, 'because he says it's the other way around.'

'*What?*' Her face contorts into disbelief.

'He said you asked him to take a look at your sink because it was blocked. And he didn't have the heart to say no.'

Priya smothers a laugh. 'That's the most ridiculous thing I've ever heard.'

'Okay,' I snap again, 'so if he wants to get back with you, then why does he keep calling and texting me?'

'I honestly don't know. But I wouldn't trust him, Willow. Honestly, I've had over two years of Gabe Walker, and you're better off out of it.'

'You went out with him for two years?'

She nods. 'Two and a half, to be precise. I hate to tell you this, but he's obsessed with me. I think he's using you to stay close to me.'

'I'm sorry, but I don't believe you,' I reply, shocked at her bald-faced lie.

'I know it's hard to believe, but why would I lie about that?' she persists. 'I like you, Willow. I don't want you to get sucked into his games. I should've told you what he was like as soon as I heard you were seeing him, but I didn't want to come across like a bitter ex.'

I curl my lip. 'Like you're doing now, you mean?'

She shakes her head. 'Believe me, I know how it sounds. But I like you too much not to warn you about him.'

I stare at my new neighbour, all the pieces starting to slot into place. She moved in here a month after Gabe and I got together. She's been overly friendly with me from the second we met. She tried to overshadow my first date with Gabe by saying he did the exact same things with her as with me. She was down at the beach both times Gabe took me to the Dolphin.

I've been such an idiot.

Priya is a liar.

'I'd like you to leave, please,' I say firmly, feeling more in control.

Hurt glistens in her eyes, but I've seen how good she is at manipulating me and I'm not falling for it again.

'*Now*,' I cry.

Chapter Twenty-Three

JASMINE

There's a clear blue sky above me and a fresh April sun glinting through the branches of a sycamore, reminding me of happier days. I pause outside the church, listening to a blackbird trilling its song from somewhere above me in the trees. I like to think it's singing specially for Gran. Or, maybe, if I let myself imagine just a little more, it could be Gran herself, come to sing me one last showtune.

But, amid the gentle breeze and the scent of spring blossoms, the reality of never seeing Gran again is a cold, sharp pain. I can't believe I'll never hear her chuckle at one of my silly jokes, or give me some of her no-nonsense advice when I'm going through a rough time. How can it be that we'll never have another one of our talks over a cup of strong tea and a plate of custard creams? She was so alive. Such a big personality. How can all that life have been snuffed out? It makes no sense. I was convinced she would live until she was at least a hundred and ten.

I regret not confiding in her about Adam. About how controlling he's become. About losing my job and not being allowed to get a new one. She would have been outraged on my behalf. She would have come round in a flash, spitting fury, giving Adam a piece of her mind. She would have told him to sling his hook and never come back. *Why didn't I tell her?* Now it's too late. I've kept too many things to myself for no good reason other than . . . *what?* Embarrassment? Fear? Worry?

I startle as Adam takes my hand, his grip firm and confident like always. 'Shall we go in?' he asks, nodding towards the church where people are beginning to file inside.

'In a minute.' I'm not able to look him in the eye. 'You go ahead. I just want . . . do you mind if I have a moment alone?'

His face tightens, but he tries to keep his voice light. 'Okay,' he replies, but I can tell he's not happy about it. He walks away from me towards the entrance, stiff-backed in his expensive charcoal suit, every inch the perfect grandson-in-law paying his respects. I watch until he disappears inside.

I'm prepared for the repercussions later, but right now, I need some time outside on my own, a few minutes with my thoughts. I need to think about Gran and what her advice would be about the mess my life has become.

I can feel her presence all around me. In the blue sky, and the whispering leaves, and the blackbird that's started singing again. I can picture her bright eyes and feel her warm hugs. She knows what I have to do. She's willing me to listen. To not be scared.

'Jasmine!' A voice cuts across the peace of the morning. The blackbird calls out a warning and flies off in a whirr of feathers. I turn to see a woman in a black dress that's just that little bit too short to be appropriate for a funeral. My mouth dries out.

Mum.

I thought she might come, even though she was never a fan of her mother-in-law. It's a shock to see her after all this time, although she hasn't changed much. She's still an attractive woman with her dark shiny hair cascading in waves and her movie-star curves, so different to my plain brown hair that's prone to frizz, and my beanpole figure. We haven't talked in almost a year, even though she only lives half an hour away. She's my mother but she feels more like a casual acquaintance, or a distant aunt. The last time we met was at my wedding, one and a half years ago.

She totters across the gravel path in towering heels and gives me a stiff hug, her perfume not quite concealing breath that reeks of gin. 'So, the old witch finally popped her clogs,' she slurs into my ear.

I clench my fists at each biting word. There's no point reacting to her comment, because we'd only get into an argument. And the last thing I want is to ruin the memory of my grandmother by listening to more bile spewed by my drunk mother. She only said it to get a rise out of me. I'm not going to give it to her.

Mum never liked Gran, and the feeling was mutual. Although Gran never outright criticised my mother in front of me – which I appreciate – I wasn't stupid. I picked up on the vibe from an early age via overheard conversations. Gran thought Mum treated Dad poorly, always finding fault with him, always frustrated that he didn't earn what she considered to be enough money. And then, when he went for promotions to get the pay rises she wanted, she would complain that he was always working. He was constantly rushing around trying to please her. He couldn't win.

After he suffered a heart attack, Mum realised, too late, how much Dad had kept our family going while she had contributed next to nothing, extravagantly spending his wages on salsa classes, and yoga courses, on holidays and house renovations we couldn't afford.

Even before Dad died, Gran was the one who did school pick-ups and gave me my tea. Dad made my breakfasts and did school drop-offs, because Mum liked to go for a run in the mornings, to 'start her day off right'. After he died, Mum's carefree lifestyle collapsed. She had never worked and didn't want to start then.

Instead, she began going out drinking, meeting men. Trying to snare a new husband to replace what she'd lost.

I remember a blazing row she had with Gran one evening when Mum had forgotten to pick me up after a school netball match because she was drunk. Gran pretty much took over raising me after that.

Mum's behaviour has always made me wonder, deep down, if maternal instincts are genetic. If I'm honest with myself, it's made me fearful to have children of my own. What if I don't bond with them? What if, despite my best intentions, I end up turning into my mother? Logically, I don't think that would happen. I don't believe I'm anything like her. But I can't push away the kernel of fear in my chest that it's a possibility. I couldn't put a child through that. Especially not now, when there would be no other support network for them. No more Gran to lean on.

'Is Lars with you?' I ask my mother, enquiring after her boyfriend.

'Lars?' She wrinkles her nose. 'I left that twat last year after I found out he was sleeping around.'

'I'm sorry . . .' I begin.

But she shakes her head dismissively. 'What about . . . what's his name . . . Adam?' she asks. 'You two still together?'

'We are,' I murmur.

'Well done.' She claps mockingly. 'Didn't think he'd stick around. Too handsome for his own good, that one. You better be careful he doesn't do a Lars.'

I don't tell her that Adam cheating isn't what I need to worry about. 'We should go in,' I say, not wanting to discuss my horrible husband with my horrible mother.

After the service, we mingle outside where Adam is charming to everyone, and Mum isn't. I knew Gran was loved, but I'm overwhelmed by the turnout. By how many of her friends, neighbours and acquaintances have come to pay their respects. The church was packed.

Adam wanted to be one of the pallbearers, shouldering Gran's coffin from the church to the grave. I couldn't stand the thought of him carrying Gran to her final resting place. Not after he gave her so little consideration in life. It would have been an insult to her memory. But there was no way I could object, not without angering him. Thankfully, I was able to speak discreetly to the funeral director, who suggested that we should have a bier – a wheeled stand that I could walk alongside instead.

Gran's neighbour, Sheila, gives me and Adam warm hugs. Adam offers his condolences to her for losing such a good friend.

'Oh, you are sweet,' she replies, dabbing at her eyes with a tissue, her blue eyeliner smudging. She turns to me. 'I'm so sorry about your gran, love. But you're lucky to have such a doting husband looking out for you. Cherish him.' If only she knew what he's really like, she'd be giving me very different advice.

I wonder how long Adam's kind act is going to last. What with Gran's death, and him trying to get me pregnant, he's almost been back to his old self. The Adam I first met who appeared loving and sweet. Even though he's treating me well right now, I can't relax. I'm constantly vigilant, balanced on a precipice. One misstep and I know I'll be done for.

The simmering dread and constant guilt mean I can't grieve properly. I'm tormented by the thought of how many days I missed being with Gran, all because Adam forbade me from visiting her. The realisation that I was too timid to stand up to him gnaws at me and sustains a silent fury. I hate that I was so weak. That I *am* so weak. But maybe that weakness won't last for too much longer.

My heart thrums with a new kind of fear. Because, hiding in among my heartache, I have a secret. One that terrifies and thrills me. Twists my stomach into knots whenever I think of it. All I need is the courage to go through with it.

Chapter Twenty-Four

WILLOW

Gabe isn't showing any signs of giving up. He's been messaging me for three days straight and now it's Monday and he's pressing the buzzer to my flat and continuing to message me – calling, texting and WhatsApp-ing. Begging me to let him in. I'm torn. Part of me is desperate to see him, but the sensible part of me knows that it's not a good idea right now, even though I finally believe he's been telling the truth about Priya.

At the same time, my mind has been racing with the dilemma of what to do about Saturday's beach encounter. Should I try to shove the memory aside and pretend nothing happened? Hope that the waves of the past might quietly recede? But how can I when my safety's at stake? My old life seems like a hazy dream, and the unexpected sight of that familiar face has brought the nightmare rushing back. Is it time to pack my bags again? The thought of starting over somewhere else makes me want to drop to my knees and cry.

The door buzzer is making me crazy. I can't think straight knowing that Gabe is here. My phone pings with yet another text message:

Just give me two minutes, Willow. I bought you a cappuccino from our favourite coffee shop. It's getting cold.

He's not giving up. Sod it. I go into the hall, press the entry button and open the door to my apartment, leaving it slightly ajar before heading back into the lounge. I pace from one end of the room to the other as I wait for him to come up.

I don't have to wait long. He must have taken the stairs three at a time. He barrels into the flat, straight towards me, but my glare halts him in his tracks. He's breathing hard, his eyes alight with hope, but the air is strained between us. He bridges the gap to hand me my coffee and he wasn't kidding when he said it was getting cold. I set it on the dining table.

Gabe unzips his bomber jacket and drops on to the sofa without being asked. I sigh and perch on the opposite arm, waiting to hear what he has to say.

'Willow, I wish you'd believe me,' he cries, pushing a hand through his hair. 'I'm not interested in Priya. It's over, but she won't accept it. This whole situation is her doing. She moved here. She befriended you. All of that happened *after* we got together. And she genuinely did ask me to look at her blocked sink, which I stupidly did.'

'I know,' I reply softly.

'You do?' His expression shifts to one of surprise.

I cross my arms over my chest and meet Gabe's gaze. 'I spoke to her on Saturday and none of what she said made any sense.'

'Thank goodness,' he murmurs. It's clearly a relief to him, knowing that I've worked it out for myself, but part of me wonders whether we can ever really move past this drama. It's been exhausting, and has had me second-guessing everything and everyone. I didn't leave my old life behind to step into these kinds of complications. I promised myself when I arrived here that I would lead a quiet existence. And this feels like anything but.

Gabe crosses the small distance between us and tries to draw me in to a hug. But I hold back, my body instinctively putting up a barrier as my mind races. Feeling my resistance, he looks disappointed by the fact I'm not falling into his arms straightaway. But he lets go and drifts over to the window, gazing out before turning back to face me. 'I can't tell you how glad I am to hear you say that about Priya,' he adds. 'This whole thing has been slowly driving me crazy.'

'You and me both,' I murmur in agreement.

In the charged silence, we both understand that Priya must have moved into the apartment because she knew about us, that she followed him here. It's so creepy to think of what she's done. Especially as she came across as so friendly and normal.

'I'm sorry you've had to go through this shit,' he says with genuine remorse in his voice. 'It's the last thing I wanted for us. I thought she'd accepted things were over. Part of me wondered if she'd moved here intentionally, but I didn't want to believe it. I'd hoped it was just a crazy coincidence.'

'It's mad,' I agree.

'And it was hard to say anything to you because it sounds so . . . out there.'

I privately wonder what each of us did to deserve such terrible exes. Maybe that's why we were drawn to one another, sensing a kindred spirit in need of some comfort.

'So . . .' He gives me a hopeful look. 'Do you think we could put this behind us, and get back to being us again?' He walks back over to the sofa, to where I'm standing, my arms wrapped around myself.

I shake my head. 'I'm glad we've got it sorted, Gabe, but I need a bit of space right now.'

'Space?' he echoes. 'As in, a day, a week?'

'I don't know yet. Just . . . can you give me some time to sort stuff out?'

Typical Gabe, he's still concerned. 'Anything I can help with?' he asks.

'Not really,' I reply, realising that I can't drag him into this. 'It's something I have to do on my own. I'll message you if . . . when I'm ready.'

Gabe looks a bit taken aback. He thinks for a beat then accepts it. Sort of. I can see the struggle in his eyes, wondering if I'll ever get back in touch. But he nods anyway. 'You're sure this isn't about Priya?' he presses.

'I promise.'

He nods, looking half relieved but still a little lost. 'Can we at least hug?'

'I'd like that.' I swallow down a burst of emotion threatening to spill over.

He pulls me into a bear hug that's warm and familiar and everything I've been craving since I started keeping him at arm's length. It's been killing me, shutting him out, but letting him in has its own risks. I wonder again if this might be the last time I see him. Because I can't be sure I'm safe here. And if I'm not – if there's the tiniest hint of doubt – I'll have to flee again. And there'll be no chance for any goodbyes.

Chapter Twenty-Five

JASMINE

I'm in the cramped spare bedroom of Mrs Bunton's meticulously kept home, struggling to lift a towering section of a beige Ikea wardrobe on to the carpeted floor. The room is filled with the overpowering scent of a plug-in air freshener overlaid with lemon furniture polish, and I can feel Mrs Bunton's critical gaze lurking in every shadow. I'm already drenched with sweat despite the open window that does little to cool the air, the weight of the furniture pieces making my arms burn.

I landed the job via Gran's old neighbour, Sheila. She's been incredible at getting me these little cash-in-hand jobs here and there. Jobs that only take a couple of hours max, so that I'm not away from home for long. Luck has held with me so far, and Adam is still oblivious to what I'm doing. As soon as he leaves for work, I race around the house, clearing away the breakfast things, making the bed and putting a load in the washing machine. Then I race for the bus to take me to whatever job I might have that day.

It's been five months since Gran's funeral. During that time, I've been working for cash and squirreling it away into an offline savings account. I also managed to keep secret from him that Gran left me just over two thousand pounds in her will. That too has gone into my savings account, and I've already accumulated just over four and a half thousand pounds in total. I would have had more if Adam had allowed me to keep my remaining wages, but they went into a joint account used for grocery shopping, for which I have to provide the receipts. He claims it's for 'budgeting properly', but I know full well it's his way of ensuring I never splurge on a simple coffee catch-up with friends.

Meanwhile, my friend Naomi has vanished from my life. Months of dodged invitations and forced excuses led to her blocking my number, leaving a raw sting of betrayal in place of the friendship I thought was unbreakable. I guess she just got fed up asking, but I can't say I'm not disappointed. I thought we were better friends than that. I'd thought we might find our way back to each other and she'd allow me to explain.

Only a few, like Chrissie, Tina and Louie, still message from time to time, and even though I haven't been able to see them in person since our impromptu breakfast earlier this year, it's nice to know they're still thinking of me.

I now rely on this burner phone that I use for my odd jobs, leaving my iPhone – complete with tracker app – at home. It's risky and I'm always scared that Adam will discover my secret. But I can't sit and do nothing anymore. I can't pretend to myself that my life isn't in danger.

I'm constantly on edge, fearful that the wrong word or movement might set off another episode of Adam's unpredictable outbursts. These little jobs are a way for me to save money so that one day I can make my escape.

Adam's gentle treatment of me, in the wake of Gran's death, didn't last very long and, while he hasn't actually hit me, he's not averse to grabbing or pushing me and calling me vile names. It's only a matter of time before his actions escalate into something more serious. And I want to be long gone before that happens.

'Knock, knock.' Mrs Bunton pokes her head around the door, her silvery hair neatly coiled at the back of her head. 'Just bringing you a cup of tea and some biscuits,' she chirps, her eyes flicking over the room as she steps in from the hallway.

'Thank you,' I reply, as she sets the tray down on the bedside table. Although, truthfully, the thought of drinking hot tea right now is far less appealing than a glass of iced lemonade.

A second figure follows her into the room – a pretty blonde girl slightly younger than me. I vaguely recognise her from somewhere, and the knowledge of that makes me nervous.

'This is my granddaughter, Sasha,' Mrs Bunton announces with pride. 'She's popped in for a visit.'

'Hi,' I say, mustering a friendly smile and wiping the sweat from my top lip. 'Nice to meet you.'

Mrs Bunton's eyes widen slightly as she drops another detail. 'Sasha tells me she knows your husband.'

I freeze. In that split second, the warm room seems to cool drastically, my skin prickling with a sudden chill, everything shifting into slow motion.

'Jasmine? Jasmine, are you all right, dear?' Mrs Bunton shifts her gaze between me and her curious granddaughter. I sink heavily on to the bed, nausea tightening my throat. 'Sasha, fetch Jasmine a glass of water, will you?'

The girl disappears and Mrs Bunton sits next to me on the bed, putting a hand to my forehead. 'Goodness, you're terribly clammy. Are you ill?'

I shake my head. 'Just a bit overheated, I think.' Although every fibre in my body is screaming otherwise.

'Yes, well, it's a sticky morning. We're having an Indian summer. They think it's going to reach the thirties today. I'll bring the portable fan upstairs.'

I can't tell her the real reason I feel faint. What if that girl tells Adam she saw me here?

'I did ask Sheila if you were up to the job,' Mrs Bunton continues, her lips pursed. 'I warned her that it was a large wardrobe, but she assured me you could manage it.'

Her voice is an annoying buzz in my ear. I'm more concerned with what her granddaughter might do or say. The door opens again and she reappears with a tall glass of water. It's lukewarm but I sip it gratefully. 'Thanks,' I murmur.

She gives me a smile in reply that's as tepid as the water.

'How do you know Adam?' I ask, forcing myself to look up with a friendly smile.

'My boyfriend, Marc, works with him,' she replies blandly.

'Oh, yes, Marc,' I say, picturing his face – good-looking, but knows it. 'I met you at a work drinks thing a couple of months ago,' I add, recalling that she and her clique weren't particularly friendly.

'Oh, yeah,' she replies. 'Chaplin's Wine Bar.'

'That's right. Marc and Adam sometimes play golf together,' I add, hoping to steer her away from more personal enquiries.

'That's how Marc and I met,' she says, her voice warming a little. 'Our dads both belong to the golf club.'

I force a laugh. 'Nice,' I offer, my brain scrambling to come up with any plausible reason for her not to mention me to her boyfriend. But I can't seem to think of a single thing. 'How long have you two been together?'

'Almost six months.' She perks up as she starts talking about him. 'He's so good to me. He's taking me to Malaga next week and we're staying in this amazing four-star hotel. I literally can't wait.'

I press the glass against my forehead, desperately trying to ward off the rising heat and the dread of what might happen next. 'Sounds amazing,' I muster.

'Going bikini shopping this afternoon,' she adds.

'Great.' I pause for a moment and swallow before continuing. 'Look, I know this sounds weird, but would you mind not mentioning to Marc that you saw me here?'

Sasha frowns and looks at her grandmother, who mirrors her expression.

'It's silly really,' I continue, stumbling over my words as I try to justify a half-baked explanation. 'It's just that . . . well . . . I'm saving up to buy Adam this really . . . expensive drill that he wants. It's a surprise and I don't want him finding out.' Even to my ears, my reasoning sounds absurd, but it's the best I can come up with.

Sasha's eyebrows raise and she shrugs. 'Um, yeah. Course.'

Panic lodges in my chest. I'm getting seriously bad vibes from Sasha and I think my excuse has made it more likely that she'll say something to Marc. In fact, I know she will. I should have just kept my mouth shut.

'How are you feeling, dear?' Mrs Bunton asks. 'Ready to get back to it? Shall I make you a little sandwich to keep your strength up?'

I shift my gaze to the older woman. 'Would you mind if I finish the job tomorrow? I'm almost done. I'm just really not feeling very well.'

She frowns. 'It looks like there's still quite a way to go. Why don't you come downstairs and take a little break. Have something to eat and then perhaps you'll perk up. My good friend's visiting from Canada tomorrow and I really need to have this room finished tonight so I can concentrate on the rest of the preparations in the morning.'

'I'm sorry, Mrs Bunton,' I say, getting to my feet and gathering my things, realising I can kiss goodbye to the forty quid this job would have paid. 'I'm going to have to go.'

'What if you're still ill tomorrow?' she asks, mild panic lacing her voice.

'Sorry,' I repeat, heading towards the door with a stab of guilt that's quickly drowned out by an incoming rush of fear.

Mrs Bunton turns towards her granddaughter. 'Sasha, darling, are you able to finish putting this wardrobe together for me? There's cash in it for you – a hundred pounds.'

Wow, that's more than double what she was going to pay me. But, right now, I wouldn't finish the job for a thousand.

I slip out the bedroom door, catching Sasha's terse reply as I hurry down the stairs. 'I would, Nan, but I've just had my nails done and I'm meeting Layla in town in a bit.'

I fly through the front door and race towards the bus stop, my heart thumping, sweat sliding down my back. I check the timetable, swearing under my breath when I see I missed the previous bus by five minutes and the next one isn't for another half-hour. The sun climbs higher overhead. It's almost 10.30 a.m. and, with Adam not due home until after four, I'm briefly reassured that I have a decent window of time.

I sit at the bus stop under the generous shade of an oak tree. But the minutes are trickling by too slowly. I really do need to get home. My thoughts grow frantic again. Maybe I should call a cab. But my burner phone is basic, without internet connection, and I don't know the number of any taxi firms. I'm in a residential street so there are no shops for me to go in and ask. Worst-case scenario is that Sasha calls her boyfriend in the next hour and tells him she met me at her nan's house. And if Marc is with Adam when she calls him, then . . .

Shit.

The idea of fleeing with nothing but the clothes on my back crosses my mind, but my savings passbook is hidden in the wardrobe, and I need to bring clothes and toiletries with me, although those aren't as essential. But money's going to be tight. My plans are dependent on saving six thousand pounds and I only have four and a half right now. It's doable. But only just. And I definitely can't leave without my savings book.

Finally, the bus pulls up alongside me. I wait for a couple of passengers to disembark before climbing on with shaky limbs. I pay with a five-pound note. My fingers fumble the change and I watch it fly in all directions. I'm trying not to lose it. Trying not to cry. An elderly gentleman, seated at the front of the bus, reaches down and retrieves a pound coin which he hands me with arthritic fingers.

'Thanks,' I manage to croak as the bus lurches forward. I spot a twenty-pence piece by the luggage rack, but I can't see any more. A girl catches my eye and straightens up before sliding her gaze away. Pretty sure she's just pocketed the other pound coin, but I have more worrying issues on my mind so I let it go, walking past and sliding into the first available seat.

I need to think of a good excuse as to why I was at Mrs Bunton's house, just in case Adam *is* at home. Nothing will save me from his anger, but as long as I come up with something that sounds believable, I can hopefully spare myself the worst of it. Trouble is that all my excuses sound so flimsy. I wouldn't believe me, so why would he?

As the bus rumbles inexorably towards home, my mind frantically tries to map out a plan of action, but my brain is too cloudy, my thought processes too clogged with fear to be of any use.

I'm going to have to wing it.

Chapter Twenty-Six

WILLOW

Minutes after Gabe leaves my apartment, there's a sharp rap on my front door. I sigh, frustrated that he's back so soon. It was hard enough for me to say goodbye the first time, without having to drag it out.

I open the door, ready to let him down again, but it's not Gabe. It's my neighbour, Elsie, leaning on a wooden walking stick in the dim light of the hall. Her lined face is a mixture of irritation and confusion.

'I don't know what's been going on with you lately,' she grumbles, 'but I've been hearing all sorts of commotion coming from your flat. I used to think you were such a nice, quiet neighbour. I was thankful there's been hardly a peep out of you since you moved in two years ago. Now, all of a sudden there's running up and down the corridor, arguing, crying, knocking on doors. It's like a bloomin' madhouse!'

To my horror, I burst into tears. Not the quiet kind that slide down cheeks and can be wiped away with a swipe of the hand. But the noisy, sobbing kind that can't be stopped until they're done.

'Oh my Lord,' Elsie says. 'I knew I should have stayed home.'

'I'm sorry. I'm really sorry,' I sob, walking back towards the living room with Elsie following. 'It's just everything is so complicated and awful. And I think I might have to leave. And if I don't leave, then I might be in danger. But even if I'm not, then I'll always be worrying and looking over my shoulder. It's just – it's not fair! Why is this happening to me?' I sink down on to the sofa and cover my face with my hands, too upset to be embarrassed by my outburst.

Elsie stands there, leaning on her stick, unmoving, not saying a word. After a few long moments, my sobs start to quiet, and I lift my tear-stained face.

Her eyes are unblinking and devoid of sympathy as she gazes back at me. 'You finished?' she asks.

I sniff and manage a hesitant nod, bothered by her brusque tone.

'Right. Well, I don't know what's going on. And, quite honestly, I don't want to know. But . . . if you're in trouble, you need to pull up your pants and sort it out.'

I shake my head, irritation at her callousness making me forget my tears for a moment. I'm here, worrying about my safety, and this grumpy old woman has barged into my flat and is giving me a hard time about it.

'After my husband died,' Elsie continues, oblivious to my mood change, 'I realised everything was down to me. If someone wronged me, or if I was struggling, I didn't have anyone to help me out. I had to sort things for myself. It's not easy, Willow. It's brutal sometimes. You just have to claw your way through it until you manage to carve out a bit of peace and security. Looks like you were doing that quite well until recently, but you seem to have lost your grip. I think you need to remember who's in charge of your life.'

'Well, thanks for the advice,' I reply, pushing myself up from the sofa, 'but, like you said, you don't know what I'm going through.

So why don't you just go back to minding your own business, and let me mind mine!'

Elsie's face crinkles into a wry smile as she pats my arm lightly and chuckles. 'There's that fighting spirit,' she says, before turning to leave. Just as she reaches the lounge door, she stops and turns back, slowly. 'In case you ever need it, I keep a key under the mat.'

My mouth falls open at her out-of-the-blue offer, but I'm too stunned to reply. By the time I stammer out a feeble 'thanks', she's gone, closing the front door behind her.

What was all that about? The flat feels empty after she leaves, like it's holding its breath, waiting. I wander over to the window and gaze down at the street below, at the yellow leaves swirling to the ground, leaving the only home they've ever known.

Drawing a deep, steadying breath, I think I know what I have to do. I have to call him. I know he recognised me on the beach and I'm terrified in case he comes back or, even worse, he's still here. But I can't hide from the situation. Burying my head in the sand and hoping for the best isn't an option. I learned that the hard way once before, and it led to disaster. The only way to handle situations like this is to confront them head-on.

I do a quick online search, pick up my phone and tap in the number with trembling fingers.

A woman replies. 'Hello, Sonia speaking, how can I help you?'

I swallow down my fear and ask if he's there, my heart thumping erratically.

'Of course,' Sonia replies, her tone polite but brisk. 'Who shall I say is calling?'

'Tell him it's Jasmine Owens.'

Chapter Twenty-Seven

JASMINE

It's just after 11.30 a.m. as I turn into our road, feeling as though I've just run a marathon. My eyes strain to see our house, praying Adam isn't back. I stop and exhale when I see his van is missing from the driveway, almost crying with relief. Perhaps I've unfairly maligned Mrs Bunton's granddaughter. Maybe she'll keep my confidence and won't tell Marc she saw me today. I still feel that's unlikely, but if she has plans with her friend in town this afternoon, perhaps she won't speak to her boyfriend until afterwards, which will give me plenty of time to make my getaway.

Now that my hand has been forced into leaving early, I'm desperate to get going. I curse myself for waiting this long. The money I've saved is surely enough to get me started. I feel a rise of optimism as I head towards the house that, hopefully, I'll never have to set eyes on again.

Unlocking the front door, I throw a quick glance over my shoulder before slipping inside. It's blissfully cool compared to the midday heat out there. I wonder if I might have time for a shower. But maybe that's pushing my luck. No. I'll just grab my things and go.

'What's this doing here without you?'

I yelp in surprise as Adam emerges from the kitchen holding my phone. My pulse skitters as I try to appear calm even though my heart is racing like an express train. His van wasn't outside. What's he doing home?

I force out a relaxed smile, trying to improvise. 'Thanks, Adam, I thought I'd lost it! Got halfway down the street and had to double back.'

'Halfway down the street?' He gives me a bemused look.

I'm getting a bad feeling, but the most important thing right now is to get hold of my savings book. 'I'll be back in a sec, I just . . . I really need the loo.' I start climbing the stairs as fast as I dare.

'I'm talking to you, Jasmine,' he snaps.

'I know, sorry, just need to pee and I'll be straight back down,' I call from the top of the stairs, praying he doesn't follow me. As quick as I can, I slip into our bedroom and ease open the wardrobe door, grabbing my fake-fur jacket, bringing it into the bathroom with me and locking the door just in time to hear Adam's footsteps thud up the staircase.

Piss off, piss off, piss off! I cry in my head.

In the bathroom, with shaking hands, I remove my savings book from the hidden pocket in the lining and hang my jacket on the door hook. I think about putting the savings book in my handbag, but worry in case he snatches it off me. Instead, I shove it inside my padded bra and readjust my top in the mirror, ensuring it doesn't show. If I can only placate Adam, get him comfortable enough to return to work, then I'll be able to pack up some stuff and leave. If not, I'll have to run. And the thought of it makes me retch. I flush the toilet and run the cold tap, splashing my face over the sink, then stare at my blotchy skin, at my hair, damp with sweat, and my wide, scared eyes.

Calm down. You can do this, Jasmine. Just act natural.

Adam is waiting outside the door, but I walk past him and down the stairs. 'Have you got time for an early lunch? I can make us some cheese toasties, if you like? Or maybe just a regular sandwich. It's a bit hot for toasties,' I babble, trying to sound as normal as possible, but I think I'm coming across as manic. 'Where's your van?' I ask, lingering in the hallway as he stands at the base of the stairs.

'At work,' he replies, his gaze locked on to mine, his voice dangerously low. 'Marc dropped me home.'

My insides turn to water. 'Oh, yeah? How's he doing?'

'Fine. He had an interesting call from his girlfriend, Sasha, this morning.'

That bitch. Adam knows. He knows where I was, and he's going to make me pay for it. I open my mouth, but I can't speak.

'She said you were at her nan's house this morning' – Adam smiles – 'putting together a *wardrobe*. She said you asked her not to tell her boyfriend. Why would that be, Jasmine? Why would you not want me to know?'

I swallow and take a subtle backwards step towards the front door, trying to calculate if I can open it before he reaches me. But I'm too late.

Adam lunges forward and grabs a handful of my hair. 'Earning money on the sly?' he hisses in my ear. 'Leaving your phone at home on purpose so I won't find out?' He twists my hair so it pulls at my scalp painfully.

I suck in a cry.

'Where's the cash, Jasmine? What have you done with it?'

'I was saving up to buy you a birthday present,' I gasp through the pain as he yanks my hair again. I'm sticking with the line I gave Sasha. 'Don't have any money of my own. Wanted to buy you something special so I did a couple of tiny odd jobs, that's all.'

'Liar!' he roars into my face, shoving me away from him towards the kitchen, where I lose my footing and slide to the ground. My scalp burns and my hip throbs from where I've just landed on the hard tiles.

Adam's face is mottled with rage and he strides over to me, leans over and punches me hard in the stomach. The pain is instantaneous, deep and grinding. I can barely breathe and I'm so shocked I don't even feel like I'm here. Adam is yelling something at me but I can't make out his words. All I can feel is the white-hot throb of pain in my belly.

If I don't do something now, I genuinely think he might kill me. I don't know if I can move, but I have to try. Pushing away the screaming pain in my stomach and the fire in my hip, I stagger to my feet to face my husband, his features contorted with fury. Then, with every ounce of energy that remains in my battered body, I knee him in the groin as hard as I can.

His eyes widen and he doubles over, but I don't hang around to see any more.

I snatch up my dropped handbag and fling open the front door.

'Get back here!' he croaks, his voice hoarse.

But I head out the door, slamming it behind me. If he recovers quickly, and gives chase, I'll never be able to outrun him, but I have to at least try.

I stagger down the path and on to the pavement, clutching my stomach, a whimper of fear erupting from my mouth as I try to decide which way to go.

I turn at the sound of my name to see my neighbour Carol standing in her doorway, her dog, Alfie, behind her barking relentlessly. 'In here!' she hisses. 'Quick!'

I halt, confused, my body still telling me to run, but my gut telling me to trust Carol, so I slip into her driveway. She motions to me to hurry up and I stumble along the path into her arms, where she ushers me over the threshold just as our front door flies open and I hear my husband roar my name.

Chapter Twenty-Eight

WILLOW

I stand by the living-room window and gaze unseeing through the glass, my phone clamped to my ear, my brain whirring. There's a click and a loud burst of muzak as I wait for the receptionist to put me through.

Saying my old name out loud to the receptionist has got my heart thumping. I haven't used it since I left, and it makes me feel vulnerable. Am I doing the right thing? After seeing him on the beach, I don't trust the police to keep me safe. I don't want to confide in Gabe. I can't trust my mum not to blab to Adam, and anyway, I haven't spoken to her in over two years. The last time was to tell her I was leaving the country. Of course, I didn't leave England, but I wanted her to think that, just in case Adam got in touch and she ended up telling him where I went.

As my fears spin around like a carousel in my head, Elsie's words come back to me – that I'm the one in control of my life. Her blunt phrasing mingles oddly with Gran's advice that I shouldn't be scared of anything, that I can do anything I want. In a strange way, Elsie reminds me a little bit of Gran. Although she's a lot more prickly – I can't imagine ever getting a hug from Elsie. I try to channel Gran's confidence. Try to let it guide me.

I reason with myself that this is me taking charge. This is me not being passive. I don't want to run again and neither do I want to live in fear. As much as it scares me to make this call, I need to do this.

A minute later, the line clicks again and I hear a breath on the end.

Despite my inner pep talk, my heart stutters.

'I wondered if you'd call,' he says, a teasing lilt to his voice.

My mouth is dry, the taste of adrenaline making it hard to swallow. I resist the urge to hang up.

'I thought it was you on the beach the other day, but I couldn't be certain,' he continues, the words flowing easily, unlike my own frozen vocal cords. 'Your hair's a bit of a mess now, if you don't mind me saying. Why did you cut it? You've let yourself go, Jas.'

I clench my jaw, refusing to let his words get under my skin. I've spent months perfecting the art of hiding my emotions, but now I feel old wounds reopening. My fingers are pressed against the cool glass of the window, its smooth surface a sharp contrast to the jumbled mess inside my head.

'You still there?' he asks, amusement in his voice.

'I'm here.' I grind out the words.

'Look,' he says, his voice softening, 'I don't want to talk about all this on my work phone. Why don't we meet up?'

'I'm not meeting up,' I reply, the thought filling me with dread.

There's a beat of silence that has me second-guessing how he's going to respond.

'Yes you are.' That maddening smirk still laces his voice. 'Because if you don't, I'll just give Adam a call.'

My skin goes cold at the threat. 'Fine,' I mutter, realising I don't really have any other choice. It looks like I'm going to have to swallow my fear and meet up with Bertie.

Chapter Twenty-Nine

JASMINE

The front door clicks softly behind us as I stand in Carol's hallway, gasping for breath. I think she might have just saved my life. Alfie noses my hand, and I stroke his silky head. Am I safe now?

'I'll call the police,' Carol says, tucking a lock of hair behind her ear.

'No!' I cry.

Carol's eyes widen. She puts a finger to her lips as Alfie starts growling, deep and menacing, his hackles rising. Through the frosted door pane, I see a blurry figure coming up the path. I'm trapped in Carol's hallway, which is safe in theory, but it's nowhere near safe enough. I wish there were an escape tunnel running out of her house like in those old prisoner-of-war movies.

Without pausing, Carol ushers me into a room at the back of her house – a comfy space done out like a library, with floor-to-ceiling bookcases, a squishy sofa and a red leather recliner. She pushes the door until it almost clicks shut, draws the curtains and motions to me to sit on the sofa. But I can't sit down, I'm too tense. Alfie's nose is pressed against the door, his growls interspersed with sharp barks.

I jump as the doorbell rings, echoing throughout the house, and Alfie goes berserk.

'Don't answer it,' I whisper, although I can't be heard over Alfie's barking.

Carol shakes her head, having read my meaning. 'Don't worry. We'll stay here until he leaves,' she tells me. 'Alfie, quiet!' she hisses, and puts a hand on the back of the dog's neck. He does as he's told but lets out a low whine.

Carol frowns in my direction, her gaze taking in my hunched position, straying down to where my hand rests on my stomach. 'Are you hurt?'

'I . . . I don't know,' I reply. 'He . . .' I trail off and bite my lip, still in disbelief that Adam actually punched me. I shake my head, unable to voice what happened.

'Should I call an ambulance?' Carol asks. 'Can I see?' She reaches over, but I step away from her, horrified by the thought of her looking at the damage my husband wrought on my body.

The doorbell rings again and I flinch. 'What about your windows?' I whisper. 'And doors? Are they locked?'

'I think so. Apart from the ones in my bedroom,' she says. 'Once he's gone, I'll close them.'

'Carol!' Adam bellows through the letterbox. 'Carol, I need to speak to you!'

My neighbour heads towards the door and I tug on her sleeve. 'No, please stay,' I beg. 'Carol!'

'I'll tell him I'm calling the police. That should get rid of him.'

'Better to pretend you're out,' I say. 'Then, if you see him again, you can act dumb.'

'Let me call them now,' she insists. 'It's safer that way. We can't stay hidden in here. He could try to break in the back door.'

'Oh, God,' I stammer. 'I'm so sorry to get you mixed up in this mess.'

'Nonsense! I should have got mixed up in it a long time ago. I had a suspicion about him, but I never did anything. I'm sorry.'

'He's gone quiet,' I say.

'Hmm, that's what worries me. Stay here. Alfie will look after you, won't you, boy?' She rubs his head and he wags his tail.

'What are you going to do?' I ask.

'Just going to check if he's still out there.'

'Hang on,' I hiss. But I'm too late to stop her. She disappears beyond the door and Alfie whines, turning in a tight circle.

I hear her steps as she creeps up the stairs. Meanwhile, I'm down here spinning out, imagining Adam jumping our fence and breaking in through Carol's back door. Did he actually see me come in here, or was he just hoping Carol might know where I am?

The door opens again and Carol gives me the thumbs up. 'I peered out of the spare bedroom window and saw him jogging off down the street,' she says triumphantly.

I exhale. 'Thank goodness. But he'll come back when he doesn't find me.'

'Did he hurt you?' she asks again, seeing me gingerly patting the side of my head where Adam yanked my hair.

'Pulled my hair and shoved me,' I mutter. 'And then he . . . he punched me in the stomach,' I blurt out, the admission bringing a fresh wave of pain deep in my gut. I pray he hasn't done any lasting damage.

'No!' Carol cries. 'That evil so-and-so.'

'But I'm fine,' I add, wanting to believe it. 'It was just scary, that's all.'

'I should say so,' Carol replies. 'What a nasty bully. Please let me call the police for you. I'll be a witness that he's been abusive.'

I think about letting her do it. I really do. But the thought of speaking to them, explaining all the little things he did . . . They might not take it seriously. They might think I'm making it up. But, most of all, I'm terrified of what Adam will say or do. He'll twist it. I know he will. And he'll get Marc and Sasha and Mrs Bunton to say that I'm unhinged. I can't take the risk of everyone dismissing it, and then I'd be left to deal with the consequences. And I don't have the strength for any of that. I just want to disappear.

'Carol,' I say, my voice still shaky. 'I'm so grateful to you for saving me just now, but I have a plan. I'm going to leave. So you don't need to call the police, okay?'

'He should face charges. He can't get away with how he's treated you. It's assault. And why should you have to leave your home while he gets to stay?'

'It's not my home anymore. More like a prison,' I murmur. 'I *want* to leave. It's what I want more than anything.'

'Where will you go?' she asks.

'I . . . I'd rather not say. I trust you, but . . .'

'No, I understand. It's safer if nobody knows. What about your belongings? I don't think it's safe for you to go in there right now. He could come back at any moment.'

I shake my head. 'It's fine. I don't want any of that stuff anyway. I'll start again.' I think about Gran's jewellery that I inherited. I'll be gutted to leave it behind. I'm wearing her wedding ring on a chain around my neck, but the rest of it is in a box on my dressing table. It's not worth much, but it holds memories. I'd love to get my passport too, but Adam keeps both our passports locked in a safe and I don't know the combination.

'Money?' Carol asks. 'I can give you a bit to get you started . . .'

'Oh, no, you're really kind, but I've been saving.'

'Good girl!' Her eyes shine with admiration and I feel a little better. 'I really do think we should get you to a doctor,' she adds.

'I'll see someone if the pain continues, but right now I need to get away.'

'I understand,' she says.

'Thank you,' I reply, grateful for her acceptance.

Carol gives me some ibuprofen to help dull the pain, and then insists on packing a small suitcase for me with toiletries, pyjamas, and even her pink fluffy dressing gown. 'I know it's too hot to wear right now, but you'll want something cosy and comforting.'

'Are you sure? I'll pay you back.'

'Not necessary. It's my pleasure to give you a few things to make you more comfortable.'

I wish I could say more to express my gratitude, but I think I'm still in shock. This morning at Mrs Bunton's feels like it was several weeks ago rather than an hour or so.

I don't think Adam will report my disappearance to the police because that would risk me spilling my guts about his abusive behaviour. But, just in case he does, Carol insists on giving me a lift to the train station at Havant, an hour away from Guildford. Carol's reasoning is that, if Adam does report me missing, the police might not check CCTV cameras that far away. She's also given me a pair of sunglasses, and a jacket with a hood, so I can disguise myself a little. It all feels a little over-the-top, but when I imagine the possibility of Adam finding me, I realise I'm grateful for anything that could help keep me safe.

After she's checked the road outside to make sure Adam is nowhere to be seen, we sneak into her little silver Citroën where she makes me lie down on the back seat. 'Don't sit up until I give you the all-clear,' she instructs.

'Okay,' I reply, my heart racing once again. She's left Alfie at home and I already miss his gentle doggy presence, guarding me.

As she pulls out of the drive, I have visions of Adam rushing over and banging on the car windows, chasing us down the road. But we manage to leave Guildford without seeing him again. Carol stops at a garage so she can fill the tank with fuel and I can switch to the front passenger seat. She refuses my offer of payment for the petrol and I think about arguing, but I need to be careful with money right now, so I gratefully accept, vowing to someday pay her back for all the kindnesses she's shown me.

At Havant train station, she hugs me briefly in the drop-off bay.

'I'll never forget what you've done for me, Carol. You've saved me.'

She waves away my thanks. 'I just wish I could do more. Let me give you my number in case of emergencies.'

I take my burner phone from my bag and tap in her details, grateful to have at least one person who knows what I've escaped from.

She nods towards the platform. 'Keep your head down, remember. Until you get to where you're going. And then see a doctor as soon as you can.'

I give her another quick hug and stride away towards the ticket machine. I only have ten minutes until my train, and I wait in the toilet until the very last second.

Once on board, I allow myself to relax a little. Have I done it? Have I finally escaped my marriage? I find a double seat and sit gingerly by the window, placing Carol's case on the chair next to me to deter anyone else from sitting there. I face away from the window until the train has left the station and is heading south.

I fleetingly considered relocating to Southend-on-Sea, where Gran grew up, but I worried that Adam might remember where she's from, and go looking for me there. Instead, I picked a place with no personal ties. A small, unassuming town where I could quietly rebuild my life. It's a town Sheila once mentioned because her son, Jim, owns several rental properties there.

Once I arrive, I'm planning to change my name by deed poll to Willow McAllister, inspired by the graceful willow tree outside Gran's kitchen window. The one she loved so much. The surname is a tribute to Miss McAllister, my primary school teacher who was sweet to me after my dad died.

Once settled, I'll contact Jim using my new name. Hopefully, he's as nice as Sheila says and he'll rent me one of his flats. I'll have to book a B & B for now, but that's okay. I'm sure I'll get sorted with a proper place soon. I don't need much – just a basic studio flat would be great.

Aside from getting my accommodation sorted, the first thing I'm going to do is get my ridiculously long hair cut into a bob. Adam wouldn't ever let me cut it and I hate its long, drab straightness. I can't wait to get it cut properly into a style of my choice.

As the train approaches Hinton Admiral train station, only a stone's throw from the seaside town of Highcliffe, I clutch the case Carol packed for me, and make my way to the end of the carriage. It's just me and a young lad waiting by the doors. He gives me a nod and a half-smile, and I nod back. My body is just one dull ache now, rather than in any terrible pain, and I think I might have managed to escape serious injury. For now, I just need to concentrate on getting a safe place to stay.

I've already done a little research on the town – Highcliffe is pretty, with a castle, a beach, lots of green space, and some nice shops and restaurants. Everything a person could need.

The plan is to keep myself to myself, but my most pressing issue is to build my savings back up. I think I have enough to last me a couple of months, but I need regular work. I have an idea to get myself started, but it's a bit of a gamble as I don't know anyone here who can give me references and, for obvious reasons, I can't contact anyone from back home in Guildford. So I'm going to put up signs locally, advertising myself as a handywoman and decorator, working only for women. Hopefully I'll earn enough to scrape by. I don't need much. Just a roof and some transport. I can exist on the basics. It will feel like a luxury after the past year of hell.

I step on to the platform, deserted except for me and the young lad, who heads over to a bike stand. Hanging flower baskets sway in the warm evening breeze, while wrought-iron pillars stand like sentinels in the twilight. Old-fashioned street lanterns spread a soft, yellow glow across the platform, lighting up the red-brick building that looks more like someone's house than a station. The scene is so peaceful, such a contrast to the panic and chaos of the past few hours. The violence, running from Adam. Carol's place. Fleeing in her car. The train.

I'm exhausted, but a faint glimmer of hope flutters inside me like a timid butterfly. Maybe this is it. Maybe this is the place that will finally set me free.

Chapter Thirty

WILLOW

The hotel's drab facade does nothing to help the churn of unease in my stomach. It's one of those bland chains you see repeated in every town. I refused to go to Guildford to meet Bertie, so we've compromised, meeting halfway, in Winchester. Although knowing I'm this close to Surrey gives me the jitters.

I park my van in the car park at the rear, mechanically feeding change into the ticket machine. An hour should be enough, although I'm hoping it won't take as long as that. All I need is for him to understand that my life is in danger if Adam ever discovers where I'm hiding. Bertie might be as trustworthy as a cracked mirror, but I cling to the hope that even he wouldn't consciously wish actual physical harm on me.

Every base instinct screams not to meet him. The safest thing would be to move on again. To leave Highcliffe and head north. Maybe settle in Scotland or Wales. Or apply for a new passport and go abroad. But I realise, with a jolt, that I like my new life – my snug flat, the growing bank of clients that has given me financial security – and I might be building something genuine with Gabe. Can I really throw all that away? Is it absolutely necessary? I worry that I won't be able to recreate this life elsewhere. It's taken me just over two years to rebuild this one. To shape it into something I'm proud of. What's more, I've done it alone, with no help from anyone else. I can't believe I might have to give it all up and start over. Again.

When I first moved to Highcliffe, I was still on high alert. Still jumped at every car door slam. Still froze every time I caught a glimpse of a dark-haired man coming down the street. But, gradually, as the weeks turned to months, and I started settling in to my new apartment, my shoulders began to relax. I was never fully comfortable, but I was getting there. And now . . . *this*.

I push open the hotel's heavy glass door, its cold surface swinging silently aside to reveal a deserted reception area with stark overhead lighting. My heart clatters as I approach the lift directly ahead, pressing the button, a cocktail of nerves and dread starting to build as I wait for it to descend.

The lift doors part and a loved-up young couple spill out, giggling and kissing, wrapped in their own bubble. They don't notice me standing here. I step inside, the smell of perfume and air freshener getting down the back of my throat.

I exit on the second floor and walk along the carpeted corridor until I reach room 23. Standing at the door, I feel an overwhelming urge to turn around, get back in my van and drive home. But I force my feet to stay planted, recalling Elsie's words that I need to pull up my pants and sort out my problems. Even though every part of me is rebelling. I knock before I can change my mind.

When Bertie finally opens the door, there's a moment of surreal familiarity that tightens my chest. Clad in his work suit with his tie casually loosened and a drink in hand, he greets me with a forced ease. 'Jasmine! You look a hell of a lot better than you did on the beach.' He's drunk.

It's strange hearing my old name. I don't like it. It feels . . . unsafe.

'Sorry, where are my manners? Come in.' Bertie holds the door open wide, waving me in theatrically.

The room is as I imagined – clean and inoffensive, a hardwearing patterned carpet, a modest TV on the wall next to a framed print, a double bed, and an armchair in the corner by the window. I head for the chair and perch on the edge.

'Drink?' Bertie offers, nodding to a bottle of whisky on the bedside table.

'I'm driving,' I reply, my voice taut.

He smirks at that, and my stomach dips.

'What were you doing in Highcliffe?' I ask.

He shrugs and sits on the edge of the bed. 'Meeting a girl.'

'Does she live there?' I probe.

He takes a slow sip, his eyes unfocused. 'Yeah.'

'She your girlfriend?' I need to know if he's going to be making a habit of visiting my new home town.

'No,' he admits. 'Went to Bournemouth for a mate's stag, and ended up going back to hers. Went to the beach the morning after. Saw you.'

I silently curse my bad luck. Why, why, why did I choose that time to go to the beach? Of all the days.

'Couldn't believe it, when you walked past,' Bertie says, shaking his head. 'Nice place to move to though. I can see why you chose it.' He reaches over to grab the bottle and tops up his drink. 'You know, Adam went mental after you disappeared,' he continues, lowering his voice into a conspiratorial tone. 'Wouldn't want to be in your shoes if he catches up with you.'

'Does he know?' I ask, mentally packing my bags and giving notice on my flat. 'Did you tell him you saw me?' I swallow hard and cut to the chase. 'I came here to ask you not to mention it. Please don't tell him you saw me.'

Bertie falls silent, a slow smile spreading across his face as he watches my reaction. 'Don't get your knickers in a twist, Jas. I haven't said anything to Adam . . . yet.'

'You know he was abusive, right?' Every word is laced with memories of pain. 'You know that, don't you?'

'Adam's just . . . traditional, that's all,' he quips, as if that excuses everything.

'So, by "traditional", you mean locking up your wife and making her existence a living hell?'

'Don't exaggerate, Jas. Just because he likes his missus to stay home and keep the place nice doesn't mean he's abusive.' Bertie rolls his eyes. 'Talk about overreacting.'

'Am I?' I challenge, my eyes hardening.

'So . . . what did he do? Hit you?' Bertie's tone is incredulous. 'I don't think so.'

'You think wrong,' I reply. 'There was grabbing and pushing. He nearly ripped my hair out just before I managed to get away from him. And then . . .' I swallow, remembering his fist as it smashed into my belly. 'The bastard punched me in the stomach.'

For a fraction of a second, Bertie's eyes widen in shock before his expression reverts back to neutral. 'Why should I believe you, over my best friend?' he challenges. 'Got any photos to prove it? Adam said you were cheating on him. Said you cleared out all the cash from the safe and ran off with another man.'

'*What?*' I cry in disbelief. Adam's lies are absurd. 'I didn't even know the combination to his precious safe. If I did, would I have left my passport behind? The one he confiscated, by the way. And I never knew there was any cash in there.'

Bertie shrugs. 'So how did you set yourself up in a new town without any money?'

'I'd been saving up so I could escape him,' I say, the words tumbling out as I begin pacing the cramped room. 'My life was a living hell. And, what other man? There was no *other man*. Adam didn't let me out of his sight long enough for me to start an affair. Did you know he put a tracking app on my phone?' Annoyingly, my eyes start to fill with tears. But they're tears of frustration and anger. This is exactly why I didn't call the police. Because it would have ended up as a 'he said, she said' situation with all Adam's friends and colleagues sticking up for him. To everyone else – including my work colleagues – Adam was charming, sweet even, a mask that hid his true nature. Only I, and perhaps Carol next door, ever witnessed the truth behind that smile.

'Fine,' Bertie declares, pouring the rest of his drink down his throat and setting his glass on the bedside table with a harsh clatter. 'I won't tell him. Happy?'

Relief washes over me and I can't quite believe it was that simple. Perhaps Bertie isn't as bad as I thought.

'Be a shame to let this hotel room go to waste though, wouldn't it?' he adds, his tone shifting to something dangerously playful.

'Yeah, right,' I snap, getting to my feet, not finding his joke very funny.

'No, Jas.' He steps in front of me, blocking my exit. 'I'm serious. I've always thought you were hot – in a nerdy librarian kind of way. But obviously I wouldn't have done anything while you were with Adam. Now though . . . I feel like you kind of owe me.'

A sinking, familiar dread crawls over my skin. Before I can protest, Bertie slips a hand on to my back, guiding me closer as his intentions become unmistakably clear. When his lips meet mine in a clumsy, drunken kiss, raw confusion surges in my gut. I understand what he's after, yet every fibre of my being recoils. I didn't flee one nightmare only to stumble into another.

In that suffocating moment, terror grips me fully, and I shove him aside, bolting from the hotel room towards the lift, my steps frantic, my heart pounding. One hand repeatedly slams the lift button while I wipe my mouth with the other, throwing panicked glances over my shoulder, but Bertie hasn't left his room. He isn't chasing after me.

The lift door opens and I step in, terrified that I'm doing the wrong thing. That by rejecting Bertie I'm opening myself up to an even bigger danger. But the thought of sleeping with that man makes me sick. I can't do it.

I press the ground floor button in a haze of fear, caught between two terrible scenarios. I have to hope that Bertie was simply trying his luck with me. That he wouldn't be so cruel as to tell Adam about me after what I told him.

The lift reaches the lobby and I flee the hotel, bursting back out into the chill night air, regretting ever having come. Have I just made the biggest mistake of my life? Do I now need to leave my home and disappear once again?

Chapter Thirty-One

The knife glides through the ripe avocado as I slice it into neat wedges and add it to the salad. Gabe's due to arrive for dinner at seven, and although I promised myself I'd delay his visit until I sorted out this Bertie mess, Gabe's concerned calls and messages have made me realise how nice it is to have someone who genuinely cares about my well-being. I worry that the more I push him away, the greater the risk of losing him entirely. I can't help thinking about how different Gabe is to Adam. How kind and funny he is. How safe he makes me feel, allowing me to be myself and live my life, rather than twisting me into a version of what he wants in a woman.

My heart flutters erratically as I try to shake off the unsettling thought that Adam might still be a lurking threat. The air feels heavy with all my unspoken fears, and I can't help but wonder if tonight might be the last time I see Gabe.

It's been three days since I visited Bertie at the hotel in Winchester, and I'm still in shock at his drunken attempt to sleep with me. Every minute since then I've been on tenterhooks waiting for him to call. He doesn't know my new name or my address, but if he tells Adam I live in Highcliffe, I'm sure it won't be too hard for him to track me down. I realised, too late, that after Bertie saw me on the beach, I should have pretended I was simply visiting the area. I should never have revealed that Highcliffe is my home.

My few possessions are already stuffed into a case – the same one Carol gave me – and I've been meticulously scanning web pages and maps of quiet, remote villages in the Lake District.

I should have moved further away from Guildford to start with. I was naive not to expect that someone I knew would spot me eventually. But I wasn't thinking straight at the time. My mind was in panic mode. And then I found my little flat, and fell in love with the area. More fool me.

I'm still holding on to a glimmer of hope – if Bertie were to tell Adam that he's seen me, then he runs the risk of Adam discovering that he tried to blackmail me into sleeping with him. And Bertie has to know that Adam would not take kindly to that. So maybe I'm safe after all. If only there were a way to know for certain.

A rap at the front door interrupts my swirling thoughts. I glance at my phone to see it's only six thirty. Gabe's half an hour early, and I'm not changed yet. I rinse my hands in the kitchen sink and dry them on a tea towel before heading into the hall and checking my reflection in the mirror. I smooth my hair, straighten up and answer the door.

My heart drops when I see who it is.

'Sorry, Priya, I'm busy right now.'

She isn't her glamorous, lively self today. Her normally glossy hair is lank, and her skin is dull. She's dressed in oversized grey sweats with a brown stain at the neckline. 'Could I just have a couple of minutes of your time, Willow?'

'Like I said, I'm busy.' I try to close the door but she wedges her foot in the gap.

'Please,' she begs. 'Just one minute.'

I mutter an expletive under my breath. The last thing I need is for her to be here when Gabe shows up. But I guess I still have half an hour. 'Fine,' I relent. 'Just one minute.'

She brightens a little and follows me through to the living space, where she stands awkwardly by the sofa.

I don't invite her to sit, because I need her to leave as soon as possible. 'What is it?' I ask, my patience too thin for any of her games.

Fidgeting with her fingers, she finally murmurs, 'I just wanted to ask if we could start over? I'm sorry we disagreed over Gabe and, of course if you still want to see him, then that's your choice.'

I shake my head in disbelief. 'Well, thanks for giving me your permission, Priya. Very kind of you.'

She flushes and quickly adds, 'I didn't mean it like that.'

She's doing a good job of playing the innocent act, but this time I'm not buying it. 'Okay, is that all?'

After a brief pause she confesses, 'I just . . . I wanted us to be friends.'

'So did I, Priya. But then you went all weird on me, telling me about your first date with Gabe and how you did the same things as we did. It wasn't just uncomfortable, it felt like you were trying to sabotage us. To ruin all our first moments.'

She nods. 'I get it. I shouldn't have said those things. I . . .' She trails off and then swallows. 'Just, be careful, okay? I don't want you getting hurt.'

'Noted,' I reply, fighting the urge to roll my eyes. 'Well, I think that's your one minute up.'

She nods again, her eyes huge, like a puppy dog's, but I'm not falling for the act. And I really want her gone before Gabe shows up.

Right on cue, my buzzer goes. Priya's gaze shifts towards the hallway intercom.

'You can leave now.' I step forward to open the front door and watch her retreat down the corridor, taking in a few deep breaths, trying to regain what little equilibrium I had before she showed up at my door.

I ignore my buzzer for now. I'm not letting Gabe in until she's safely back in her flat. The last thing I need is a conversation between the three of us, ruining the whole vibe of the evening.

Too late, the landing door swings open and someone steps into the hallway. But it's not Gabe. It's a young, uniformed police officer, followed by a slim woman with dark hair pulled back into a ponytail. She's dressed casually in black jeans, boots, and a navy puffa. Priya turns back to look at me, curiosity flickering in her eyes. I wonder if they're here for her or me. They stride past her and head my way. I feel strangely numb, like nothing they could say would shock me. But maybe that's because my brain is already on overload.

Or . . . maybe they're here to see Elsie? But that hope is short-lived as the officer fixes his gaze on me and asks if I'm Willow McAllister.

'Yes,' I reply.

'Do you mind if we come in for a chat?' the officer asks, his tone polite but firm.

'What, *now*?' I ask, my gaze flicking to the older woman who's beside him, wondering if she's also a police officer. All thoughts of preparing dinner for Gabe have fled. Why do the police want to talk to me?

'Yes please,' he replies.

'Um, fine,' I murmur, blinking rapidly as I step aside and invite them into the hall and then through to the lounge. In the dim light, they seem to loom almost larger than life, radiating authority.

The woman clears her throat and introduces herself. 'I'm Detective Sergeant Katherine Lin and this is my colleague PC Martin. Would you like to sit down,' she adds.

'I'm fine.' I choose to remain standing as tension grips my body. Asking me to sit down can't be good.

DS Lin's tone turns grave as she continues, 'Well, I'm sorry to have to tell you that on Tuesday morning, we found the body of a Mr Bertie Grierson in a hotel room in Winchester.' She pauses, waiting for me to digest the news. But it doesn't sound real. She continues, 'And our investigation indicates that you may have been there the previous night to visit the deceased.'

As her words gradually sink in, my vision blurs. 'Bertie's dead?' I whisper.

'We don't believe it was due to natural causes,' DS Lin explains evenly. 'So I'm afraid we'll have to ask you to accompany us to the station.'

My voice catches as I stammer, 'You think I had something to do with it?'

'Let's talk about it at the station,' she replies.

I shake my head in disbelief, unable to comprehend what's going on. Someone *killed* Bertie?

Chapter Thirty-Two

I didn't realise that when DS Lin said they wanted to talk to me at the police station, they meant the one in Winchester, not locally here in Dorset. They suggested I travel with them in their squad car, but I decided to take my own van so I could get home more easily afterwards. Although now, as I grip the steering wheel with sweating palms, I'm beginning to think that was a bad idea. I can barely concentrate on the drive, my head too consumed with the shocking news that Bertie is dead.

I can't pretend I didn't hate the man, but would I have wished him dead? Well, maybe I did for a while. But that's hardly surprising. I thought he hadn't called because he was toying with me, making me suffer before letting me know he was going to tell Adam he'd seen me. Instead, he was lying dead in his hotel room. It hardly seems real.

Does that mean the killer showed up right after I left? If I'd stayed even the tiniest bit longer, perhaps I could very well be dead now too. My head spins from the thought. I open the window and gulp down freezing air that makes my eyes water and my chest tighten. Still, the sharp, cold blast helps clear the fog of panic and I manage to drive the rest of the way to Winchester without any mishaps.

My phone pings with a text from Gabe. Before leaving Highcliffe, I sent him a quick, apologetic message to cancel dinner at my flat. I didn't go into details, but I realise that if I want to have a real relationship with him, I might have to tell him about my past. I'm not quite ready for that just yet though. I have too much to deal with right now. Gabe didn't reply to my text straightaway which made me think I might have blown it with him. But now I pull over briefly to read:

No worries about dinner. Maybe see you later? xx

Two kisses and no recriminations. I exhale and feel a smile tug at my lips, which is crazy considering what's going on right now. I've got it bad. I'll message him after my interview. Provided it all goes well.

The police station is an eighties red-brick building on the corner of a narrow street. All the on-street parking is reserved for permit holders, so I find a multistorey car park further up the road and then make my way back to the station on foot. I head to the front desk, and I'm immediately shown to an interview room that smells of sweat and cleaning products. The desk officer is polite and brings me a cup of tea. I also manage to beg a couple of biscuits, wolfing them down, crumbs scattering as I'm joined by Detective Sergeant Lin and another plain-clothes officer who introduces himself as DC Sean Corrigan.

It was a fifty-minute drive to get here, which I guess I should be grateful for, because it gave me a sliver of time to think about what I should say to them. And I think I know what I have to do. Even though the thought of it brings me out in a cold sweat.

'Am I under arrest?' I ask immediately, wanting to put my mind at rest. To know what they're thinking.

'At the moment, you're helping us with our enquiries,' DS Lin replies, her eyes dark and steady. 'You're not under caution and you don't need a solicitor. This is just a witness interview.'

My heart thunders so loud in my ears, I'm sure the officers can hear it echoing around the quiet, sterile room. I wish Gran were here to tell me everything's going to be okay. I don't think I've ever felt this alone in my life.

'We'll be recording the interview,' DS Lin continues, pointing out the black box on the table between us, 'and DC Corrigan will take notes, too, all right?'

'Fine,' I reply, as if I have a choice.

Corrigan presses the record button and clears his throat before stating the date and time, and where the interview is taking place. One by one, we introduce ourselves formally.

'You said it wasn't an accident,' I start, hesitantly. 'Do you know who did it yet? Who killed Bertie?'

'We're in the process of establishing that, Mrs Owens,' DS Lin replies, her tone clipped but not unfriendly. 'Or is it Ms McAllister? You changed your name by deed poll just over two years ago, is that correct?'

My breath stutters in response. The fact that I changed my name somehow makes me sound already guilty. 'Yes. My name's now Willow McAllister. You can call me Willow.'

'Okay, Willow,' DS Lin says. 'Did you meet with Bertie Grierson on the night of Monday 27th October?'

'I did,' I reply firmly. 'But I didn't want to be there. And I didn't stay for long. How do you know I was there? CCTV?'

'That, and we listened to Bertie's recorded work phone calls from that day. Yours was one of those calls. He asked to meet you at the hotel at 8.30 p.m., correct?'

'Yes,' I confirm, taking a sip of tea that's already cooled.

'Would you like to explain your reason for the visit? And what occurred there?' she continues.

I blow air out through my mouth, my fingers trembling in my lap as I remember the events of that night. And all the events leading up to it. Am I really going to have to tell them everything? I guess I am. Maybe Carol was right two years ago when she urged me to call the police and report my husband. If I'd done as she suggested back then, perhaps I could have avoided all this. But there's no point thinking like that. I'm here now, and I realise that this is my opportunity to tell them the whole truth. About Adam's abusive behaviour, and how I had to leave him and change my identity. About how I saw Bertie on the beach and how he tried to blackmail me into sleeping with him.

I just have to hope that they believe me. And that after I tell them, they're able to keep me safe from my husband.

'All right,' I say slowly, looking from one to the other. DS Lin hasn't let her eyes drop from my face and DC Corrigan's pen hovers above his notepad, waiting for me to begin. 'I'll tell you everything from the start. But it might take a while, if that's okay.'

DS Lin gives a nod.

I pause for another second, like I'm giving myself one last chance to change my mind, but then I take a breath. I'm already in so deep: I can't stop now.

Chapter Thirty-Three

After a long evening spent talking to the detectives under the harsh fluorescent lights at Winchester police station, and an equally long, tense drive home, I finally find myself dragging my weary body up the stairs to my little apartment.

I feel wrecked – physically and emotionally. Events have left me famished, chilled to the bone, utterly drained, and all I can think about is sinking into a hot bath to wash it all away. Sadly, the small space I call home only has a shower, but that's going to have to be enough. A hot shower is better than nothing. Anything to help me shed this grotty, exhausted feeling.

After sitting with DS Lin and DC Corrigan, recounting the grim details of my abusive marriage to Adam followed by my desperate escape, and then Bertie's revolting attempts to get me into bed, they finally let me leave the station. But, before walking out the door, they made it clear that they would almost certainly need to talk to me again. Their parting words were a warning not to disappear anywhere.

That's perfectly fine by me. Disappearing is the last thing I have the energy for right now. The only disappearing I want to do is into my little cocoon of an apartment, away from everything and everyone. As I unlock the door and step inside, I wish I could stay here forever, shutting out the rest of the world completely.

Before I left, DS Lin also asked a question I wasn't expecting – whether I would want to press charges against Adam for domestic assault. They explained that things like psychological, emotional and financial abuse are all part of it. It struck me then, like a sudden epiphany, that, aside from him punching me, Adam had no legal right to control my life the way he did, dictating my every move and preventing me from ever leaving the house. He had no right to stop me from earning a living, something I'd never truly realised until she put it that way. Not to mention the shoving and pushing and throwing me to the floor when he was in one of his rages. I told her I'd think about it. It's all too much for now. I don't have the bandwidth to make that kind of decision tonight.

I head straight to the bathroom, eager to settle my mind, to blank it all out for a while. I peel off my clothes and step into the shower with a sigh, allowing the water temperature to reach just short of scalding, letting the steam fill the room in a comforting fog.

After I finished painting Tansy's hallway last week, she gifted me a box of Sanctuary pampering products. I break open the shower gel now and lather it on generously, its fresh scent cleansing me from the outside in as all the grime and stress of the day swirls down the drain. I realise I forgot to message Gabe back about coming over tonight, but I'm too exhausted to do it now. I'll call him tomorrow to apologise.

Finally, when my hair and body are squeaky clean, I grab a towel and head into the bedroom where I dry off, slap on some body lotion, and slip into my cosiest pyjamas. I unhook my pink fluffy dressing gown from the back of the door. Or should I say *Carol's* pink fluffy dressing gown – whenever I wear it, I always think of my lovely ex-neighbour who saved my life that day – and slip it on.

I guess the one good thing in all this, the silver lining, is that Bertie being dead means I'm off the hook with Adam. Bertie now won't get the chance to scurry off and tell him he saw me alive and well in Highcliffe – unless he managed to get a quick call to him before he was murdered. As it stands, my location is safe. At least for now.

But I can't stop wondering about Bertie. Who on earth hated him enough to kill him? He wasn't the nicest person, that much is for sure, but murder is such a leap. It wouldn't surprise me if he pissed off a long list of people, but to actually go so far as to kill him? That's a whole different level.

I head for the kitchen and rummage around in the freezer for something quick to eat. I take out a frozen margherita pizza and almost swoon at the vision of thick crust and bubbling cheese, before realising I'll have to wait for the oven to heat up. Ugh, I'm so hungry. I turn on the oven and butter a couple of slices of bread, hoping the carb overload will keep me going while I wait.

The half-finished salad from earlier sits wilting and limp on the chopping board. I slide it all into the bin, suddenly sad that my dinner with Gabe was thwarted yet again. Maybe we're just not meant to be. It's disappointing how often I seem to be figuring that out, and I hate myself a little for caring so much.

A loud rap on my front door startles me. I check the time on my phone. Just after eleven thirty. Who the hell would be calling round at this hour? Surely not the police again? It must be Gabe. I vaguely remember his text saying something about seeing me later. *Damn.* Much as I'd like to see him, I'll have to put him off. Right now, I just need to eat something and to fall into bed.

I readjust the tie on my dressing gown, and head to the door.

He's standing in the dark hallway, turned slightly away. The bulb in the hall must have gone. I'll have to call the landlord. 'Hey, Gabe,' I say, apologetically. 'Sorry I didn't message back, but it's been a crazy evening.'

He turns and I think I'm having an out-of-body experience when I see who it is.

'*Adam*,' I breathe, my whole system going into shock.

Chapter Thirty-Four

I need to close the front door! *CLOSE IT!* I scream in my head. But I can't seem to move any part of my body. Adam doesn't speak. He just pushes the door wide, brushing past me as he steps right into my flat, gazing around with a glint of danger in his eyes. Taking it all in, cataloguing the shabby furniture, the lack of decoration.

He looks dishevelled, his stubble patchy, his shirt crumpled. He has dark rings beneath bloodshot eyes and his hair is lank. The Adam I knew would sooner die than go out looking anything less than immaculate.

I'm shaking. I can't breathe. Questions crowd my mind. How did he get here? How did he find out my address? The front door stands wide open behind me. I want to run, but fear streaks through me, stopping me cold, my mind racing with grim scenarios. If I run and he catches me, what will he do? Maybe I should scream for help. Would Elsie hear me? Priya? I'm trapped. Caught between the need to run and a paralysing terror.

Doubt and desperation jostle inside me until, as if he can read my mind, Adam circles slowly back around and closes the door with a click, silently motioning for me to go into the lounge with a nod of his head.

Everything I've done to escape him is slipping away, falling apart. I do as he asks and move towards the sofa, standing frozen and stupid, watching his face as he takes in my little sanctuary. *He found me. He found me. He found me.* I should have gone further away, hidden better. I thought I'd been so careful. I ignored all the little voices that told me I hadn't been clever enough.

I can't move. I can't speak. Everything is crashing down around me and I'm still standing here like an idiot, doing nothing.

Adam turns, his lips parting. 'I saw you,' he states, his voice so tight and low I have to strain to hear it. This is the most dangerous Adam, the one that simmers slowly and can explode into violence at any second. It doesn't feel like two years since I last saw him. It feels as though the years that separated us have collapsed into moments.

'I saw you going into Bertie's hotel room,' he continues. 'And I saw you tonight going into the police station.'

My stomach drops. He's been trailing me for days. Maybe longer. These past few nights I thought I was safe, when all this time he was watching me. I reach out and grip the back of the sofa for support as his words slash through me.

He roams around the room like he can't quite believe I'm here, like he's thinking about the best ways to drag me back to the life I left behind, the life that nearly broke me.

I'm ready to cry and scream, but I know that any outburst from me will only make things worse. I remember what I have to do, like a dog who's been well trained.

He stops pacing and turns to me, his eyes narrow. 'How could you leave me, Jasmine? Running off like that, making me think you were dead?' Adam's words are sharper now, hot with a slowly building fury. 'Were you seeing Bertie this whole time? Did he install you in this shitty flat so you could be together?'

Adam thinks Bertie and I were having an affair!

'He was my best friend, Jasmine,' Adam continues. 'It's such a fucking cliché – my wife and my best friend.' He throws me a filthy look. 'Of course, Bertie denied it when I confronted him, but I could tell something was off. How long has it been going on? Years? Did it start before you left me?'

It's an accusation. It's a dare. He's trying to see if I'll lie to him, if I'll deny it, if I'll cry and beg for forgiveness. He expects me to crumble. I want to. I want to drop to the floor and weep, but I can't let myself collapse like that – not again. I'm terrified, but I have to do something to stop this. I have to find a way to stand and fight. I can't live like this, not anymore. I want my words to be strong, but my mouth is dry, fear and dread coating my tongue.

'Me and Bertie?' I respond, hoping I'm managing to mask how afraid I am. 'I wouldn't touch him with a bargepole.' I hope he believes me. I don't know what he'll do if he doesn't. I want to disappear. I want to hide. But I refuse to cower anymore. He brought this fear to my door; I'm not letting him coat me in it and walk away with me.

'Why were you at the police station in Winchester?' he snaps next, pulling at the collar of his shirt. 'What lies did you tell them about me?'

It suddenly occurs to me with the force of a truck smashing into a wall – *Adam killed Bertie*. It's so obvious now. He thought we were sleeping together and so he killed him. Maybe he was planning on killing us both. The thought sends shards of fear through my veins. Is that why he's here now? To finish the job?

I need to think fast. To calm him. Convince him that I didn't sleep with his best friend. And then I need to get out of here and call the police.

'I promise I never slept with Bertie,' I answer softly, as though trying to calm a vicious animal. 'I couldn't stand the man, so why would I ever want to sleep with him?'

'Do you think I'm an idiot?' Adam retorts. 'You met him in a hotel room at night. What else would you have been doing? Hosting a Tupperware party?' He rolls his eyes, his temper rising again.

'Look, Adam, can I just talk honestly with you?'

'That's why I'm here,' he declares coldly. 'To find out why you left me and why you betrayed me with my best friend.'

I take a slow breath, hoping I can say the right thing. The right words that will keep me safe from his anger. From his fists. 'Like I said, I wasn't sleeping with Bertie. The reason I left Guildford was because I was scared of you. You kept me prisoner and wouldn't let me go out, or work, or see my friends, or earn any money. Of course I loved you, but I couldn't live that way, locked up in the house. Surely you understand that?'

My words hang between us for a moment, trembling with the weight of past pain and present fear.

He shakes his head dismissively. 'You're exaggerating. It wasn't that bad. I just . . . I thought we were supposed to be starting a family, and you working and getting stressed would have got in the way of that.' He gives a bitter laugh. 'Remember, it was you who told me that stress can ruin a couple's chance to conceive. That's the only reason we decided that you'd stay home.'

'Work wasn't causing my stress, Adam. It was fear.'

His lips tighten and I realise I have to reel it in a bit. I have to flatter and cajole. Lie for all I'm worth. 'Adam, do you think I haven't missed you these past two years? Of course I have. I loved you. *Love* you. It's been . . . awful here on my own, without you.' My hands shake and my eyes glisten with tears, but they're tears of terror, not of the emotion I'm trying desperately to fake.

He doesn't reply and I can't tell if he believes my words or not. I press on anyway.

'The reason I met up with Bertie,' I continue, 'was that he spotted me on the beach last Saturday, and he recognised me. He was with some girl he met. We didn't speak, but I was worried he was going to tell you he'd seen me. So I called him at work to ask him not to say anything.'

Adam's gaze is still fixed on me and I try to disguise a shiver of fear by clearing my throat and continuing.

'Bertie said we should meet up and gave me the name of a hotel. So, I drove there on Monday night asking him to pretend he never saw me. He agreed, but he wanted me to sleep with him in return.'

Adam's jaw clenches tighter. He opens his mouth to speak, but I cut him off before he starts.

'I didn't – of course I didn't. I left immediately and came home. Then the police showed up earlier this evening telling me Bertie was dead. That's why I had to go to the police station tonight – because they think I was the last person to see him alive.'

'Bertie's dead?' he echoes, but he doesn't sound too surprised.

'Someone killed him,' I say, forcing my voice to sound casual. 'Probably mistaken identity or something.' I can't let Adam know I suspect him.

There's an abrupt shift as he eyes the kitchen. 'Okay, well – that's . . . Are you going to cook that pizza?' He gestures towards the defrosting packet on the counter. 'I'm starving.'

I cross the room, tearing off the packaging and sliding the pizza into the hot oven, my mind still a whirl of conflict and fear.

'Haven't eaten all day,' he adds. 'Once we've had something to eat, we'll hit the road. Go home. Forget all this ever happened and start again.'

My heart plummets. He wants me to go back to Guildford with him. Of course he does.

'I'm willing to put all this behind us.' He comes into the kitchen area and puts a hand to my cheek. It takes every ounce of my willpower not to flinch away from his touch. 'This time, it will be different,' he promises, his tone soothing. 'You can get a job, if you want. We'll just tell everyone that you made a mistake. That you begged me to come back. How does that sound?'

I nod, unable to speak.

'Jasmine? I asked you a question. How does that sound?' he presses.

'Good,' I whisper, the word sounding hollow as tears roll down my cheeks.

'So why don't you look happy?' he growls. 'Why are you *crying*?' His eyes narrow and he shakes his head slowly. 'You're still the same fucking liar that you were back then, aren't you? I don't know which words are true and which are fairy tales. Do you think I'm an idiot?' he yells.

I edge away from the oven and around the breakfast bar. But he's faster, striding past, and he's now standing between me and the lounge door. Why didn't I run when he first came into the flat and my exit was clear? I could have made a break for it and screamed blue murder, woken everyone up in the block. Instead, I froze like the weak, pathetic fool I used to be.

And now Adam's eyes are glinting with malice, getting meaner. I think this time he might actually kill me.

Chapter Thirty-Five

'Willow? Are you okay in there?'

In the lounge, Adam and I both freeze at the muffled sound of a voice outside my apartment door. I catch a flicker of worry in his eyes and the sight of it makes my heart leap.

Priya! It's *Priya*. Her voice is a lifeline, but it's one I don't dare to reach for.

I should scream for help – but Adam shoots me a look, vicious and full of warning, as though his hand is already around my throat. My lips clamp shut.

'Say anything and I'll end you,' he hisses, drawing closer, until he's a dark wall between me and the exit.

'Willow!' Priya's persistent cry echoes from the landing. 'I heard shouting. Are you all right?'

Despite everything, despite her endless interference and her fixation on Gabe, I could hug her right now. She's my only hope.

'Piss off and mind your own business!' Adam yells, acting like he's in control of everything – me, Priya, our fate, the very air in the room.

'Gabe, is that you?' Priya calls out, confusion in her voice. 'Willow, are you in there?'

'Her name's Jasmine, you stupid bitch,' Adam grinds out, too quietly for her to hear.

I open my mouth to call out to her, but he's already one step ahead, already moving faster than I can think.

He lunges for a tea towel lying on the breakfast bar and starts stuffing it into my mouth until I gag, my protests silenced by fabric that tastes of stale water.

Priya's voice grows louder now. 'Willow, just let me know you're all right? And I'll leave, okay?'

Adam grabs my upper arm with bruising force that flashes me back to the day I left him. He shoves me down on to the sofa, sending shooting pains up my back as I land awkwardly.

Silence looms from outside now and I'm terrified that she's gone. That she's not going to force the issue. Unless, maybe, she's doing exactly what she threatened to do and is finally calling the police.

I yank the tea towel from my mouth, gasping. 'Adam,' I manage to choke out. 'Let me tell her I'm okay, and then she'll leave. If you don't, she'll call the police.'

'It doesn't matter,' he snaps back, his shoulders dropping like he's decided something crucial. 'We're leaving now, come on.'

'Leaving? To go where?' I'm stalling, desperate to buy time, praying Priya hasn't really gone.

'Home, of course,' he sneers. 'It's obvious you never told your neighbour who you really are and where you're from, so it won't matter if she talks to the police.'

I don't tell Adam that I've already given the police his name. That I've already informed them about his abusive behaviour. That, hopefully, when they discover I'm missing, they'll come looking for me in my old home.

That's if Adam doesn't kill me first.

How did I end up with a man like him? A monster. When we first met, I thought he was so kind, so strong. I thought he would love and protect me. I never imagined that one day his strength would turn against me.

'Get up,' Adam commands. 'I told you, we're leaving.'

I move slowly, willing Priya to call the cops, to get them here quickly, before he drags me away.

'Quickly,' he orders, jerking me to my feet.

I wonder if I can summon the nerve to bang on the wall in the hope that Elsie might hear it. But what if she does, and comes round, and then Adam hurts her? I can't risk it. Another idea hits me as I remember Elsie keeps a key under her doormat, but how would I get to it? I'd need to trap Adam in here for long enough to get out into the corridor, let myself into Elsie's flat and lock the door. It's impossible.

'I need to go to the bathroom,' I blurt out, searching desperately for another way to delay.

'You'll have to hold it,' he retorts, pulling me towards the door.

'Let me at least get dressed,' I plead, gesturing to my pyjamas and dressing gown.

'We'll be in the car, you don't need to get dressed. All your clothes are waiting for you at home anyway.'

'What about shoes?' I'm frantic now.

'No shoes,' he replies, his voice flat and final.

No, no, no. I can't let this happen. I can't let Adam take me to his van. I can't leave here with him. The very thought of even seeing our old house again makes me sick with fear. I have to at least try to get away from him between here and his vehicle. If I don't, I'm as good as dead anyway.

Adam prods me through the lounge and into the hall, towards the front door of what used to be my haven. I'm praying to God that Priya is still out there on the landing. Still concerned about me – even if her concern is more to do with Gabe than with me.

Adam slips ahead and presses his ear against my front door, listening intently. Hearing nothing, he cracks the door open and peers out.

'All clear.' He smirks and my hope dies.

My heart thunders as I consider my next desperate move.

As he eases open the door fully, I summon every ounce of strength and shove him aside with both hands before making a run for it, sprinting along the corridor, terror clawing at me, fear stabbing at my chest. I call out for help, but my voice is weak and breathless, and barely a sound comes out.

I daren't look back. I pray my shove knocked Adam off balance enough to give me a good head start. I approach Priya's door with a tug of longing, but I can't risk precious seconds banging on it, waiting for her to open up. If only she was still out on the landing. Where did she go? I chance one desperate thump on it with my fist as I pass, hoping that's enough to draw her out and witness the danger I'm in.

Memories crash over me of the last time I fled from my husband, when Carol was my saviour. I wish she were here now. Perhaps wearing her dressing gown will bring me some luck.

I shove open the landing door and race down the stairs, hoping I don't trip and go tumbling. And now, as I reach the next flight, I hear the sound of footsteps clattering behind me, ratcheting up my terror another notch.

I crash through the lobby and stumble out into the cold night. My bare feet slap against the cold, unforgiving stone steps and then the gritty pavement, but I can't care about that. His footsteps ring out behind me as a loose plan forms in my fear-drenched brain.

I'll head to the beach. To the Dolphin restaurant. I'll burst in there and scream to anyone in earshot that I'm being chased, that I'm in danger. Surrounded by people, he won't dare abduct me.

Adam's footsteps keep pounding behind me, loud and relentless. I can't tell how close he is. The gravel path is torture on my bare soles, crunching into my skin with jagged bursts of pain, but I keep going until my feet finally hit the smooth, damp sand.

He's closing in – his breaths now merging with my own – but I cling on to the hope that I can outrun him. That I can get to the restaurant before he drags me back to darkness. My lungs burn and my legs ache, but I force myself onwards.

Up ahead, the faint outline of the restaurant appears. I'm nearly there – so close I can almost taste relief.

But something is horribly wrong.

There's no light spilling from its windows. It should be illuminated! Why is it shrouded in darkness? Too late, I remember Gabe mentioning that it's only open at weekends during the winter.

It's closed.

And I'm stranded on a dark, deserted beach.

With Adam bearing down on me.

Chapter Thirty-Six

My bare feet pound the cold, damp sand as I sprint, the muscles in my legs screaming with pain as fear blurs my vision and sweat coats my skin. I don't know how much longer I can keep running. My heart is a jackhammer in my chest as I risk a glance back to see his shadowy figure not far behind. He's gaining on me. I feel the panic rising and it chokes me, but I force myself to keep going.

The dark outline of the Dolphin restaurant is coming up on my left. Do I keep heading along this deserted beach? It's a bad idea. He'll catch up with me. I know he will. He's faster, fitter. I don't think I can keep going. But if I stop . . .

'You can't outrun me, Jasmine,' he snarls, his voice dangerously, terrifyingly close.

I stumble in shock. He's almost on me. A sob erupts from my chest. But I'm not giving up. I'm not stopping so that he can kill me, like he killed Bertie, or take me back to a life of misery. I won't let it happen. I can't.

I decide to make for the Dolphin anyway, even though it's closed. Maybe somebody's up there – the owner or another member of staff. *Anyone*. I just need someone to see me. To help me.

Suddenly, I'm not running anymore as my feet are knocked from under me. His hands are on my ankles. He must have lunged for me. I feel myself falling, my knee cracking as I land with a sickening thud on the hard sand.

There's a moment of silence before I find my voice and scream, praying that someone might hear me. 'Help!' I cry. 'Help me! *Please!*'

'Shut up,' Adam growls as he crawls along my body until he's on top of me, the smell of stale alcohol, sweat and aftershave tainting the clean ocean air. 'There's no one out here. I told you I wasn't going to let you run away from me again, you stupid bitch. And don't think for a minute that I believe that story about you and Bertie. If you're going to lie, you need to do better than that.'

'I wasn't lying,' I plead.

'Shut. Up,' he repeats, his breath hot on my face. 'I never want to hear your whiny little voice again.'

In what feels like slow motion, Adam's cold hands wrap around my neck and I know there's no way I'll be able to fight him off. He's going to strangle me. I kick upwards and tug at his jacket, but I don't seem to have any strength. I can't shake him off. He's an immovable object, and my attempts to escape are laughable.

'Please,' I croak. But the air is being squeezed from my lungs, and my throat is on fire. My vision blurs and I know I'm on the edge of blacking out. I don't want to die. My heartbeats thud in my ears, mingling with the roar of the waves as I desperately try to breathe. But I'm fading. It's too late.

A dark cloud blocks the inky sky and I hear a dull thud.

The pain in my throat suddenly eases and I wonder if I'm already dead.

I blink and try to focus as Adam rolls off me. Why did he stop? Has he miraculously had a change of heart?

'Willow! Willow are you okay?'

'Priya?' I gasp. 'Is that you?'

'Oh, thank God,' Priya cries, sinking to her knees beside me. Her fingers press into my shoulders as if to reassure herself that I'm still here, still breathing. Her chest heaves from exertion, or maybe it's just the panic of what she's done. 'You're still alive,' she pants, her voice urgent, relieved, and full of disbelief at the same time.

I put my trembling hands to my throat, patting the bruised skin. I can barely swallow. As well as my throat, my knee is on fire and my back feels bruised. But I'm somehow grateful for the pain and discomfort. It means I'm not dead. I struggle to sit up. 'Is he . . . ?'

'I bashed him on the head with a rock,' Priya replies, gulping air as she glances nervously over her shoulder. Her eyes are wide with shock, catching the moonlight as she stares at Adam's motionless body on the sand. 'Was he trying to kill you? Who is he, Willow? Do you know him? Are you okay?'

I scoot away from him on my bottom, my whole body shivering and shaking, whether from the cold, the shock, or the fear that he might get up again. 'Is he dead?' I croak, my voice barely audible, the words ragged and frayed.

'I don't know,' Priya replies with a shake of her head, her mouth forming a worried line. 'Oh, God, what if he is? It wasn't a big rock, but at least it was enough to stop him.' She reaches for my hand and eases me to my feet.

I feel unsteady, like I don't know how to stand anymore.

'Let me call the police back,' she continues. 'Tell them where we are. I called them already so they should be at the flat by now. It shouldn't take them long to get down here. Are you okay to walk?'

'I think so.' I test my knee and wince at a flare of pain, but I think I can hobble.

Priya puts a call through and talks fast while we put some distance between ourselves and Adam, our feet shuffling and slipping in the sand. I almost expect him to leap up and come charging after us, to hear his footsteps gaining on us once more. I'm numb with cold, and I feel like my mind is barely clinging on as I try to block out the screaming pain in my knee and the raw ache in my throat.

'I thought I was dead,' I whisper.

'They're on their way,' Priya says, putting the phone back in her pocket and wrapping an arm around my shoulders, holding me close as if warming the life back into me.

'Thank you,' I manage to say, my voice still rough, my body so fragile and exhausted it feels like it's breaking apart.

'I thought I was going to wet myself when I saw him on top of you like that,' she replies. 'But you're safe now. He can't hurt you.'

I swallow and try to speak again, but it just comes out as a hoarse whisper. 'How did you know where to find me?'

Priya shakes her head as though she still can't believe what's happened. 'I heard raised voices coming from your flat and I thought it was you and Gabe having an argument. But it sounded really bad, so I knocked and asked if you were okay. When you didn't reply, I went back to my place and decided to call the police. I didn't know what else to do. I worried I might be overreacting, but I thought – better to be safe than sorry.'

'Thank goodness you did,' I reply.

'After I ended the call, I heard a thump on my door.'

'That was me!' I cry.

'Well, it's a good job you did that because I opened the door and peered out to see that man flying down the stairs. I didn't know what was going on, but I checked your flat and saw that the door was wide open and your smoke alarm was beeping. I thought maybe there was a fire, so I went inside to look for you. I called out, but you weren't there so I turned off the oven and ran down the stairs and out into the street, where I saw that man disappearing around the corner at the end of the road.' Priya keeps going. A torrent of words spilling out.

'I didn't know if I should follow, but I got a bad feeling, so I chased after him. When I reached the beach I saw that he was after you! I nearly died. I couldn't believe it. So I grabbed a rock from the breakwater and carried on chasing.' She puts a shaky hand to her mouth. 'It was the only thing I could think of. To just run and hope I caught up in time.'

'I can't believe you did that, Priya. You saved my life.'

'You'd have done the same for me,' she replies.

I guiltily think about all the uncharitable thoughts I've had about Priya recently. She may be Gabe's ex, but, from now on, I'm going to make sure she's also my friend.

'Who is he?' she asks.

'I . . . he's . . .' All that comes into my mind is a looming shape. A terrible fear I can't put into words right now.

'Don't worry,' she soothes. 'You don't have to say anything.'

I'm glad she doesn't press me on who Adam is. I don't ever want to think about Adam Owens ever again. About the terrible years I spent running from him. I know I'll have to explain all this at some stage very soon, but first I need to let my brain try to process everything. I cling to the hope that it might finally be over, that this might be the end of the horror he's inflicted on me for so long.

'I will tell you,' I reply. 'Just . . . not right now.'

We continue in silence, the only sound the waves rolling back and forth. My throat is still on fire and I seriously wonder if I'll ever be able to talk properly again. But at least I'm alive. *I'm safe*. My head spins with the knowledge of it, dizzy with relief.

I throw an anxious glance over my shoulder, but it's too dark to see anything back there, to work out if Adam is still on the sand or not. We keep moving. We keep going. Facing forward again, I see flashlights up ahead, getting closer.

It looks like the police have arrived.

I allow myself to relax a little, blowing air out through my mouth and letting a few tears fall. Then I just focus on putting one foot in front of the other, until I don't have to anymore. Until the beams of light are right on us, and we're surrounded by people in uniforms, and the fear trickles away into nothing. I clutch Priya's arm, soaking up her friendship and letting myself believe it might be over.

'My friend's hurt,' Priya cries. 'A man tried to strangle her. We need an ambulance.' Her voice seems to be coming from a million miles away as we crumble against each other.

'Ambulance is on its way,' replies a broad-shouldered officer with a Dorset accent. 'Be here any second now.' He guides us to a clear spot on the sand, sits me down, and drapes a blanket over both our shoulders. I can't stop shivering, shaking, crying. 'Where's the perpetrator?' he asks.

Priya points back down the beach. 'I . . . I hit him with a rock,' she says. 'He was trying to kill my friend.'

The officer nods and turns to speak to his colleagues before two of them take off along the beach towards the spot where we left him.

'Do you think I killed him?' Priya asks me. 'Do you think I'll go to prison?'

'If they send you to prison, they can lock me up too,' I hiss, taking her hand and squeezing it.

She nods, and we sit, side by side, waiting to hear whether my husband is dead or alive.

Chapter Thirty-Seven

FIVE DAYS LATER

I knock on Priya's door, and I don't have to wait long before she opens it, with a tired smile. The skin beneath her eyes is bruised and a rash of acne dots her chin.

'Come in,' she says softly.

We hug briefly before I follow her into the lounge, where she invites me over to her deep, squashy sofa. I nudge a couple of silk cushions aside and sit down. 'How did it go?' I ask, my voice still hoarse but definitely improving. 'You should have let me come with you, Priya,' I add. 'I could have driven you.'

'Thanks, but Dad dropped me back,' she replies. 'You just missed him.'

Priya's been at the police station all day, waiting to hear if they're going to bring charges against her for saving me by hitting Adam with a rock. I've been going out of my mind with worry and frustration for days, feeling helpless, despite pleading with the police to realise that I would be dead if she hadn't done what she did. Thankfully, her parents know a good lawyer who's been fighting her corner, but it's been a stressful time for Priya and her family.

'I'm in the clear,' Priya says, her voice breaking and her lip trembling as she says the words.

'Ohhh, thank goodness.' I stand and give her a proper hug this time, relief flooding my body.

After a moment, I sit back down and Priya sinks down beside me and elaborates. 'After all our police interviews and then seeing the hospital report of the injuries to your neck and throat, the DS agreed that my use of force was lawful. That you would probably have died if I hadn't acted. They won't be prosecuting me.'

'I should think not!' I cry. 'I'm so relieved.'

'And now I'm absolutely knackered,' she says, letting her head tip back against the sofa and closing her eyes.

'I bet you are. Same here. I feel like I could sleep for a month.'

'Of course,' she adds, opening her eyes again, 'it helps that I didn't actually kill the bastard.'

'I guess so,' I reply. The fact that Adam only suffered a minor head wound and concussion is a blessing for Priya. But I feel uneasy knowing that Adam is still alive in the world. Especially as he now knows where I live. Of course, he's currently in police custody and my solicitor says that he'll probably be locked up for a very long time, if not for the rest of his life. So I should be able to rest easy. Trouble is, I've been on edge for so long now that it's hard to make my brain believe that I'm finally safe.

'Honestly, Priya' – I look into her tired eyes – 'I know I keep saying it, and the police obviously agree, but if it weren't for you, I'd be dead right now. Probably floating out to sea somewhere being nibbled on by fish.'

'Ew, Willow, that's a horrible image.' Priya screws up her face in disgust.

I laugh at her reaction. 'Oh, *now* you're squeamish. You weren't so icky about things when you were clubbing Adam over the head with a rock.'

She lightly shoves my shoulder. 'Stop it.' She smiles and attempts to get to her feet. 'Want some tea?'

'Stay there, I'll make it.'

'Thanks,' she replies with feeling. 'I don't actually think my legs work anymore. Or my arms for that matter. Or my brain. Also, I'm still calling you Willow, but that's not even your real name is it?'

I sigh and walk over to her kitchen area. 'Actually, it is my legal name now. I changed my name by deed poll after I escaped from my marriage. I didn't want him tracking me down.'

'So, which do you prefer?' she asks with genuine curiosity.

I start opening cupboards to look for the tea things. 'Good question. My parents gave me the name Jasmine, but it somehow feels tainted by Adam. He spoke my name in all kinds of horrible situations and when anyone says it now, I . . . well, it sounds stupid, but I hear it spoken in his voice.'

Priya shakes her head, and I notice a tear drip down her cheek. She swipes it away. 'I'm so sorry for what you went through with him. I can't even imagine it.'

I shrug away the thoughts that have started to crowd my brain again. 'At least it's over now. Well, aside from the court cases.'

'*Cases*, plural?' she queries.

I nod. 'DS Lin is going to help me bring charges against him for all the domestic abuse I suffered. We're going to throw the book at him. I was too scared to do it before, but now that he's in police custody, I feel like it's safe for me to be honest about what he put me through. The problem is that if he was found guilty of just domestic assault, he'd only get put away for a short time, so I'd be worried about him being released in a year or two and coming after me. Now that he's charged with my attempted murder, he'll go away for much longer.'

'Good!' she replies. 'So, I'm guessing you're going to keep the name Willow?' she asks, raising a brow.

'Yes. Willow,' I confirm. 'After my gran's favourite tree. And McAllister after a lovely teacher I once had. I've grown used to it and I feel like it suits me.'

'It really does,' Priya agrees with a nod. 'Now, where's this tea?'

I throw her a playful glare and put the kettle on.

Priya's voice dips into a quieter, more hesitant tone. 'I do have a bit of a confession to make,' she says sheepishly.

I slosh milk into our mugs, silently hoping it's nothing too bad. But at this stage, I'd forgive her pretty much anything.

'I'm not proud of myself,' Priya admits as I bring our mugs over to the sofa and set them on the carved wooden coffee table. She pulls her feet up under her and shoots me a worried glance.

'Go on,' I prompt.

'Okay, well, that night, when Adam was there, the reason I knew something was up was because . . .' Priya swallows and licks her lips, cringing slightly. 'I was listening at your door before I heard the shouting.'

My eyes widen at her admission.

'Not because I was up to anything sinister,' she quickly clarifies. 'I just . . . I thought Gabe was with you, and I wanted to hear what he was saying. I was worried about you.'

I kind of wish she hadn't told me that, because it reminds me that before the whole *rescuing me from Adam* drama, we were no longer friends. In fact, I didn't even trust her. I realise that I don't entirely believe her motive for listening at my door, but that's okay. I understand that she did what she did because she was in love with Gabe. Probably still is. And that's not a crime. It's sad.

'Willow,' she prompts. 'Do you hate me?'

'Of course not,' I reply. But in this moment, I feel as though our friendship is going to be tricky while I'm still seeing Gabe. Unless, perhaps, I move out of this block and find somewhere new to live. That way, I can still be friends with Priya without worrying that she's watching our every move.

'I hope that's true,' she says sadly. 'I promise you, promise, promise, promise, that I'm not in love with Gabe, but I still want you to be careful, because—'

I gently lift my hand to halt her mid-sentence. 'Priya, please stop.'

She clamps her mouth shut and looks chastened.

Taking a slow, steady breath, I continue in a gentle yet firm tone. 'I think, if we're going to be friends, we might have to agree not to talk about Gabe.' The last thing I want to do is offend Priya, but I can't listen to her attempts to split us up. It's just too uncomfortable. And I've promised myself that I'm not going to put up with shabby behaviour from anyone anymore. I'm going to look after myself and cut toxic people out of my life. I don't think Priya's toxic, I just think she's been blinded by love, and I want to give her a second chance.

She bites her bottom lip and takes a breath. 'Okay. You're right. It's a deal.'

My shoulders drop in relief. I hold out my hand and she shakes it, our eyes locking in what I pray is mutual understanding. I just have to hope that, despite all the complications and unspoken tensions, we can make our friendship work.

Chapter Thirty-Eight

'I'm sorry I haven't been able to see you in a while,' I say, feeling a little awkward.

Gabe pushes himself off the leather bar stool to give me a hug, and I get a wave of his lemony and cedar aftershave. I've missed that smell. He pulls me in to a gentle yet firm embrace, grounding me in the moment. I exhale and relax.

'Don't apologise,' he replies, his voice low and reassuring in my ear before we move apart. 'You said in your voicemail you've been having a stressful time. Anything I can do to help?'

'No, it's just nice to see you.' I slide on to the bar stool next to him. I've come straight from Priya's flat to a bar in Highcliffe, where I'm meeting Gabe for the first time since Adam attacked me five days ago. It's early Tuesday night and the place is quiet aside from a gentle hum of background music, and the clink of bottles as the barmaid refills the shelves.

'Hungry?' Gabe asks, picking up a menu. 'They do great chilli fries here.'

'No, but I could murder a glass of rosé.'

'Coming up.' He signals to the barmaid and orders my wine before turning back to me, his eyes narrowing with concern. 'Have you been ill? Your voice sounds a bit . . . croaky.'

I let out a sigh. 'I'll explain, but I really need a drink first.'

'Sounds ominous,' Gabe replies, the corner of his mouth lifting in a half-smile.

'You have no idea,' I murmur.

Once my wine arrives, I clink glasses with Gabe, who's ordered a fresh pint. My first sip hits the spot, and I savour the cool, crisp taste, followed by the burning warmth of alcohol as I swallow. I feel Gabe's eyes on me and I hesitate, wondering how to begin explaining who I really am, and the chaos that's followed me from my previous life.

'You don't have to tell me if you don't want to,' Gabe says gently, taking my hand.

I shiver at his touch, realising that I still really like this man. 'I want to,' I reply firmly. 'I think I need to explain. I couldn't before, because . . . well, truthfully, it wasn't safe to tell anybody. But now . . . now I can hopefully start from scratch, living a proper life.'

Gabe's eyes widen at my cryptic words.

I realise that I don't know how he'll react, but I can't not tell him. If it puts him off, then I guess he isn't the man for me. I take a larger sip of rosé before continuing.

Gabe is quiet while I spill out the details of my terrible marriage. How Adam's controlling nature and physical abuse led me to escaping and hiding out here in Highcliffe with a new name to start a new life. Gabe's expression darkens as I go on to tell him about the events of the past couple of weeks. The shock of seeing Bertie on the beach, followed by his revolting attempt to blackmail me into sleeping with him. And, finally, Adam's recent reappearance in my life. Followed by his attempt to kill me.

Once I'm finished, Gabe exhales slowly and shakes his head. 'I had no idea the hell you've been going through,' he replies. 'I'm so sorry. That's . . .' He runs a hand over the top of his head and exhales. 'I wish you'd told me sooner – but I understand why you didn't. I like to think I could have helped though. I would have kicked Adam's arse for starters.'

I smile at that. 'Priya did a pretty good job of that.'

'She really did, didn't she?' Gabe massages his stubbled jaw with both hands.

I take a deep breath before adding, 'I'll understand if you'd rather stay friends than anything more. I know it's a lot to take in, especially as I'm going to be going through a court case in the next few months, so . . .' My voice trails off – I'm unsure of how much more to say.

'Willow,' Gabe interjects firmly. 'Um, should I still call you "Willow"?'

'Definitely. I'm keeping my new name.'

'I'm glad,' he says. 'It suits you.' And then, with a twinkle in his eye, he adds, 'Although "Cappuccino Girl" suits you better.'

'Haha, I'm never losing that nickname, am I?'

'Definitely not.' He grins before turning more serious. 'So, what I was about to say, before, was that I really like you.' He pauses and gives me a look that melts my insides. 'I'd still like to keep seeing you as more than friends, if that's okay? I want to be here, supporting you through all of it. But, totally understand if you want to be just friends, or take it slow. Whatever you need.'

My heart swells at his words, the warmth of his offer wrapping around me like a soft blanket. It feels so good to be with someone who's happy to give me space, but also wants to be there for me. 'I'd like us to be more than just friends too,' I reply.

Gabe leans forward and presses his lips to mine in the softest of kisses. I blink and feel an overwhelming surge of peace and happiness. Something I haven't felt in years. I put a hand to his cheek and we smile at one another.

'Another drink?' he asks, his voice light as he lifts his empty pint glass.

'I'll get these.' I reach for my bag on the back of the stool.

'No, tonight's on me,' he insists. 'You deserve to be pampered after what you've been through.'

'Thank you,' I murmur.

'So, about that ex of yours,' Gabe says, signalling the barmaid for another round. 'He's in police custody, right?'

I nod, feeling a mix of relief and lingering apprehension. 'Yes. Don't worry, he should be facing a very long prison sentence.'

'I'm not worried for me,' Gabe clarifies. 'Just thought, if you're feeling at all anxious and want me to stick around, I'm happy to crash on your sofa. I'd invite you to stay at mine, but my flatmates are pretty annoying. It wouldn't be much fun for you.'

'That's really sweet.' I'm touched by his offer. 'But, weirdly, I feel quite safe in my flat. I probably shouldn't, after what happened, but I have Elsie next door, and Priya down the hall, both looking out for me. Plus, I got a safety chain fitted and extra locks. Although I know the words "horse" and "bolted" come to mind.'

'Okay.' Gabe nods. 'Cool. Just want you to know the offer's there.'

I take a long, reflective sip before replying, 'I've actually been mulling over moving somewhere new – still in Highcliffe though.'

'Really?' Gabe asks. 'That would be a shame. It's such a great apartment.'

'I know. Anyway, it's irrelevant – it's a fixed-term tenancy. I'd have to wait almost a year till it's up before I can move out and find somewhere else.'

'Well, if you wanted to leave sooner, I'd be happy to take over the tenancy for you?'

'Really? You'd do that for me? Even with Priya living down the hall?'

'Oh – yeah, maybe not.'

We both laugh, and I feel a bit disloyal. Priya saved my life, even if she is obsessed with my boyfriend.

Gabe's expression turns serious again. 'I mean it though. If you really want to leave, I will take it over, despite Priya.'

'That's kind, but I'd never expect you to do that,' I reply. 'I think it's actually a good thing that I've been forced to stay. My flat is my sanctuary. It would feel weird living somewhere else. Plus the rent's reasonable and my landlord's decent.'

'I'm glad.' Gabe hands his card to the barmaid.

I hug my happiness to myself, letting the possibilities dance in my mind. Maybe, next year, if things are still going well, Gabe and I could rent a new flat together. I know he hates the place he shares with his three flatmates. He has virtually zero privacy. And he's as good as said he's not averse to living with me in the short term, so maybe, down the line, it could become more permanent.

I wouldn't want us to live at my place together though. It would all feel too much – Gabe, me, Priya. No. It would be better for me and Gabe to have some distance from her.

I resign myself to the fact that, until my tenancy's up, I'm just going to have to hope Priya stays true to her word and gives us some space. No more listening at my door, or offering up unsolicited advice. Not if I want this thing between me and Gabe to work out. Which I very much do. More than anything.

Chapter Thirty-Nine

FIVE MONTHS LATER

Adam Owens found guilty of killing best friend in Winchester hotel after wrongly suspecting affair with wife
Frank Hayward
Winchester Herald

A man has today been jailed for 32 years after he was found guilty of the murder of Bertie Grierson in Winchester.

Adam Owens, 33, of Brisbane Drive, Guildford, was convicted following a trial at Winchester Crown Court.

Officers were called by the ambulance service just before 9 a.m. on Tuesday 28 October last year to a report of a stabbing at a hotel in Winchester where Bertie, from Guildford, was confirmed dead at the scene.

Jurors were told Owens had armed himself with a knife and deliberately inflicted the fatal stab wound to Bertie's chest after showing up at the hotel late Monday night, wrongly believing that his estranged wife, Jasmine Owens, had been having relations with him. He later tried to strangle Jasmine, who suffered serious but not life-threatening injuries.

On Tuesday 7 April, Owens was convicted of murder, attempted murder, non-fatal strangulation and attempted kidnap, after a jury deliberated for just over two hours.

Following Owens's arrest for murder, he was also charged with coercive and controlling behaviour, when his wife, Jasmine, along with his former girlfriend, Joss Mariner, disclosed previous domestic-related incidents that took place in Guildford.

After completing a house search, officers discovered evidence indicating Owens intended to imprison his wife, including newly fitted locks on internal doors and a brand-new internal CCTV system.

Owens denied the offences but was convicted following a trial at Winchester Crown Court.

Detective Sergeant Katherine Lin said: 'Owens is a violent individual whose behaviour had a huge impact on the women he was in relationships with. They suffer with frequent nightmares and anxiety following the abuse they were subjected to.

'The victims showed great courage in supporting a prosecution, working with police and CPS to ensure a murderer and violent domestic abuser is in prison.

'I am extremely grateful for the evidence they provided, and I hope seeing Owens put behind bars will bring them some form of closure.

'No one – whether that be a woman, a man or a child – should ever be subjected to domestic abuse within an environment that they perceive to be a safe space.

'We understand that it's not always easy to report incidents of this nature to us, especially when you have to relive any trauma faced at the hands of an abuser, but we encourage victims to come forward and report incidents.

'If you are being abused, or you know someone who is, please call 101 and report it to the police. If it's an emergency, dial 999 immediately.'

Today, Owens was jailed for a total of 28 years. He was sentenced to life imprisonment with a minimum term of 28 years for murder, as well as 22 years for attempted murder, and 2 years for coercive and controlling behaviour. All sentences will be served concurrently.

Chapter Forty

Chrissie grins as she refills the bowls of posh crisps, nuts, and olives, her eyes sparkling with approval. 'You look genuinely happy,' she says to me, popping a salted cashew into her mouth. 'And your hair really suits you short like that. It frames your face perfectly.'

I tilt my chin upwards, striking a Madonna pose, and we both pout and lean in for a selfie that's ruined by Louie and Tina's last-minute photo-bombing. Laughing, I pull them in for a proper picture, but soon we're all contorting our faces into silly expressions.

I've thrown an impromptu party this afternoon, having invited my old friends from Guildford to come to Highcliffe for a visit. Chrissie, Tina and Louie were all furious with me for vanishing off the face of the planet for so long, believing Adam's lies about me leaving him for another man. But once they heard the true reason for my disappearance, they were devastated and full of self-recrimination for not realising what had been going on. It's been fantastic to see them again. To hear what they've been up to. And to realise that I'll be able to visit them whenever I want, without Adam's terrifying restrictions.

The irony isn't lost on me that Adam is the one who's ended up behind bars, when it was me he wanted to imprison. Now that the court case has ended, I'm determined not to let the past wreck my future. I don't want to give Adam the satisfaction of ruining the rest of my life. Of keeping me scared. But it's easier said than done.

I've been speaking to a counsellor to help stop the nightmares and the random bursts of fear that still plague me daily. His ex-girlfriend Joss got in touch with me too, and we spent a long evening comparing notes. She lives in Northern Ireland now, having wanted to get as far away from him as possible. She apologised to me for not reporting him to the police. For leaving him free to repeat his abuse on someone else – on me. But I reassured her that it was understandable. That I'd done the same thing. At the time of our escapes, we'd each been mentally exhausted, wanting to hide away rather than bring the spotlight down on our trauma.

Much as it was good to meet her and bond briefly over our shared experiences, I don't think we'll be staying in touch – too many painful memories.

I turn to notice my ex-neighbour behind me at the sink, meticulously washing up glasses and bowls. 'Hey, Carol,' I call out over the music, which has suddenly gone up in volume. Louie's in charge of the playlist. I'll have to ask him to turn it down a bit. 'Leave that lot and come and have a selfie with me. It's supposed to be a party. The washing-up can wait till later.'

'I like to keep busy,' Carol replies, drying her hands on a tea towel before coming to stand next to me. I hold my phone up and tilt my head towards hers, but she looks stiff and serious.

'Smile, Carol,' I urge.

She smiles, but her expression is more stern and bemused than happy. I tap the screen to capture our quirky friendship and then we crouch down to include her beloved red setter, Alfie, in the next photo. She and Alfie are staying with me. I've given her my bed, while I sleep on the couch. There's not enough space for my work friends to stay here too, so they've rented an apartment around the corner for a couple of nights.

Carol sold her house soon after I left Guildford. 'Didn't fancy living next to your creepy ex-husband,' she admitted.

'Don't blame you!' I replied.

Now, she lives in a bigger place on the outskirts of town, with a third-of-an-acre garden for Alfie to run around in. But she says it's a bit isolated and that she hasn't managed to settle there. 'You did well to end up in this spot,' she remarks. 'I like it down here.'

'Well, you're always welcome to come and stay, anytime,' I offer, knowing I'll never be able to repay her for helping me to escape my marriage, and for giving evidence to help put Adam behind bars.

'Thanks,' she says, a genuine smile transforming her features. If only she'd smiled like that for our selfie. 'I've discovered today that Alfie absolutely adores the beach. We might have to consider moving down. I'm sure I could get a transfer,' she muses.

'That would be amazing,' I cry, meaning it. 'Although, I don't even know what you do for work, Carol,' I admit shamefacedly.

'I'm a project manager at a banking firm,' she answers, catching me off guard. It's not what I expected.

'Cool. You should talk to Priya's brother. He's in banking too.'

'Hmm,' she murmurs, noncommittally.

'Oh, and I've still got your dressing gown,' I continue, pushing out the traumatic memory of the day she gave it to me. 'Would you like it back?'

'Oh, no.' She shakes her head dismissively. 'I bought myself a new one – it's got pink and white stripes and I much prefer it. You can keep my old one.'

'Thanks,' I reply. 'It's been through a lot, that dressing gown. I'm quite attached to it.'

Carol pats the back of my hand as Priya's soft voice pulls my attention.

'Hey, Willow,' she says. 'Sorry to interrupt. Can I talk to you for a sec?'

My heart drops at her serious expression. I wonder what she wants to discuss. I hope it's nothing to do with Gabe.

I recently broached the idea with him of us looking for a flat together. He was open to it, but he wants to contribute fifty-fifty and everything is either too expensive for him or an absolute dive. So we've decided to try living together at my place, as it's cheaper than everything else we've seen. He's round here ninety-nine per cent of the time anyway, so it makes sense for him to give notice on his shared apartment and move his stuff in here.

I also haven't mentioned to Priya yet that Gabe's officially moving in with me, but I'm hoping the two of them will at least be civil to one another. Gabe reiterated that he's willing to leave the past behind and forgive her, so I hope she can do the same. And I hope that she meets someone new who'll take her mind off him. I never did find out what happened between them. Gabe said they just drifted apart, and Priya was evasive when I asked her.

She guides me over to the window, where the light has begun to dim into a soft, twilight glow, and she lowers her voice. 'I just wanted to let you know that I won't be renewing my tenancy on the flat.'

My heart gives a little flip. 'You won't?' I echo, feeling relief, tinged with sadness. Despite everything with Gabe, I still really value our friendship.

She tosses her dark hair back over one shoulder. 'I think we both know it's an awkward situation, even if we're pretending it isn't.'

'I'm sorry,' I reply softly. 'I hope you don't think I want you to leave.'

'No, not at all. But I . . .' She trails off, shaking her head as if dismissing a thought too heavy for the moment. 'Never mind.'

I press lightly. 'What were you going to say?'

She shrugs with a tight smile, changing the subject. 'No. Just, it's a great party. Your friends are lovely. Chrissie and Louie are hilarious.'

'Aren't they?' I grin, feeling the tension dissolve, glad that Priya's dropped whatever it was she was going to say – probably something about Gabe. He's here too, somewhere. Last I saw, he was in the hallway chatting to Louie, who was shamelessly flirting with him.

It's been tricky for Gabe this afternoon, being in the same room as Priya and her family, but he's keeping a low profile and being his usual lovely self with my friends, who all adore him.

'Also,' Priya adds, 'Nik wants to talk to you about a business idea.'

'Really?' I frown, confused. 'But I'm a handywoman – I thought he was in banking.'

'He is, but he hates it. Wants to get out,' she explains, steering me towards the dining table where her brother, Nikhil, and their parents are chatting with Elsie from next door. 'He's been hunting for new investment ideas and wants to talk about the possibility of franchising your business. Anyway, I'll let him fill you in.'

I'm a little taken aback by the suggestion, but I can't help feeling intrigued too.

Priya's brother is over from New York. He's handsome, smart and funny, and I'm sure Priya's been trying to matchmake us. I'm worried it's a ploy to get me away from Gabe, but I'm ignoring all the unsubtle hints from her and her parents. Maybe, if I wasn't already in a relationship, I'd be happy to be set up with him. Anyway, it's irrelevant as I'm committed to giving things a proper go with Gabe, which will be much easier once Priya moves out.

Despite her insistence that she's completely over him, I'm still not convinced, but I have to respect what she says. After all, she did save my life. And we've been getting on well. Aside from a few

Gabe-related comments, there's been very little weirdness between us, which is a relief.

She and her mum have even offered to help me redecorate my flat. It's funny that I can see other people's spaces and instantly know how to make them come to life, but with my own, I'm useless. Or maybe it's just that I hadn't felt settled enough until now to make it a home. Urmila suggested going for a simple beach vibe, with lots of natural materials, jute rugs, cream knitted cushions, and wicker lamps. I have to admit, I love the idea, and my landlord, Jim, has even agreed that I can replace the saggy grey sofa with a sofa bed – thanks to some cajoling from Urmila. I don't think anyone could ever say no to her.

'Here she is,' Priya's mum says, pulling me into a warm hug. 'The brilliant Willow herself. Your business is such a fantastic idea. I can see it going global.'

'It's really smart,' Nikhil adds, his brown eyes filling with admiration.

'Tell her what you told us, Nik,' Priya pushes.

He tuts. 'Not now, Pri, it's a party.' He turns back to me. 'Maybe we could meet up in the week and I could pitch you my idea in full?'

'Sounds good,' I reply, earning an excited squeal and a round of claps from Priya.

'Come round to the house,' Urmila says.

'Good idea,' Nikhil replies. 'Since I've been home, she's made more food than I could ever consume in three lifetimes. You need to come and help me eat some of it.' He pats his stomach as though it isn't washboard flat.

A smile tugs at my lips. 'Count me in. I've tried your mum's cooking and it's sensational.'

I turn at the sound of raucous laughter behind me. It's Elsie and Sheila, currently giggling away like schoolgirls.

Having Sheila, Gran's old neighbour, here, too, makes me feel as though a bit of Gran has come to visit. She and Elsie have been getting on like a house on fire. I don't think I've ever seen my grumpy neighbour laugh, but something Sheila's said has really tickled her.

'Oh, Jas – I mean, Willow,' Sheila says, catching my eye. 'This one is such a hoot.' She wipes her eye as tears of laughter escape.

'Are you going to share what was so funny?' Urmila chips in.

'Absolutely not,' Elsie replies, and they collapse into giggles again.

Priya and Elsie were surprised when I introduced Sheila and told them she's our landlord's mother. I wanted to invite Jim too, but Gabe pointed out that it might be harder to relax, having our landlord here.

As I gaze around my tiny apartment, I'm filled with a warm glow. A deep sense of belonging. Of optimism and hope. Of gratitude. I'm not related by blood to any of these people, but they all feel like family. Like we would do anything for one another.

The only people missing today are Naomi and my mum. After Naomi blocked my number, I thought that was it for our friendship. But after she heard about Adam, and realised the real reason I'd neglected her, she got back in touch and was devastated and remorseful that she hadn't tried to help me. I reassured her that there wasn't anything she could have done – even if I know that's not strictly true – but I value our friendship too much to let it slide for a second time. We've since met up for lunch and it was nice, but it did feel a little forced. And, although we made promises to catch up again soon, I think we both know it probably won't happen.

As for my mother, I got back in touch with her, but she was too busy to come down this weekend. It's a friend's birthday, apparently. We haven't spoken since I fled Surrey and she never even reached out when the news about Adam was in the papers. All she offered when I contacted her last week was a detached 'I hope you're over all that Adam stuff now.'

I didn't even dignify that with a response. Just told her to take care and enjoy the birthday party, before hanging up. I knew I shouldn't have risked calling her, but there's still this needy, annoying part of me that wants to try. That wonders if this time she'll be different. That maybe she'll care enough about my well-being to be interested and ask questions. But I refuse to wallow in self-pity now. Not when I'm surrounded by so many wonderful souls. People who've chosen to be in my life and who genuinely care.

'Hey.'

I look up to see Gabe's blue-eyed gaze on me, his arms snaking around my waist as he pulls me in for a kiss. I told him beforehand that we shouldn't be too touchy-feely around Priya as I don't want to rub it in. But I feel powerless to pull away. He's everything I want right now.

'Hey yourself,' I murmur back with a smile, gently disentangling myself from his arms. 'We shouldn't.' I tip my head in Priya's direction.

'I know.' He sighs. 'But you're just too irresistible.'

'Priya just gave me some good news, actually.'

'Oh?' He raises his brows.

'She's given her notice on the flat,' I announce quietly.

Gabe frowns. 'Really?'

'Yep. She's moving out. So we don't need to worry about any more weirdness.'

'I'll believe it when I see it,' he replies, pulling me in for a proper hug. 'But, if it really is true, then, of course, that's amazing news.' He kisses the top of my head and I feel like no one has the right to be this happy.

'We should have another drink to celebrate,' I say, stepping back. 'Beer?'

‘Please.’ Gabe nods, but seems distracted suddenly. I mean to ask him about it, but he interrupts my train of thought. ‘Actually, don’t worry, I’ll get them.’ Before I can respond, he heads over to the kitchen, to the ice bucket in the corner that’s stacked with bottles as there’s not enough room in my tiny fridge. I watch, drinking in the sight of him as he pulls out two bottles of IPA and dries them with a tea towel.

I can’t wait for him to get to know all my old friends better. Gabe and I are showing them the sights of Highcliffe tomorrow. We’re planning to explore the castle followed by a long beach walk complete with ice creams, and then later a fish-and-chip supper. I truly feel as though this is my home now. Gran would have loved it here. She always said she wished she could live nearer the coast again. How the sea always lifted her spirits.

‘Well, now I’m doing it, Gran,’ I whisper, imagining her warm smile as she sees that I’m living just a stone’s throw from the most beautiful sandy beach. Maybe I’ll have kids here and they’ll have the kind of upbringing that Gran had. The sort of childhood she always wanted for me. Walks on the beach, sandcastles, a proper family life. A life where, I think – no, where I *know* – I can finally be happy.

Somewhere outside, above the low hum of the party, I’m sure I hear a bird singing.

Epilogue

SEVEN MONTHS EARLIER

I stand in the lobby talking to Jim, a balding, middle-aged man with a friendly smile, who agreed – after a bit of persuasion – to meet me at the block to discuss renting one of his flats. I'm dressed smartly, my hair's freshly washed, I have all my references and have even managed to scrape together a hefty deposit along with my first month's rent. It's way over my budget and I've eviscerated my overdraft, but I don't care. I'll deal with the fallout from the bank later.

'I know we're here to talk about one of your New Milton flats,' I begin, 'but I was actually hoping to rent something in this block.'

Jim's brow creases. 'Like I said on the phone, this block's full. The last unit went in July – my new tenant moves in next month.'

'I'm happy to wait in case another one comes up,' I plead. 'I have great references.'

'So, you're not interested in the New Milton flat?' Jim's friendly smile evaporates and now he just looks pissed off. 'Is that why you wanted to meet here? And not there?'

'Sorry.' I grimace. 'Thing is, I work in Highcliffe, so I was hoping to rent locally. I'm happy to pay a bigger deposit though,' I persist.

'And I'd be happy to take that bigger deposit,' Jim replies, his frown deepening. 'If. I. Had. A. Flat. Available. Not sure how to say it any clearer.'

I'm annoying him now, which isn't the best way to go about renting one of his properties. 'Sorry.' I flash him an apologetic smile. 'Would you be able to get in touch if one comes up in the block?'

'Sure. Fine,' he replies in a tone that implies he's never ever going to call.

I've blown it. 'You've got my number, right?' I check anyway.

He nods wearily. 'Are we done?'

'Thank you,' I reply, disappointment flooding my veins. 'Sorry again.'

'And this is why I need a new managing agent,' Jim mutters as we walk out of the building together and into the cool September afternoon.

'Thanks for your time,' I call as he strides off.

He lifts a hand in acknowledgement, but doesn't turn around.

I stand on the pavement, deflated, unsure what my next move should be.

A mutual friend told me that Priya has put a deposit down on this block. That she'll be moving in next month. Our break-up was painful. I haven't been able to eat or sleep properly since she left. I miss her so much, but she just won't listen. It's been five months since we split and she moved back home with her parents. I had to let our luxury apartment go as I couldn't afford the rent without her generous contribution. Or, rather, her parents' generous contribution. So I've ended up in a crappy shared flat with annoying flatmates who never clean up after themselves, and never seem to go out. It's made me realise how easy I had things with Priya. How stupid I was to take her for granted.

Now that she's back living with her parents, it's been almost impossible to see her. They won't let me in. Won't even answer the door to me anymore. Even though I've done nothing but try to prove to her how sorry I am. Her parents used to love me. We spent evenings socialising with them, even went on holiday together. I'd hoped that Ted might want to bring me into his multi-million-pound software company one day – show me the ropes, because neither she nor Nikhil are interested. It would have been a dream for me to become part of the family. To become a part of the business. But I stupidly let her slip through my fingers. I relied too heavily on my looks and my charm without putting in the effort. I won't make that mistake again. I'll prove my worth.

Of course, I don't want to come across as stalkerish. I just want her to realise that what I did wasn't the real me. It was a moment of madness. The thing is, I was only working part-time back then, and had no savings. I wanted to get her something nice for her birthday but I was skint and so – it feels terrible even admitting it to myself – I took eighty pounds from her purse. I've never done anything like that before, but she'd mentioned this necklace that she liked and I didn't have quite enough and so . . . the opportunity was there, and I took it. There was way more cash than that in her purse, and I honestly didn't think she'd notice.

But she instantly knew it was missing. And she realised it was me. Of course she did. She's not stupid. Who else would have taken it when there was only the two of us at home? I could kick myself for doing it. Such an idiotic mistake.

When she first told me the money was missing, I acted concerned, but I could tell she was suspicious. She looked at me with confusion and then disbelief, and I pretended to be confused too. But then she finally accused me, grabbing my wallet and finding the four offending twenties. I continued to deny it, but she didn't believe me. Said it was the final straw. But I didn't know we'd even reached that stage. I'd thought everything was good between us.

She started talking about my laziness and lack of ambition. About how I never helped out around the flat. How I expected her to arrange everything and do everything and that she was sick of it. It was just this barrage of criticism out of nowhere. I apologised and said that she was right. That I would pull my weight more. But it was like a switch had gone off in her head – from loving me, to not.

I never admitted to her accusation that I took the money. I couldn't do it. I was ashamed. I just kept insisting that the notes were mine and that she'd made a mistake.

The galling thing is that I only did it because I wanted to buy something nice for her. I wasn't spending the money on myself.

She never mentioned the cash again – aside from assuring me she wouldn't tell anyone about the money I took, because it was too humiliating to think about – but she didn't mention much of anything again. Because she left.

Ever since that day, I've been trying to win her back.

I got myself a proper job – okay, the pay isn't great, but at least I'm working full-time now, and hopefully it will lead to promotions and pay rises in the future. But she doesn't seem impressed that I'm making an effort. That I've taken what she said on board and I'm really turning my life around. I think her parents have been poisoning her against me, which actually hurts as much as Priya's rejection.

But the fact that she's now getting her own place means I'm in with a shot again. Without her guard-dog parents, we'll finally be able talk without their interference. The problem is, I can't just hang around outside the building all the time. It will look suspicious and there's bound to be some nosy tenant who'll want to know who I am and what I'm doing, loitering.

So, my brilliant idea was to rent a place here too. Try to win her back that way. It would be so much easier if I was living in the building. I can't afford it at all, but my plan was to stretch to a couple of months – that would have given me enough time to win her back,

I'm sure of it. But now, the landlord has crushed my hopes, so I'll just have to be discreet and try to chat with her while she's coming and going from the block.

I stand aside as two women walk by me: an old lady and a much younger woman – she's pretty in a low-key kind of way, with brown hair and a sweet face.

'I told you, Willow,' the old woman rasps, 'you need to tell him that's your parking spot and not his. If he doesn't move his car, you should go ahead and key it.'

'Elsie!' the young woman chides. 'You'll get me arrested.'

'Well, it's him that should be arrested for parking in your space,' Elsie quips back, fumbling in her bag. 'Where's my blasted keys?'

'Don't worry, I've got mine,' Willow replies, waving them at her.

As I surreptitiously watch her slip the key into the lock and walk into the lobby with Elsie, something clicks in my brain. My pulse starts to race as I feel the stirrings of another brilliant idea.

There's no need for me to stretch my finances trying to rent a place I can't afford. Not when I can date someone who already lives here. And with the help of a girlfriend who lives in the block, I'll have a legitimate excuse to be around. I'll be able to see Priya every day. Plus, there'll be the added bonus of making her jealous. Win-win.

I just have to make sure I start this new relationship before Priya moves in so that I can pass it off as a wild coincidence.

However long it takes – days, weeks, months – I'm not giving up until Priya takes me back. She's the only way I can see my life truly improving. I can move back in with her, win round her parents and then I'll propose. She's the only future I want. And I'm not losing her again. I'm not going to spend my life in crappy flat shares, in crappy jobs earning minimum wage and working long hours.

'Willow.' I murmur the name aloud, liking the sound of it on my tongue. 'How do you feel about becoming my new, temporary girlfriend?'

If you have been affected by the issues raised in this book, help and support is available in the following places:

UK: www.nationaldahelpline.org.uk/

US: www.thehotline.org/

AU: www.1800respect.org.au/

CA: www.domesticshelters.org/en-ca/domestic-abuse-help-in-canada

ACKNOWLEDGEMENTS

It definitely takes a team to publish a book, and I'm very grateful to mine! A huge thank you to my wonderful editor, Sammia Hamer, for being so supportive and flexible. Endless appreciation to my developmental editor, Hannah Bond, for all the brilliant ideas and tweaks that made this story shine. Gratitude to Eoin Purcell, Rebecca Hills, Nicole Wagner, and the fantastic team at Amazon Publishing for bringing this book into the world. I'm eternally thankful.

Hats off to Sadie Mayne for her fantastic work on the copy-edits, and to Gemma Wain for proofreading like a pro. Thanks both for your patience and red penmanship.

Thank you to The Brewster Project for creating another stunning cover. Major thanks to Jonathan Pennock, Clare Corbett, and the team at Brilliance Publishing for producing another audiobook worthy of a standing ovation.

Endless thanks to author and police officer Sammy H. K. Smith for advising on police procedure. Any embellishments or errors are entirely mine.

I'm deeply grateful to my beta reader, Terry Harden, who explores my books like a treasure hunter – thank you for your patience and insightful feedback. Huge thanks to the truly awesome team at Tandem Collective for all your incredible support and infectious enthusiasm. Thanks also to my wonderful readers, bloggers, reviewers, supporters, recommenders, and posters – you're the driving force behind my writing, and I'd be lost without you. Special thanks to the fabulous Mark Fearn and his Facebook page BOOK MARK! It's such a great bookish community and you always manage to make me laugh out loud.

Lastly, a huge, heartfelt thanks to my dear, darling friends and family for your unwavering love and support, especially my husband, Pete, who's always the first to read my books, and reassure me through my many meltdowns, and somehow still love me afterwards.

A LETTER FROM THE AUTHOR

I just want to say a huge thank you for reading my latest psychological thriller. I hope you enjoyed it.

If you'd like to keep up to date with my latest releases, just sign up to my newsletter via my website www.shaliniboland.com and I'll let you know when I have a new novel coming out. Your email address will never be shared, and you can unsubscribe at any time.

If you enjoyed *The Ex*, I'd be really grateful if you'd be kind enough to post a review online or tell your friends about it. A good review absolutely makes my day!

Shalini xx

ABOUT THE AUTHOR

© *Shalini Boland 2018*

Shalini Boland is the Amazon and *USA Today* bestselling author of over twenty psychological thrillers. To date, she's sold three million copies of her books.

Shalini lives by the sea in Dorset, England, with her husband, two children and their increasingly demanding dog, Queen Jess. Before kids, she was signed to Universal Music Publishing as a singer/songwriter, but now she spends her days writing (in between restocking the fridge and dealing with endless baskets of laundry).

She is also the author of two bestselling sci-fi and fantasy series as well as a WWII evacuee adventure with a time-travel twist.

When she's not reading, writing or stomping along the beach, you can reach her via Facebook at www.facebook.com/ShaliniBolandAuthor, on TikTok @shaliniboland, on Bluesky @shaliniboland.bsky.social, on X @ShaliniBoland, on Instagram @shaboland, or via her website: www.shaliniboland.com.

Visit Shalini's website to sign up to her newsletter.

Follow the Author on Amazon

If you enjoyed this book, follow Shalini Boland on Amazon to be notified when the author releases a new book!
To do this, please follow these instructions:

Desktop:

1) Search for the author's name on Amazon or in the Amazon App.
2) Click on the author's name to arrive on their Amazon page.
3) Click the 'Follow' button.

Mobile and Tablet:

1) Search for the author's name on Amazon or in the Amazon App.
2) Click on one of the author's books.
3) Click on the author's name to arrive on their Amazon page.
4) Click the 'Follow' button.

Kindle eReader and Kindle App:

If you enjoyed this book on a Kindle eReader or in the Kindle App, you will find the author 'Follow' button after the last page.